PRAISE FOR
The Gift of Hope

"McKanagh's story sparkles with humor and hope."
—Charlotte Hubbard, author of *Morning Star*

"Kristen McKanagh's *The Gift of Hope* is pure joy to read, with endearing Amish characters and heartfelt relationships!" —Rebecca Kertz, author of *Finding Her Amish Love*

"Upbeat and sweet. . . . I can't wait to read Kristen's next book. Truly a gift that will stay in my heart."
—Emma Miller, author of *A Summer Amish Courtship*

"As with anything written by this author, readers are treated to an amazing offering. . . . If you want something different and need an escape from the worries of life, get your hands on *The Gift of Hope* and enjoy." —Fresh Fiction

"The story is magical, well described, with a wholesome romance and believable characters you want to root for. I loved this book!" —Romance Junkies

The Unexpected Gifts Series

THE GIFT OF HOPE
THE GIFT OF JOY
THE GIFT OF FAITH

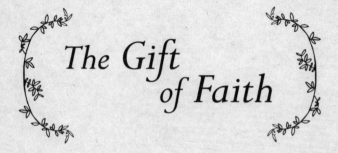

The Gift of Faith

UNEXPECTED GIFTS

Kristen McKanagh

BERKLEY ROMANCE
New York

Berkley Romance
Published by Berkley
An imprint of Penguin Random House LLC
penguinrandomhouse.com

ISBN: 9780593199909

First Edition: April 2023

Printed in the United States of America
1 3 5 7 9 10 8 6 4 2

Book design by Gaelyn Galbreath

To the McHams, the Wardens & MESA—
the biggest influences on my personal faith journey

Chapter One

✳

PUSHING A LITTLE harder than she meant to on the screened back door of her parents' house, Faith Kemp tried to catch it before it banged closed. No need to let the ladies inside know they'd gotten under her skin.

The problem was, a sleeping baby strapped to her chest meant she had to be careful as she moved, and the bag of baby things made her even more awkward . . . so she missed. With a wince at the loud crack of wood on wood, Faith paused on the steps, shocked the baby hadn't woken, and winced again at the hole of silence in the house.

Jah. They'd heard.

She sighed. The brisk Indiana autumn air blew through her dress and cloak, counteracted by the warmth of the bright sun. She still hesitated. Maybe she shouldn't go out when the weather was so windy?

For a second, she debated sneaking back into the house to grab the library book she was reading so she could go to the empty dawdi haus across the graveled courtyard to

read. One of the three primary structures on their farm—
the main house, dawdi haus, and barn—the small set of
private rooms where her grossdawdi had lived before his
death was her favorite quiet escape.

I'll probably get caught.

She couldn't face another second with the ladies who'd
come visiting. Most were kind enough, but several were the
doubters in their Amish community. The ones who hadn't
been quick to welcome her back. Especially Martha Gick.

But ignoring them wasn't easy when they were in her
house.

"Faith!" her mother called from inside. "If you're determined to pick blumes, make sure the boppli is warm
enough."

As if she would have done anything else. Faith looked
down into the baby's angelic face, her rosebud lips pursed
in sleep. She'd taken care of this baby from the day her
sister, Mercy, had given birth. She'd traveled across the
country with her. Loved her. Cared for her. Even named
her, because Mercy could hardly bring herself to look at
her own child. In her heart, Faith knew that her sister had
already decided to give the baby away and probably didn't
want to bond with her. Faith, on the other hand, had found
her calling with motherhood. Every second with Rose was
precious.

Mamm is only caring for her only kinskind, grandchild.

Faith managed to force lightness into her voice. "All
bundled up," she called back. "And I have a bag with her
things."

"And try not to trip." Worry laced the words.

Hanging on to her patience took effort. "I'll be extra
careful." She always was with the baby.

A pause greeted that, followed by a reluctant and yet still brusque, "Oll recht. Don't stay out too late."

Only late enough for the bevy of ladies gathered in the kitchen to leave. They were making applesauce from the fruit harvested from her parents' small orchard. It would take them a while. Faith planned to stay away until they were gone.

Was it terrible of her to be happy that little Rose had fussed and fussed, meaning Faith couldn't be of much help?

The baby scrunched up her face and let out a protest at Faith for standing still too long, even as she remained asleep. With a grin, Faith started down the stairs, out past the barn, and along the fenced fields of larger produce. The pumpkins and squash had both grown wonderful gute this year, ripe and round in the fields. Dat would need more help harvesting.

But she wasn't going to worry about that right now.

The nattering women in the kitchen, with their probing comments and speculative glances, were too fresh. How Mamm missed the intent behind those glances and questions was a miracle, but she always gave people more credit than they deserved. Faith had been that way once, too.

And yes, she'd known when she'd returned home that it would take time to regain some of her community's trust, but she hadn't expected it to be this hard. She was the gute girl. Mercy was the one with all the dreams and plans and disdain for their upbringing. Meanwhile, Faith was paying the price for both of them all the same.

So much speculation.

Beyond telling their local community of Amish in

Charity Creek, Indiana, that Rose was Mercy's child, they hadn't shared much else about Faith's return with the baby. Mostly because Faith had refused to share the details with her own family, not wanting her parents to be more upset than they had to be.

And they would be, if they knew where and how Mercy was living.

Many in their church had been welcoming, but a few were unaccepting. They thought of Faith as a girl who'd jumped the fence and returned only when she realized she couldn't make it in the Englischer world. She was fairly certain some wondered if Rose was actually her baby and she'd lied, pinning the sin on her absent twin sister.

But Rose wasn't a sin and she wasn't a mistake. She was perfect and innocent. She deserved love and a gute life.

Whatever path Gotte had intended for her, Faith never in a thousand years would have pictured this one. Although maybe this hadn't been His plan for her. Maybe He'd had other ideas and Faith had taken a wrong turn. Or maybe her sister's tornado of a life had carved a path through Faith's decisions and forced her down a different road.

But Rose was the light of her life, and she wouldn't change a thing. Except maybe Mercy coming home, too. Not that that would ever happen.

Her mater's words ringing in her ears, Faith carefully made her way over the steps at one of the fences— coordination was not one of her blessings—and headed out into a large, untilled field beyond. One full of autumn wildflowers.

Goldenrod lit the entire area in happy yellow that glowed in the sun. Most would consider it a weed, but not only could it be used in herbal teas, it would be perfect for the autumn door wreath she was making as a donation for the upcoming Harvest Festival.

But first she had to find the perfect spot to lay Rose down. She didn't want to risk scratching the baby as she plucked the flowers.

Lifting her skirts and the bag of baby paraphernalia, she hiked through the tall grasses to a spot at the edge of their property where the grasses were short, thanks to a large oak spreading its limbs wide and providing protection from the wind for the baby. There Faith spread out the blanket she'd brought, then carefully managed to wiggle Rose out of the straps and lay her in the center of the blanket. Thankfully she stayed asleep through the transition for once.

If she woke up and started crawling, she wouldn't go past the edges of the blanket, so she would be safe enough. Pressing a kiss to Rosie's soft cheek, Faith took up the flat basket she'd brought, along with gardening gloves and a pair of shears, and got to work cutting flowers, never going where she couldn't see Rose, checking on her frequently. Despite the chill in the air, the day was perfect, with sun bright and warm on her face between gusts of wind.

She hummed softly to herself. No tune in particular.

"My bees need those blumes."

On a gasp, hand flying over her heart, Faith whirled around at the deep baritone voice close behind her.

Letting out a sharp breath of relief when she recognized her intruder, she huffed a laugh. "Daniel Kanagy, you about gave me a heart attack."

He said nothing to that. Instead, he stood there, studying her in that quiet way he had. Though, if she wasn't mistaken, a tint of red warmed his cheeks.

Willing her still-racing heart to calm down, she offered

him a smile. Even though she'd been home almost two months now, beyond one brief greeting—the first time she'd attended Gmay after returning to Charity Creek—she hadn't talked to Daniel directly. Nothing beyond a nod on Sundays at Gmay or if they crossed paths. He'd always been a nice boy, if somewhat withdrawn, when they'd been in school together.

But he was that way with everyone.

She had no reason to expect him to greet her with harsh words or suspicious stares, but she'd started guarding her heart against people's reactions to her since coming home.

"We haven't had a chance to talk much since I got home," she said. "How are your family? The store?"

She'd heard already through others, of course, but she didn't know what else to ask. The Kanagys, who owned a family-run, all-Amish-made gift shop in town called A Thankful Heart, had three boys—Daniel, Aaron, and Joshua. The younger two had each recently married local girls, Hope Beiler and Joy Yoder, both of whom Faith liked.

Daniel made a face like he'd sucked on a lemon, and she almost smiled. He'd never been much for small talk, as she recalled.

"Fine," he said. Then crossed his arms over what had become a broad chest.

The kind of strength that could weather any storm. The errant thought, and a fanciful one for her, sent heat into her cheeks. What a silly thing to think about a man she hardly knew.

Granted, he'd always been one of the best-looking boys in the district. All the Kanagy boys were, with their dark hair and dimples. Daniel had his mother's rich brown eyes, but he was the only one with a cleft in the middle of his chin, which Faith had always thought made him seem trustworthy for some odd reason.

And his quietness, instead of being awkward, gave him an air of confidence and mystery. At least that's what all the girls said.

The girls he ignored. Faith included. Maybe even more so, given who and what she was now.

At twenty-five, she was older. Now with a baby who was not her own to care for.

Not exactly a great prospect for marriage. Widowers with kinder of their own to raise . . . now, those had been buzzing around her like a swarm of bees. However, much to her parents' dismay, taking on a husband who might pass away while she was still relatively young, leaving her with even more children to care for on her own, was not something Faith would consider. Which meant she needed to figure out how to support herself and a baby. Her parents loved her, but she had trouble picturing a future where she was anything but a burden to them, and Dat needed help on the farm.

She shushed the small voice in her head touting her faults.

"I'm glad you are all well," she said. "I've been meaning to visit the shop. Has it changed much?"

"Some." Another one-word answer.

Faith didn't take it as rudeness or as anything against her. This was just his way.

"What are you doing out here?" she tried.

"Tending my bees."

Right. He'd said something about bees when he'd startled her. At least that was more than a one-word answer. Faith smiled brightly. Daniel blinked. A long, slow one, like he wasn't quite sure why she was bothering to aim her teeth in his direction.

"I thought bees went dormant as it got cooler?" she said, undeterred.

Mercy might be the wild one, the fun one, but Faith had always thought of herself as the easy one to be around. She liked people. Usually.

Daniel shrugged. "Honeybees overwinter, but only after it drops below fifty degrees."

That was the longest sentence she'd gotten from him yet. Did she push her luck? "Overwinter?"

He took the bait, shoulders visibly dropping as he eased into a topic he clearly enjoyed. "The drones die off and the queen and female workers huddle in the hive and shiver to generate heat."

Faith leaned forward, sincerely interested. "They shiver? I bet that's something."

Humor tugged at the corners of Daniel's mouth for half a heartbeat until she ruined it by saying, "Maybe you can show me sometime."

The corners turned into a frown. "Maybe."

She stiffened. He wasn't exactly jumping at the chance. Perhaps he was more wary of her than she'd thought.

Then he said, "But right now they are still foraging to build their honey stores for the winter . . . and you are taking their flowers."

Faith startled, glancing around her. She hadn't even thought about bees—just the arrangement she was planning in her head. "I'm so sorry." She studied her half-full basket.

After a moment of hesitation, Daniel gave her a wave, then turned to leave.

"Is there an area where I can safely cut flowers that won't disturb your bees?" she asked.

She wasn't even sure why she did, beyond a sudden urge to not be alone, and Daniel Kanagy, of all people, was . . . nice . . . to be around. Comfortable.

Before he could answer, a tiny wail of protest sounded from under the tree. "Uh-oh. Sounds like someone's awake."

Faith left Daniel to hurry over to the tree, except halfway there she managed to stick her foot in a hole and fell to her hands and knees with a muffled *oomph*.

"Are you oll recht?" Big hands at her waist scooped her up to deposit her on her feet.

Faith sucked in sharply at Daniel's sudden nearness. Not in alarm, but in the way she suddenly wouldn't have minded a hug, too. To hide such a thought from him, she stepped back with a forced laugh. "I'm fine. It happens a lot."

"I know."

She peeped at his face, expecting censure, only to find a kind sort of worry there. To make him feel better she held up her glove-covered hands. "Gute thing I was wearing these."

Another cry from Rosie brought her swinging around to continue hurrying to the baby. Sure enough, Rose was wide awake, had wriggled out of the blanket Faith had wrapped her in, and was scooting around, stopping at the edges of the blanket like she always did. Rosie didn't seem to like the feel of leaves and grass on her hands and feet. All tangled up, and her face scrunched up and red, she was definitely angry that Faith had dared to leave her someplace where she couldn't get away.

Did it make her a bad mother that she sort of dreaded

the day when Rosie realized she could go past the edges of a quilt?

A shadow fell over them as Faith unwound the baby from her wrappings. She glanced up to find Daniel had followed. "What's wrong?" he asked, staring at Rose.

"Nothing. She's just hungry and"—Faith patted Rosie's bottom—"and needs a change."

Quickly she had the baby in a dry, clean cloth diaper, which was a feat all by itself. The child was never still, and a small sheen of sweat lined Faith's upper lip by the time she'd finished. She needed to get a bottle ready, but she knew her Rose. At eight months old, she cried if she wasn't held or crawling. No in-between. Faith glanced around for a safe place to tuck her, but the only available safe spot was Daniel, who hadn't moved. With a mental shrug, she held a wiggling, protesting Rose up to him. "Do you mind?"

She nearly laughed at the panicked expression that stole across Daniel's otherwise stoic features. She'd seen him play with kinder at various community gatherings, but never babies. And neither of his brothers had given him nieces or nephews yet. Maybe he wasn't comfortable with them?

He didn't reach for the baby, taking a step back even.

"Please?" Faith jiggled Rose midair, arms starting to ache. "It would help me so much."

That did it. With visible reluctance, he scooped the baby out of Faith's hands and up against his chest. At first, he tried to hold her like a regular baby, cradled on her back in the crook of his arm.

Rose was having none of that.

She thrashed her little legs and arms until he sat her up, then did everything she could to push and scoot up his chest to his shoulder.

Out of the corner of her eye, as she prepared the baby's

food, Faith kept watch on the pair. When she finally looked up, she couldn't help the chuckle that tumbled from her. Rose was standing on Daniel's arm while he held her safe with his other arm. She'd pushed up so that they were eye to eye, and she was exploring Daniel's clean-shaven face with her hands.

A tiny, unexpected twinge of an emotion she couldn't put her finger on struck. Daniel was letting Rose get that close to him, and it left Faith suddenly breathless.

Which made no sense.

Granted, she used to have an almighty crush on Daniel when they were scholars. It had been years, though. Amish finished school after eighth grade, after all, and she'd been away since she was nineteen, tracking Mercy all over the countryside at first before staying close to her sister. Now she was back with a baby. It would be verhuddelt, so foolish, for her to even think about how gute she remembered Daniel being at arithmetic, or how he never let the other bigger boys bully the smaller children, or the way no girl could catch his eye.

You included, Faith Kemp.

Rose reached out with her tiny, chubby hand and managed to knock off his hat and grab a hank of his dark hair, giving it a yank.

"Ouch," Daniel rumbled.

Rose's eyes flew wide, then she broke into an irresistible baby grin that took up most of her face and giggled—the precious baby giggle that stole Faith's heart every single time she heard it.

Daniel stilled.

Not that he wasn't already holding pretty steady, but this was different, like he was fascinated all of a sudden. Then he narrowed his eyes and said "Ouch" again in exactly the same way. The adorable moment sent a skittering of shock through Faith.

Rose's giggle this time was even longer, making Faith's lips twitch. Clearly her baby was delighted with Daniel.

The man lowered his brows like a ferocious bear and did it again. Faith never, ever would have pictured Daniel Kanagy like this. Rose's giggles soared up into the trees, and Daniel softly chuckled with her, dark eyes alight with laughter.

Then he glanced up and caught Faith staring.

The smile disappeared and he handed the baby back to Faith mid-giggle. Rose cut off the laugh and reached for him with a little whine. Before that whine could turn into a full-blown cry, Faith flipped her around, tickled her tummy, then popped the bottle into her mouth.

"Are the flowers for anything in particular?" Daniel asked abruptly.

She raised her head, blinking at the fact that he'd asked her a question at all. "I'm making a dried door wreath to sell at the Harvest Festival."

Daniel considered her silently. "You made that arrangement for Joy and Joshua as a wedding gift, didn't you?"

Amish didn't carry flowers or decorate for weddings the way Englischers did, but Faith had been to one wedding while she'd been out in the world and had loved the bouquet the bride had carried. So she'd made a smaller version for Joy and told her she could let it dry as a keepsake. She couldn't believe Daniel remembered that. "Jah. I did."

"She loves that thing." He scrunched up his nose like he couldn't figure out why.

Faith grinned. "I'm glad."

He fell quiet, but she didn't mind. Sitting here in the

field with Rosie slurping away and Daniel standing over them like he was keeping them safe was peaceful.

"The southern part of this field is well enough away from my bees." Daniel pointed, answering the question she had asked right before Rose woke up. Then he turned and walked away.

Faith's mouth dropped open as she stared at his departing back.

Then she dropped her gaze to find Rosie's clear blue eyes—the same as her and Mercy's eyes—trained on Faith's face. "Rosie Posie," she whispered. "You could charm the birds from the trees." She glanced back up at Daniel, who was already a spec on the horizon. "I, on the other hand, clearly can't."

Chapter Two

✳

DANIEL TRUDGED THROUGH the field back to his bees. He'd been drawn by the sound of Faith's humming and had stood behind her enjoying the soft sound for longer than was proper. Then he'd gone and made a fool of himself. First about her disturbing the bees and then with the baby. He'd just been so surprised to find her out there. Not ready for it. Of course the first time he finally got a chance to talk to her alone, he'd mess it up.

His steps slowed.

Having grown up with Faith, he'd gone to school with her and her twin sister, Mercy. He had also encountered them at various gatherings and frolics around their Amish community, as well as at church every other Sunday. Before she'd run off, she'd been the only girl in the district who hadn't tried to catch his attention. She'd never brought him baked goods, or come into the store several times a week, or tried to get him to ask to drive her home from singeon on a Sunday evening. He'd gotten over that crush a long time ago, while she'd been gone.

Vanity would be to wonder why, so he tried not to wonder.

He had no idea if, since her return, she'd started going to any of the singeons or frolics meant for die Youngie, those in Rumspringa mostly, though unmarried Amish were welcome, too. But he'd quit attending after his brothers had gotten married. He'd grown too ault for those anyway. Twenty-six felt . . . old.

Too old for the need to get anything out of his system. Too old for the boys who had yet to grow up. Too old for the giggling girls, many still in school or fresh out of school. Just too old.

Then again, maybe he'd always felt that way. Dat used to say his soul was beyond his years.

Faith's clear blue eyes—like the sky at twilight—lingered in his mind while he checked the bees. The memory of her smiles and the way she'd sincerely seemed interested in his bees stuck with him all the way home, right in time for Mamm and Dat to arrive from the store in the buggy. Daniel greeted them, helping put Frank, their buggy horse, away while his parents set to work, Mamm to start dinner and Dat to go feed the chickens. Daniel also fed and settled the other horses for the night before heading inside.

He had rid his mind of Faith Kemp by then.

"Mamm?" he called out as he took off his shoes at the back door.

"In the kitchen," she called back. It had been months since she'd been sick, and she still sounded winded when she talked. He didn't like that.

Daniel found her cooking and gently pushed her aside

so that he could take over stirring the homemade apple-sauce she'd made over the weekend and was warming. She patted his arm and moved to the propane-heated oven to check the noodles she had baking.

"Mamm?"

"Hmmm?"

"Do you know the flowers from Joy and Joshua's wedding, the ones she keeps in their family room?"

Apparently, he hadn't kicked Faith Kemp out of his mind after all.

"Of course. They're lovely."

He agreed, though he wouldn't admit it out loud. "Do you think something like that might sell well in the store?"

The fact that Faith thought they might sell at the Harvest Festival had ticked off the idea in his head.

"Oh!" Mamm straightened, adding another twist to the egg timer on the counter. "I should have thought of that myself." She turned a beaming smile on him. "What made you think of it?"

Usually his mother dealt with finding goods women might be more prone to like in the store—quilts, kitchenware, lotions, and such. Dat brought in stuff like leather goods and farrier-forged items. Daniel shrugged. If he told her he'd bumped into Faith in the field and actually talked to the girl, Mamm would have them married off by Christmas.

Used to him, his mother barely noticed the shrug, clearly already thinking through the idea. "Faith Kemp made that, jah? I'll have to ask if she is interested in doing something for the shop when I see her at Gmay on Sunday."

A small kernel of warmth bloomed in his chest, but

Daniel put it down to having a wonderful gute idea that would be something new for the store. Nothing to do with Faith herself.

Except that he'd overheard her father, Henry Kemp, discussing how he wasn't sure what Faith was going to do to support herself and the baby.

Daniel frowned over the memory. Henry had seemed to imply that she needed to support herself. That he needed help on the farm. These days, with good land being more and more scarce, all Henry had to do was throw a rock and he'd hit ten men willing to give up their factory jobs and work a farm.

But why did that mean Faith needed to support herself?

Not that it's any of your business, Daniel told himself firmly.

If the Kemps, Faith included, needed any help, they would reach out to the gmay or to close family and friends.

The front door opened with a thump that could be heard through the house. "We're here!" Joy's voice rang out cheerfully. Daniel smiled—or his version of it, at least. He'd forgotten tonight was family dinner night. Joshua and Joy lived in the dawdi haus, but Aaron and Hope lived with her family a short enough walk away. Each week on Friday, his brothers and their wives joined him and their parents for dinner. Mamm would be in heaven, as always.

IT HAD BEEN a week. A week of checking his bees more than they needed, given the season. A week of using that as an excuse to be near that field and see if Faith was there picking her flowers, then wondering why he'd bothered to look when she wasn't. Daniel was stocking some of Aaron's new carved wooden toys on the shelves in the shop. His brother was blessed with talent when it came to wood-working, which was why he'd left the store to become a carpenter making furniture in the Troyers' store down the street, while also continuing to provide toys for their family shop.

Daniel whistled softly to himself, not paying much attention to Joy and Hope, who were helping customers while Mamm was in the back room. As long as *he* didn't have to help customers, he was fine. He preferred working in the background, organizing and lifting, even working on the computer. They'd gotten permission from their bishop to have one for the shop.

He glanced at the shelves carrying honey from his bees. Gute business, but he'd never pressed Mamm or Dat about wanting to do more with it.

Now that Aaron had left the family business to be a carpenter, Joshua had left to train horses with Joy's dat, and both their wives now worked at the store in their places . . . Daniel didn't feel right asking to be in the shop less. Especially when bopplin started coming and Joy and Hope couldn't be in the shop as much. A Thankful Heart had been in their family for generations now. Someone had to carry on the tradition.

Daniel was the only brother left.

So he'd continue the way he had been and thank Gotte for his blessings. Even if he wanted different blessings. Who was he to question Gotte's plan?

"Wie gehts, Daniel?" a friendly voice said from behind him.

He paused with his hand on a tiny rocking horse, recognizing Faith's voice immediately and taking a moment to will his heart to beat a little slower.

Straightening, he turned to find her standing close

enough that he could smell the lavender of her shampoo. She was carrying a wreath made of dried flowers. He recognized the goldenrod she'd been picking when he'd found her in the field.

Mamm must have talked to her about arrangements for the store. Gute.

Faith was wearing a green dress today, which looked nice with her blue eyes and light brown hair. Faith had always reminded him of an adorable mouse, one he wanted to put in his pocket and keep safe. Daniel made a face, because even he knew that was not a comparison Faith would appreciate.

Except she mistook the frown, taking a small step back. "I didn't mean to bother you. I was looking for your mamm?"

She hadn't bothered him, but he didn't correct her. If he did that, she'd probably ask why he was frowning. "She's in the back."

Faith glanced in the direction in which he nodded, then back to him. Before she could say anything, Martha Gick and her two daughters, Barbara and Clara, walked in. That's when he saw it. The way Faith stiffened ever so slightly. If he hadn't been looking directly at her, he would have missed it.

After a nod of greeting, she turned away from the women and offered him a smile that didn't reach her eyes. This close, he could see the strain around her mouth yet. "Denki."

"Where's Rose?" he asked when she'd only taken three steps toward the back room.

She paused before turning back to him, her gaze flicking over his shoulder and back. "Rachel Price is watching her for me. Her dat gave me a ride into town and she came along."

Oh.

Another glance over his shoulder, then something in her expression shifted. Almost like she'd decided not to let herself be bothered. Suddenly she grinned and lifted the wreath. "Wish me luck."

He didn't look away until she called out tentatively before going through the curtains that blocked off the storefront from their back rooms. He'd always thought of Faith as one of those people who liked everyone, chatting easily, warm and welcoming and comfortable in her own skin. He glanced in Martha's direction. A bit of a stickler for strict rules, Martha had a tendency toward a sharp tongue. So, for that matter, did her daughters. Had Faith been on the receiving end of it?

None of my business.

Faith was a big girl and could take care of herself. Before he could turn back to the restocking, he caught both his sisters-in-law watching him from across the store.

Daniel raised his brows in question.

Joy and Hope exchanged a glance, and the sinking feeling in his gut told him he knew exactly what they were thinking. The last thing he needed was sisterly matchmakers.

Ignoring his sisters-in-law, Daniel went back to his stocking. So what if he was also listening for any sign of how it was going in the back room?

"Hi, Daniel."

He hid a wince and glanced over his shoulder at Clara Gick. Pretty as a picture in a purple dress with her honey blond hair tucked neatly under her kapp, she offered him a smile. She was always offering him smiles, and to help with the store, and to bring him a pie or treat.

"Hi," he said.

"I've burned clear through the wonderful beeswax candle you made me," she said.

He hadn't made it for her. If she had one, she'd bought it here. "Oh?"

She clasped her hands before her, lowering her gaze shyly. "Only I can't find more."

Right. He would have called Joy or Hope over to help, but both were engaged with the other Gick women. "We moved those," he said, then walked away, expecting her to follow. The candles had only been moved to the other side of the shelf, but he pointed.

"Denki," she said, color raising in her cheeks.

He went to return to what he'd been doing, only she cleared her throat. "If you don't mind my asking, are you dating Faith Kemp?"

Daniel blinked several times. While girls tended to try to catch his eye, they were rarely that direct. "No," he said.

"Oh." She directed her gaze to her shoes. "Gute. I'm glad. I mean for you. She's . . . well, she has a baby now."

Why would that matter?

She didn't give him a chance to find out, though, taking a candle from the shelf and walking back to her mother.

Shrugging off the moment, he went back to what he'd been doing and finished restocking Aaron's toys. He'd hardly picked up the first item before Rachel Price rushed into the store with a red-faced, crying Rose in her arms.

"Is Faith Kemp here?" she asked Hope in a flurry.

Hope pointed to the back room with wide eyes, no doubt because Rachel was visibly upset and had a big tear in the sleeve of her dress. "Is everything—"

Rachel rushed away before Hope could finish asking her question.

Without hesitation, Daniel followed her into the back room. She was handing Rose over to Faith. "I'm so sorry," Rachel was saying.

"No, no," Faith assured her. "I'll be fine. Go look after your dat."

Seeing him, his mamm explained, "Zachariah Price's buggy was hit by a car."

With Rose inside? His gaze shot to the baby now in Faith's arms, but she appeared unharmed, except for all the crying. Faith, though, had gone pale as she checked Rose from top to tail.

"Rose and I just got knocked about a bit, but we're fine," Rachel said.

After another second, Faith nodded, holding the infant close and jiggling her. Reassured the baby wasn't injured, Daniel turned to Rachel. "I'll help."

But she shook her head. "Plenty of helpers already, but Dat needs to go to the hospital. We think he broke his arm, and the buggy is busted up something awful."

"Go be with your dat." Faith laid a hand on her friend's shoulder. "I can find my own way home."

"Denki," Rachel said, then rushed away.

Despite what she'd said about plenty of help, Daniel followed her all the same. Another pair of hands never went amiss. Sure enough, they needed another man to help roll the buggy with one busted-up wheel out of the street and down a nearby alley, where it would be out of the way until it could be retrieved.

By the time he returned to the shop, only Mamm was in the back room.

"I helped get the buggy out of the street," he told her.

She patted his arm. "Always doing the right thing, my Daniel."

"Where's Faith?"

He didn't like the way his mother's brows beetled with concern at the question. "Rose wouldn't settle, poor bop-pli, and so she decided to walk home." His mamm tsked, shaking her head.

The Kemp farm, while relatively close to town, was farther out than their own house and would take her a good long while to reach by foot.

"I'll go find her and give her a ride."

Mamm brightened at that. "What a wunderbaar idea. I'll feel much better knowing she got home faster and safely."

He didn't bother to do more than nod before heading out the back entrance of the shop, which led into an alley the width of a car, across from which a wide fenced-in field sat full of Amish buggies and horses. The Troyers, one of the first families with a storefront in town years and years before, had had the sense to purchase an open field that backed up behind the shops. Amish used the field to park, and those who worked in town might even unhitch their horses.

Which meant it took a little time to get Frank hitched up and head out, hopefully in the direction in which Faith had chosen to walk. If she had used any shortcuts through fields or woods, he'd never find her.

He didn't breathe easy until he spotted a woman in a green dress and white sweater up ahead on the side of the road. Faith stepped into the grass, no doubt at the sound of the distinct *clop, clop, clop* of his horse's hooves, eyebrows lifting when he slowed Frank to a stop beside her. "Get in," he said.

Only she glanced back toward town with a frown. "Are you headed home?"

"No."

The frown deepened and she absently patted Rose's back. "I hope you didn't come all this way for me. I'll be fine."

"It's no bother." That's what his mother always said when people protested a kindness.

It didn't seem to work. "Nae, really. I'm sure you have so much work, and I—"

"Faith." She stopped talking at the sound of her name. Only he had no idea what argument might make her get in the buggy. "I'm worried about the baby," he tried.

Rose wasn't crying anymore, so that excuse seemed awfully weak. He cleared his throat and tried again. "She must have been wonderful scared."

Faith rubbed her cheek against the top of the baby's head, then finally gave in. "Denki. I appreciate it."

Setting the brake, he got out. When Rose saw him, she immediately held out her arms, opening and closing her chubby baby fingers and leaning so hard toward him, Faith had to hurriedly scoop her closer or risk dropping her.

Giving the baby a chuck under the chin, he helped them both into the buggy. But when he got in himself, sitting beside Faith on the front bench, Rose reached for him again, whimpering a little.

Faith chuckled. "I think you have a new girlfriend."

Which sent heat up his neck and into his face. Rose continued to reach for him, straining against Faith's hold on her. She truly was precious with those big blue eyes, just like her aendi's—darker hair, though, and a stubborn little chin.

"Kumme." He drew the baby into his arms and handed

Faith the reins. With a happy gurgle Rose settled right down on his lap, holding on to his forearm as he wrapped it around her belly.

Faith raised her eyebrows, but said nothing, merely snapping the reins to get them started. "You should be honored," she murmured, not looking away from the horse and road. "She doesn't like to be held by just anyone."

Daniel glanced down at Rosie, who turned her head to stare right back at him. He wrinkled his nose, and she gave him a gummy grin in return. He was pretty sure she knew she was adorable.

"Your mamm is going to sell my flower arrangements and wreaths in the store," Faith mentioned after several minutes of silence broken only by the rhythmic clopping of Frank's hooves.

Daniel nodded. He'd figured as much.

"I have a feeling I have you to thank." This time she peeked at him out of the corner of her eye.

He tried to quash the small swell of satisfaction. He hadn't done that much. Faith's craftsmanship had sold the idea for his mother. "All I did was mention Joy's flowers to Mamm."

"Well . . . denki all the same."

He nodded.

Another small silence, which she was the one to break again. "I hope you didn't hurt yourself moving that buggy."

She'd seen? "No."

Suddenly Rose was no longer happy to be sitting facing out. Wiggling and pushing against him, she managed to turn to face him, then pulled herself up with his shirt and reached for his face with those grabby hands. Daniel lowered his head so she could reach better, and she put her hands on his cheeks, then gurgled baby talk at him.

He listened until she finished and was looking at him expectantly like she was waiting for his reply.

Overly conscious of Faith right beside him, Daniel said nothing.

Except Rose wasn't having any of that, gurgling in such a way that he thought she was asking him to answer her earlier questions.

"Were you wonderful scared when the car hit that buggy?" The words were out of his mouth before he thought to say them.

Rose's eyes widened a little, like she was surprised, too. Then she gooed and gaahed as though telling him of the traumatic event. Daniel even found himself nodding along.

"I hope you didn't hurt yourself," he said when she paused.

"I checked her over."

Faith's voice was tight enough that he glanced her way to find her sitting stiff backed. Why? "I wouldn't have left to help with the buggy if I didn't think you'd already made sure she was unharmed."

That earned him a longer glance. One he held.

Faith blew out a small breath. "Sorry. I get oonbunch . . . a lot of . . . advice."

Advice? "About Rosie?"

The nickname slipped out naturally. It suited the child.

"That . . . and other things," Faith murmured vaguely as she turned Frank down the graveled drive, bracketed by white fences, that led to her parents' house.

"I think you're amazing with her."

She was. He'd seen her with Rosie during church and around town. The child was always clean and cared for, but more than that, she was tickled and kissed and hugged. Affection in public didn't come easily for the Amish, who tended to reserve such things for private family time. But Faith, he remembered, had always been a hugger.

He turned to Rosie. "You are very lucky to be loved so much."

Which seemed like a silly thing to say even as the words were coming out. But a glance at Faith showed him she'd relaxed. Was even smiling a tiny bit.

A smile that dropped away as they both spied a car parked in the graveled drive right in front of the Kemps' house. The Kemps didn't sell anything on their farm that would bring Englischers there looking to buy. So who was here?

"Looks like we have a visitor," Faith said, her tone a clear indication that she wasn't expecting anyone.

Chapter Three

❋

WHEN FAITH GOT out of the buggy and reached for Rose, she expected Daniel to hand the baby over, then leave, finished being the helpful person he was and returning to his shop. But he didn't. Instead, still holding Rose, he got down, clearly intending to follow her inside.

At the same time, a young Amish man around Daniel's age—strong and handsome with sandy brown hair and pale blue eyes, though along with what Faith thought of as a mushy jaw—stepped outside behind an older gentleman who was, by the kind of clothes he wore, clearly the owner of the car.

Immediately the younger man's gaze was drawn to Faith and his steps slowed.

She couldn't quite pin down what in his gaze made her pause. Something about the way he inspected her the same way people who came into Daniel's shop probably inspected the items on their shelves. Like he was trying to decide if she were worth the cost to take home with him.

In the next moment, though, he smiled. He had a nice smile that reached his eyes, making them crinkle around the edges the same way her dat's did, thanks to all his years farming in the sun. "You must be Faith," he said.

This man was harmless. He hadn't glanced at Daniel yet. *Not the best manners, though.*

The front door opened farther, and Faith's parents both appeared, beaming at her in such a nervous way that, standing quietly beside her holding Rosie, even Daniel raised his brows.

"Oh!" her mother exclaimed. "You're home."

Mamm flicked a glance at Daniel and blinked as if surprised to find him there, then frowning. "I thought Zachariah Price took you to town."

"There was an accident with Zachariah's buggy, and Daniel kindly brought me home—"

"That was thoughtful of you," her mother interrupted, apparently not quite catching the part about the accident.

"Is everyone unharmed?" her father asked in his slow, deliberate drawl.

"Zachariah may have a broken arm, and the Prices' buggy is damaged, but thankfully nothing more serious than that," Faith said.

She didn't mention Rosie having been in the buggy at the time. The last thing she needed was another lecture about caring for her baby properly. To her relief, Daniel didn't mention it either.

"I'm glad it wasn't worse," Dat said before waving at the man. "This is Malachi Eash. Do you remember the Eashes?"

Faith dredged her memory. "Didn't they used to own the farm down the road?"

Her mother beamed again. What were all these smiles

about? Not that Mamm was ever unkind, but a smiler she was not.

"Jah," Dat said. "They sold their farm and went to live with their oldest daughter. Malachi is Loraine's youngest son."

"Nice to meet you," Faith said.

The way he smiled, though, had her second-guessing herself again. Something was going on here that she wasn't entirely figuring out.

Dat hooked his thumbs in his suspenders and rocked back on his heels. "Malachi has been looking for his own farm to buy, because there isn't enough land for all his brothers and him to share the work on theirs."

Was he going to stay with her parents while he looked around here to buy a farm? She hadn't heard of any for sale recently.

Dat bent a pointed stare on her, though his voice was gentle. "I've sold him our farm."

Sold the farm.

Faith's heart dropped to the bottom of her gut with a dull plop. The words rattled around in her head as she stared at her parents. Not that she wanted to run the farm, or could. Dat had never taught her how.

A thousand questions crowded into her head. "When?"

Her fater seemed to understand the question. "We set this up over a year ago, long before you came home."

Over a year . . . Why hadn't they told her?

"Where will you go?" she asked in a voice that sounded unsteady to her own ears.

Dat's expression turned sheepish. "We only sold the place on the condition that your mater and I live in the dawdi haus the rest of our lives and he pay me to help work the farm as long as I am able."

I'm about to lose my home?

She couldn't force the question of where she would go out of her mouth. The dawdi haus had only one bedroom, so she couldn't stay with her parents there, and she couldn't stay in the house with an unmarried man. Raising Mercy's baby already had her under suspicion.

I'll have to find my own place.

Unfortunately, she'd seen the rents around here—on the rare occasion places went up for rent—and she was fairly certain she couldn't afford it on her own. Maybe the flowers for the Kanagys' shop would sell well. Would it be enough to support her and a child, though? Especially if she had to buy or rent a home?

Malachi, suddenly all confidence and swagger, stepped forward to shake her hand. "I'm sure this is a shock, but it's nice to meet you. Your parents wrote and told me all about you."

Really? Because they hadn't even hinted at any of this to her.

The look she shot them must have said all that, because her mater rushed into speech. "That's why we've been introducing you to eligible men."

All those widowers with mouths to feed? That's why they'd been coming around?

Faith wanted to close her eyes, cry for a bit, and sit in private and figure out what to do next. The fact that Daniel was standing beside her should have been . . . well . . . mortifying. But somehow his presence was the only thing keeping her from having a breakdown right about now.

She went to pull away from Malachi's handshake, except he grasped a little tighter, laying his other hand over the top in a familiar way. "This is very forward of me, but with a little one to care for and a need for a home, and with me starting a new life and looking to find a wife and start a family now that I own a farm, it strikes me that we could be an answer to each other's prayers."

Forget disappointment. For the first time maybe ever, Faith suddenly understood what Mercy used to talk about before jumping the fence, when she'd say she felt trapped by her life. Faith had just met this man, and he was . . . what? Proposing? Already? He didn't know her at all.

Worse, her first instinct was to turn to Daniel and try to explain that not only had she not known about the farm being sold, but she didn't want him to think she'd agreed to this situation, or think she was taken, or . . .

Was this why he'd convinced his mamm to give her work? Had he known about the sale of the farm and her new homeless state? Did everyone know?

"I—"

Malachi's smile turned suddenly charming and a tad bit chagrined. "I'm sorry. I tossed all of that at you at once. I've had a while to think about it."

She didn't dare glance at her parents. They'd been plotting this for a while because they thought she needed a husband and couldn't get her own? Or maybe because they worried that if she knew, she'd run away, like Mercy had.

But Faith was made of sterner stuff. Living with her family in her familiar Amish community was all she'd ever wanted. Was this the only way she could keep that dream?

"Let me start over," Malachi offered. "It would honor me if you would consider getting to know me with marriage as a possibility in the future."

Which at least was a kinder way to put it. Maybe he was

nervous. Faith licked suddenly dry lips, wrestling with a new disappointment. Because if it had been Daniel standing in front of her offering, she would . . .

But he wasn't and wouldn't ever.

"I would love to be friends," she finally said. "And I will . . . consider the other."

Malachi's smile—a nice smile for sure and certain, with straight white teeth—widened. "Denki. That's all I ask."

Her mater heaved a relieved sigh. "Malachi has agreed to live in the dawdi haus for a short time until things are decided."

They'd worked it all out, hadn't they?

Suddenly Daniel cleared his throat. "I'd best be getting back."

He handed Rosie, who gave a protesting squawk, back to Faith, nodded at her parents and Malachi, then got in his buggy and drove away.

Faith watched after him, feeling like she'd lost something precious.

Which was silly. You couldn't lose what you didn't have, and she wasn't even sure what she would be losing.

Turning back to face the total stranger who'd basically proposed and who now owned the farm and house where she lived, she forced a pleasant smile to her lips. "Maybe we should go inside."

"Hey," the man who'd driven Malachi here called out. "You going to get the rest of your stuff?"

Malachi at least finally stopped staring at her like she was a prize pumpkin in a county fair. Faith took the opportunity to head inside, her pleased mother and stoic father trailing after her.

"Be nice to him," her mother whisper-hissed at her.

"Our Faith is nice to awlee eppa," her father said before she could answer. To everyone.

She tried to be, and Malachi had done nothing wrong. Not really. "He's obviously a gute man. Of course I'll be nice."

Which at least made Mamm relax, nodding and smiling to herself as though this marriage were already a done deal. She'd probably moved herself and Dat into the dawdi haus in her head already.

Ach du lieva. What am I going to do?

Rosie gave a little cry. The one that usually preceded a tantrum. So Faith made her way up the stairs to her room, where Rose's crib and changing table were. The baby needed to be fed, and it was time for her nap. Then Faith needed to start working on her first flower arrangements for A Thankful Heart. Regardless of what happened with Malachi, she'd pursue this new opportunity yet. New business never hurt anyone.

"Can I help?" Her new suitor suddenly appeared beside her. In her bedroom.

Not for long, though.

"Nae, though I appreciate the offer. Rose is a bit shy of strangers." Unless they were Daniel.

"I'm wonderful gute with babies," Malachi insisted.

She glanced at him. So did Rose before looking back at Faith like, *Are you seriously going to listen to him?*

Faith shrugged. "Then denki. I could use a moment to freshen up. Her diaper needs changing."

Was it heartless that she breezed right out of the room on a wail from her niece, leaving the poor man to live up to his boast on his own? Probably. He'd only been trying to be helpful and to get to know her, and Rosie, too. But she needed a moment by herself to . . . breathe. In the bathroom, she stood, hands on her hips and mind spinning with everything that had happened today.

The opportunity from Ruth Kanagy, followed by a shock of fear for her baby, then concern for the Prices, the drive with Daniel, and now the farm sold out from under her feet and Malachi's proposal for her future.

That would be a lot for any girl to take in. Wouldn't it?

Was this Gotte's way of carving out an obvious and easy path for her life? Providing for her future? Maybe. It didn't feel quite right, but Gotte's ways were mysterious. Who was she to doubt Him when He laid a future right in her lap? She'd been praying and praying for guidance, and here it was.

A future.

A gute man and the chance to live out her days on the farm where she'd grown up. Providing for her and Rosie. Her parents would be happy. And maybe the naysayers and doubters in her community would stop watching her so closely.

"You'd be a fool not to at least consider him," she told herself sternly.

Then she nodded as if to confirm she was right, even though the knots in her stomach tied themselves tighter. Rosie's cries escalated, echoing through the house, and Faith hurried back to her room to find the baby diapered and dressed and quieting as Malachi bounced her in his arms.

See, Gotte seemed to be saying. *Trust me.*

DANIEL TRIED NOT to stare across the rows of Amish gathered for Sunday Gmay to where Faith sat on the benches opposite, grouped with the other young mothers. She was jiggling Rose, who refused to stay still or quiet like the other children. More like Mercy than Faith, if he recalled correctly. Their mother had probably scolded Mercy every other Sunday after Gmay let out during their entire growing-up years.

He glanced at Faith again and had to swallow back a smile as Rosie pulled at the string of Faith's white kapp, yanking it clean off her head, pins and all. Faith gasped, mortification making the color rise in her cheeks. An Amish woman's head was not supposed to go uncovered. They wore their prayer coverings as the scriptures called them to, as a sign of respect and obedience to Gotte.

Luckily one of the other mothers took Rose so Faith could right herself with busy hands. That baby was a handful, for sure and certain, but Faith was so good with her. Unending patience. He didn't know what made him glance toward Martha Gick, who was sitting with the married women whose children were grown, but he found her watching Faith with a small sneer curling her lip. She turned her head only to catch Daniel's gaze on her. He didn't look away. He didn't glower or glare. He simply looked at her steadily, hoping Gotte might use him to remind the woman of the Amish way—including forgiveness and kindness to others.

After a moment Martha glanced down at the Ausbund hymnal in her lap.

Another glance at Faith, and he straightened in his seat, because she was looking at him now with something akin to gratefulness in her blue eyes. Or was he being verhuddelt?

It wasn't proper to stare, especially during church, so he

glanced away. Unfortunately he glanced right at Malachi, who was watching the bishop speak, listening with what appeared to be perfect, pious intent.

Clearly Gotte's reminder to Daniel that he should be listening and not paying any attention to Faith Kemp. She had a boyfriend.

Well . . . not a boyfriend, exactly. Not a fiancé either. Maybe "beau" would be more accurate, if a bit old-fashioned. Still, Malachi had basically proposed.

It was none of Daniel's business, though. He knew that. It was not the first time he'd been too late. If anything, he should be happy for Faith. Malachi Eash appeared to be an answer for her. A future for her. He just couldn't seem to make himself feel that way, though.

Perhaps progressively, Daniel had always considered marriage should be saved for love.

Not entirely a practical, Amish way of looking at things, but his own parents had married for love, and he wanted what they had. Nothing less would do, which was why he hadn't married or dated all that much up to now. He'd rather be a dedicated bachelor than end up with a girl he couldn't look at the way his dat looked at his mamm.

But Faith had Rosie to consider. Practical was her only option.

A truth that should have put a stop to any more concerns or thoughts for Faith Kemp. So after church, why he reached out and gently took Rosie from her arms as she was moving around the table where he sat, helping to serve the meal, he had no idea. She'd been balancing the baby on one hip while filling water glasses with the other.

"Um . . ." Faith looked about to protest.

"I'll hold her while you're busy," he offered.

Rosie, bless her, made a happy gurgle and patted his

arm enthusiastically. Faith's lips twisted, like she was un-decided, but she gave in after a glance at the curious faces watching them.

"Denki. I won't be long." Then she scurried off.

He was silently kicking himself until he noticed the way Faith seemed determined to be a more productive helper than all the other women combined. As if she had something to prove. Maybe she thought she did, with the likes of Martha Gick judging her every move.

Daniel bounced Rosie on his knee and kept his plate out of her reach as he picked at his own food. The baby was a mover and didn't like to stay still, so he stood up, walking away before turning and walking back for a bite, repeating that process every few minutes. That seemed to do the trick.

On one of his trips away from the table, Clara Gick appeared in front of him, wreathed in smiles. "You are won-derful gute with bopplin, Daniel," she said, though maybe "simpered" was closer.

Before he could open his mouth to say . . . well, he hadn't come up with what to say . . . she leaned nearer. "But a woman should take care of her own boppli, don't you think?"

Any hint of the polite but succinct thanks he had been planning to utter he swallowed down. "Nae," he said with-out any tone whatsoever. "I don't think so."

Clara's expression drooped. "Oh." But she seemed to brighten in the next moment. "I could hold her for you. That way you can eat."

Something she should have offered to do for Faith.

Daniel actually turned his body away so that he was between her and Rose before he even realized what he was doing. "Nae, denki."

"Oh, but—"

"Rose and I are perfectly content." On that he left her standing there and moved back to his spot at the table to take another bite.

"No woman can resist a man with a baby," Joshua teased, watching Clara over Daniel's shoulder. "I can practically hear the wedding bells that áre sounding in her head."

Daniel glanced over his shoulder, not wanting to hurt anyone's feelings. "Not for me. Not with Clara, at least."

"Maybe you should go stay with friends in Shipshewana to find yourself a wife." Aaron was getting in on it now. Just because both his bruders were so happily married themselves, they thought every man without a wife must be miserable.

"You're looking for a wife?" The sound of Faith at his back stilled everything inside him. She'd heard that?

Daniel turned slowly to find her watching with an expression that he couldn't quite place. "Nae. Or, jah. I mean . . ."

Amusement seemed to creep over her. "Which is it?"

"Both." He was not explaining this well.

But she nodded sagely all the same. "I understand."

He had a feeling she did.

"What about you?" he asked. Then almost bit his tongue off because he'd forgotten, for a second, that his bruders were right there, listening with avid attention.

Faith's gaze flicked in Malachi's direction, and she opened her mouth. He almost thought she was going to say she was in the same position as he. Instead, she pasted a bright smile on, one that no longer reached her eyes. "Every girl would like to find a gute, caring husband. Especially when she has a boppli to care for."

She reached for Rose. He handed the baby over with more reluctance than he would have thought possible, especially when Rosie protested, her little cries tugging at his heart.

Faith left to go sit with the women to eat.

Are you going to marry him?

The words had almost slipped from his lips. But imagining his brothers' teasing if they heard him say such a thing, he'd gritted his teeth to stop from speaking out loud.

It would be inappropriate to ask anyway. Faith already had a future mapped out for herself and the baby, and that's what mattered. It was none of his business.

Apparently, he never learned where she was concerned.

Chapter Four

✳

FAITH WAS SETTLING Rosie into her crib for her morning nap when Malachi called her name up the stairs. Shouted, more like. The man didn't seem to know how to walk around to find people, instead choosing to stand in one place and raise his voice. Didn't his mamm teach him better than that? In fact, she was surprised her own mamm hadn't corrected him yet. But he was a guest, of sorts, so she probably wouldn't.

Besides, as bad habits went, if that was the worst of his, then Faith would be lucky to marry him. After all, he did know what he was doing with babies, and he'd helped wash up last night even when they'd told him he didn't have to, and he was wonderful gute with her father on the farm. Dat had a new spring in his step. She hadn't realized how tired he was at the end of the day . . . until he wasn't.

Not wanting to wake Rosie, she didn't answer. She simply finished tucking the baby in, then closed the door softly behind her. Malachi was on his third shout by the time Faith hurried down the steps, and he cut himself off mid-yell, expression turning rapidly from huffy annoyance to smiling charm. "I was calling for you," he said.

Was that petulance in his voice? She mentally waved off the suspicion. "I was putting Rose down for a nap and couldn't answer."

"Oh," he said. "That's oll recht, then."

It wouldn't have been otherwise? What if she'd been using the restroom? What if she'd been in the shower and simply couldn't hear him?

Grace. She needed to give him grace. "Did you need me for something?"

Now his smile was more sincere. "I thought we might take a picnic lunch out on the property."

Maybe he was trying to be romantic? After all, he'd said he wanted to court her, and she'd mostly decided to let herself be open to the possibility of marriage with him.

Mostly.

So she smiled back. "That sounds lovely."

He rubbed his hands together with a boyish grin. "Great. When you have the food ready, I'll meet you at the barn with a blanket. I have a few things to help your dat with first."

So *she* was getting their romantic picnic together? The farm came first, so Malachi wasn't being idle, but a little surprise she didn't have to make herself would have been nice.

She supposed it didn't matter. If Malachi had made it, she'd have had to show him where things were anyway. "It might take me a while, and we'd have to wait for Rosie to finish her nap."

He frowned. "Oh. I thought we'd go, just the two of us."

Faith bit the inside of her cheek. Of course he would

assume that. After all, how romantic could a picnic be with a baby in tow? "I'll see if Mamm can watch her."

Smiles returned and he nodded. "I'll see you soon."

He was out the back door before she could nod in response, and Faith watched from the window over the kitchen sink as he crossed to the barn, where her dat must be waiting. Malachi had a nice walk. He was tall and broad-shouldered, with strength in each step. Strength that came from working every single day on the land Gotte had blessed them with. Steady. Reliable. A provider.

And handsome—not that looks were supposed to matter.

But they make it easier, Mercy used to say.

With a nod to herself that she was doing the right thing, despite the knots in her stomach that wouldn't untie themselves, Faith went to ask Mamm to watch Rose. Something her mother was delighted to do, given the reason. Then she got started putting together a picnic.

Half an hour later, the heavy basket holding all the food and drinks she'd packed hanging over one arm, she entered the barn. The familiar scents of hay and horses and well-oiled leather surrounded her as she moved from space to space in search of Malachi. She found him outside in the back, looking over the hogs with her dat.

"It's certainly an idea," Dat was saying slowly, though the look of doubt scrunching his eyebrows over his faded blue eyes didn't quite match the enthusiasm with which Malachi was nodding.

"Redd up?" Faith called out, and both men turned to face her.

"Can we talk about this more later?" Malachi asked her father.

Her dat was mid-nod when he spied her basket. "What's this about?"

She shot Malachi a questioning glance. Had he not discussed this time off with her father first? "A picnic."

Unlike her mother, who had glowed at the idea—in her own understated way, at any rate—Dat glanced between them, totally unsmiling. Though he didn't tend to be a smiler anyway. "I see."

"I'll be back to start on the southern field in a few hours," Malachi assured him with all the confidence of someone who fully expected to get his way.

And he should, Faith reminded herself for the umpteenth time. *This is his farm now.*

"Oll recht" was all Dat said.

Malachi took the heavy basket from her arm and headed back through the barn. As Faith made to pass by her father, trailing after Malachi, he put a gentle hand on her arm and kissed her cheek. She blinked at him, because her dat wasn't typically a physically affectionate man. He didn't say anything, though, just nodded for her to go on.

Malachi talked most of the way through the fields, and she wasn't too surprised when he led her over the ladder built into the fence to the outer, untilled fields where she'd bumped into Daniel not all that long ago. Today was warmer, though, and less windy, the butter-yellow sunlight heating the top of her head through her kapp.

Eventually they ended up under the same wide oak tree where she'd laid Rosie before, and Faith spread out the blanket she'd brought, then started unpacking all the food while Malachi sat and watched her. Finally satisfied, she handed him a plate. "Help yourself."

He shook his head, smiling gently. "I like watching you. You move with grace. Why don't you dish up anything you'd think I'd like?"

I have no idea what you would like.

She barely managed to keep the words to herself; after all, she didn't know him well, which was why she'd filled the basket with a large variety of foods. And the "watching her" thing . . . well . . . she guessed that was him trying to be romantic, but she didn't find it to be. If anything, it made her self-conscious.

But he's trying. That's what matters.

Biting her lip to keep from saying all of what was in her head, she decided to make them the same plate, handed him his, then settled in to eat her own.

Though she tried not to stare, it still didn't go unnoticed how Malachi took a small bite of each item, then only ate the German potato salad Mamm had made a few nights before. Nothing that Faith had made. Suddenly, she found she wasn't all that hungry and picked at her own food.

"I bet you are wondering what your dat and I were talking about when you found us," he said around a bite of potatoes.

Not really. "Mmmm . . ." she hummed noncommittally, trying to remind herself that she should be interested. She was considering marrying this man and running a farm with him. Would they talk of such things each night after the kinder were in bed, or perhaps over dinner as a family?

"I want to replace the tobacco crops with hemp."

Faith stilled with a bite of noodles halfway to her mouth. Even the Amish had learned the terrible effects of tobacco products, but many had been growing it on their farms for generations, her family included. It was one of the better crops for them. What did Dat make of this? He wasn't one who handled change well.

"Why hemp?" She lowered her fork to ask, proud that she didn't start in on questions Malachi would probably find offensive. Like why he wanted to make such drastic changes when he'd been there only a short time. Why not run the farm for a year or two before making big, sweeping changes?

"Indiana has only recently legalized the growing of hemp commercially," Malachi explained. "Though there are some rules."

"Like what?"

"Nothing to concern yourself over."

Faith gritted her teeth.

What would Gotte think if she dumped the potato salad over Malachi's handsome head? Not a proper Amish response, she was well aware. The extra-good girl she'd been before haring off after Mercy wouldn't have even considered it. Maybe being out in the wider world *had* changed her more than she realized.

Malachi was still going on about the hemp, thankfully oblivious to her very non-peaceful thoughts. "As a cover crop, hemp enhances soil health by shading out weeds—reducing the need for herbicides—and adding diversity to crop rotations. Hemp is also versatile in the market, with thousands of uses for its seed, oil, and fiber. Plus, the market is growing by the year."

"You've clearly thought this out." Maybe she was being hasty, or even downright judgmental.

His chest puffed up a little. "My older brother Matthew says I'm quite the farmer, though I would never say so myself."

The attempt at humility fell a tad short to her ears. Which was probably why a soft, rumbled "Wie gehts?" from nearby had her looking away with relief.

Relief that turned into something warmer at the sight of Daniel approaching through the tall brown grasses. *I'm only happy because he's a welcome interruption*, she tried to convince herself.

"We're gute," she answered, getting to her feet.

With only a splash of hesitation, Malachi followed suit, and they walked over to meet Daniel in the field. The two men nodded at each other.

"David, isn't it?" Malachi asked.

"Daniel," he corrected.

Daniel didn't seem bothered, as usual. Faith, however, had to hide her frown.

"Sorry. I have a terrible memory for names" was his excuse. Then he cocked his head, brows drawing together. "What are you doing all the way out here?

"Tending his bees," Faith answered without thought.

"Jah," Daniel confirmed and shot her a smile. A small one, but for Daniel that was a lot, and the warmth from his arrival that hadn't quite left her crawled into her cheeks.

DANIEL CAUGHT MALACHI'S confused frown, but only because he'd shifted his gaze away from the pretty pink in Faith's cheeks. From the weather, or from her company?

"Bees?" Malachi asked. "Why are your bees on the Kemps' property?" He even set his feet wide, arms crossed, almost as though he had an intention to deal with this situation right away.

"They aren't," Daniel assured him.

Faith's soon-to-be-fiancé's lips flattened, consternation flashing in his eyes.

Daniel said nothing more.

"A small part of the Kanagys' property abuts ours . . .

errr . . . yours," Faith jumped in to explain. Probably taking pity on Malachi, who was new to the area, after all. Although the man should probably know where his own property began and ended. Still, Daniel should have been more gracious and explained more. But for once in his life, he didn't feel like being gracious. "Daniel's bees are right at the property line on their side."

"I see." Malachi's frown didn't let up.

Daniel glanced at Faith right when a butterfly landed on her shoulder. It was large and mostly black, with a large band of white making a U shape and smaller bands of orange and blue along the bottom of its wings.

"Faith, stay still," Daniel said quietly.

Rather than question why, she did as he asked, merely raising her eyebrows in question. Stepping closer, Daniel slowly lifted his hand, putting a finger in front of the gentle bug. The butterfly stepped up and he slowly pulled his hand back so that she could see.

"A white admiral," she whispered.

She knew what kind it was? Daniel did, too, but only because he paid attention to the other creatures that might share food with his bees.

Faith stepped nearer to Daniel, close enough that her skirt brushed against his pant legs. She bent over, peering closer as the butterfly flapped its wings slowly, making no effort to fly off. Daniel, though, watched Faith, enjoying the unadulterated joy she was showing.

"Isn't he beautiful?" She lifted her gaze to ask him but trailed off as she caught sight of his gaze on her.

Daniel didn't want to look away.

"You'll probably want to move your bees soon." Malachi broke the moment and the butterfly launched into the air, flying off into the trees.

Faith took a hasty step away, stuffing her arms behind her back as she faced her soon-to-be-fiancé, who didn't seem to have noticed anything, based on his expression. The problem was that Daniel had noticed too much. Like the lavender scent of her hair, and the dark blue ring around her irises, and the small scratch on the back of her hand—had she tripped again?—and the wisp of hair that had escaped her kapp at the back of her neck that looked so soft.

He should be ashamed of himself, when Malachi was standing right there, noticing or not.

Ach du lieva.

What was Malachi talking about again? Moving his bees? "Um . . . why?"

"Because I intend to till this field for planting in the spring."

That caught every bit of Daniel's attention. This field was the main source of his bees' food. He could move them safely enough, but nowhere was quite as abundant with flowering plants.

Malachi was still going on. "I'm going to try growing hemp, and I want to use this field as a test base. That means we need to prep it now, so that we are ready to plant in the spring after the ground thaws."

"Hemp, huh?" That was all he said, but that was all he needed to say. Not that his tone was in any way rude, but all the same he also didn't try to hide that he wasn't as immediately impressed with the idea as Malachi clearly thought he should be.

Which made Malachi bristle and Faith wince. Seeing that, a pang of guilt and disappointment in his own behavior pinched around the region of his heart. Malachi was set to be part of this community and should be made to feel welcome.

"I was just telling Faith all about the benefits of hemp," Malachi said, then went off on a long, drawn-out explanation.

Which Daniel listened to quietly and without comment, though from time to time, his glance would stray in Faith's direction. She listened with apparent interest, but her fingers were busy pleating the apron she wore over her dress. What was she thinking?

Finally Malachi wound down, crossing his arms and giving a nod as if that put paid to the subject.

Daniel waited a beat, in case the other man thought of anything to add, then said, "I assume you are aware that in Indiana last year, over twenty percent of the crops of hemp had to be burned because they were too high in THC according to the new law allowing commercial growth here?"

Hundreds of thousands of dollars of crops lost, statewide. Malachi was probably wondering how a shop owner who tended bees and didn't farm knew that. He took a moment of hemming and hawing. "I've researched it thoroughly," he finally said.

Daniel nodded, trying to be more cordial and not argue any further. "I figured as much."

He caught the way Faith was studying him. Had she caught his rude manners? He hoped not. His mamm would be mortified. Plus, Daniel wanted Faith's good opinion. Malachi, at least, took his words at face value and gave a self-satisfied smirk.

"When do you plan to till this field?" Daniel asked, already calculating in his head when he needed to move his bees.

"End of the month," Malachi answered.

Faith raised her eyebrows. "Dat agreed to that already?"

Malachi grimaced, but they all knew what he was thinking. He didn't have to ask her dat.

The way Faith buttoned her lips closed, Daniel suspected she was berating herself for making Malachi feel bad about it. Daniel cleared his throat. "I'll have my bees moved before then."

They wouldn't be going out to forage much now anyway, as they were already getting ready to overwinter, but better to be safe than sorry by moving them now, rather than waiting for spring. He didn't have much of a choice, regardless.

"Can we help with moving them?" Faith offered. "I'd love to see how you work with the bees."

Did she mean that? The interest in her soft blue eyes seemed to say she was. Had she watched Malachi with the same interest when he was talking about the hemp? Daniel couldn't be sure.

"I'm sure it won't take much to move them," Malachi assured her.

Which wasn't necessarily true, depending on where he moved them. If he moved them three feet each day, the few foragers left would find the hives again easily enough. By the end of the month he could have them in a better location with minimal disruption. But that was a lot of boxes to move each day by himself, especially between working in the shop and doing his other chores. He wouldn't mind enjoying Faith's company while they talked about bees.

"Actually—" Suddenly he spied the picnic paraphernalia spread over the blanket under the oak.

Oh, sis yucht.

They'd been on a date, and he'd interrupted, like the lumbering clod he was. Not only interrupted, but the way he'd looked at Faith . . . His face might as well be on fire. "Denki for the offer, but no help needed." He pretended not to see the disappointment in Faith's frown. "I'd better be getting home."

With a nod for them both, he turned and forced feet that suddenly felt clunky to take him back across the field. He'd seen the white of Faith's white kapp when he'd been checking his bees and had come over to say hello. It was the polite thing to do, and his mamm had taught him proper manners.

At least that's what he'd told himself.

Right up until he'd noticed all those things about Faith and then realized that he'd interrupted a date. His gut was all twisted up over the idea, when he should be happy for Faith. Obviously, he should move on—not that he had anything to move on from. Maybe his brothers were right and he should go to Shipshewana to try to find a fraa. His brothers were happy. He saw that every time he was around them and their wives. He saw his parents' marriage as well, an example of love in the home. Faith was about to be married herself, not that that should make a difference.

It was time.

Why didn't he feel compelled to act on it, then?

Chapter Five

✳

THANKFULLY, THE NEXT time Faith needed to go into town, Mamm was able to watch Rosie, and Dat didn't need the buggy, which allowed Faith to deliver her first batch of flower arrangements to A Thankful Heart on her own. Nerves danced in her stomach like the first snowflakes of a winter flurry.

She glanced back at the arrangements stacked on the floor of the buggy. *I hope these are what Ruth was looking for.*

Carefully she directed her horse up the narrow back alley behind all the shops until she found the right place. That was where she'd been told to pull up when she had goods to deliver. Setting the brake and the horse, she got out and knocked on the door that had A THANKFUL HEART stenciled over the generically tan paint that matched all the other doors back here.

A second later it swung open and Hope Kanagy, Aaron's wife, stuck her head out and grinned. "Hi, Faith."

Hope had only ever been kind to her since she'd returned—so had Joy, Joshua's wife—so it seemed silly that a thimbleful of anticlimax struck her first. Maybe because she'd pictured Daniel opening the door. That was all. She was just surprised. Ruth had led her to believe that he helped unload deliveries.

He's probably busy or something.

Or not there today.

What she wasn't going to let herself be was disappointed. Why should she be? Just because she'd had a fanciful moment in a field staring deeply into his eyes didn't give her any claim on Daniel. Especially since she'd had that moment in front of Malachi. He was who she should be having moments with.

Pushing all of that to the back of her mind, she returned Hope's smile. "I have a delivery of dried flower arrangements for Ruth."

"Wunderbaar! Joy will be thrilled. She loves her wedding bouquet so much, and she's been waiting to see what you bring. I think she might be your first customer."

Warmth bloomed in her cheeks like summer sun at noon even as she lowered her gaze, not wanting to let pride overtake her. She'd always liked Joy, who was a ray of sunshine, her dark eyes always smiling. "I'm glad."

"I'll get someone to help you unload," Hope said.

"Oh, that's not"—the door shut between them—"necessary."

Faith shrugged and moved to her buggy, pulling the first arrangement that had been on the front bench beside her closer. She was about to carefully lift it when two strong arms reached around her, hemming her in.

"I'll get that." Daniel's voice in her ear was soft and yet firm.

She should have stiffened or, at the least, found his nearness uncomfortable. Maybe there was more of Mercy's influence in her than she'd realized, because what she wanted to do was cuddle into him. His warmth surrounded her, and his strength was visible in the corded muscles of his forearms—he'd rolled his sleeves back to work, she guessed—and he smelled of sunshine and fresh laundry and maybe even a touch of honey.

And you're going to say yes to Malachi, a tiny voice piped up in her head.

A mental reminder that finally made her stiffen up. Luckily, Daniel was already lifting the large dining room table centerpiece over her head. So hopefully he hadn't noticed. She wouldn't want him to have even an inkling of the inappropriate thoughts she'd been having about him.

That would be . . . terribly embarrassing.

Faith cleared her throat and picked up a smaller box of mini-bouquets similar to what she'd made for Joy and turned to find him holding the door for her. She willed herself not to blush as she passed into the back room of the shop with him following behind . . . into an empty room. No sign of Hope, or Joy, or Ruth, or Joseph.

Just the two of them alone.

She'd been alone with Daniel before, but this felt different. Maybe because she'd just been picturing cuddling with him. "Where is everyone?"

"Hope is handling the front room. Dat and Mamm are at the house today doing chores. And Joy is giving a class on quilting in what used to be Aaron's workshop in the alley."

Which left the two of them to unload her goods.

That shouldn't make a difference to her, beyond being grateful for the help. For sure and certain, it shouldn't make her want to smile. She'd decided to marry another man. Smiling over this one was . . . wrong. Wasn't it?

"Do you miss working with your bruders?" she asked, managing to pull a normal-sounding question out of her muddled mind.

Thankfully, Daniel didn't seem to notice. "I do," he said simply. That was all. Which made her want to smile again, because that was so like Daniel. To the point. She suspected a whole host of deeper emotions lay under those two simple words.

Faith lifted the bouquets she was holding. "Where do you want these?"

"Oh . . . uh . . . Mamm wasn't sure how big they would be and wanted to see them before she put them out in the store, so we cleared this shelf back here to hold them until then."

Faith eyed the spot. The long flat items and smaller items would fit fine, but not the taller vase bouquet that she'd made using one of her mater's cracked pitchers and tied with a woven ribbon. But that was okay. They'd find a different spot for that.

She worked quietly alongside Daniel for the small amount of time it took to unload her buggy. Regret tugged at her as she stepped toward the back door, which they had propped open with a rock while they'd worked. "Ach vell . . . I put suggested prices on stickers on each item, but tell your mamm she can price them all as she sees fit. She knows better than I do what will sell. The percentage split we discussed is fine with me."

Daniel nodded, and she waved and stepped away.

"Would you like to have lunch with me?"

Faith stopped with her foot raised to climb up. "Um . . ." She glanced over her shoulder, trying to pretend the bubbles in her stomach weren't excitement but concern that he'd even ask. He knew she was all but promised.

Daniel looked about as comfortable as a pig in a hat. "It's just that it's my break time, and while you're here, I thought I might give you details about how things have worked with our other vendors in the past. Some tips that might help."

Oh. All the excited bubbles burst. *Pop. Pop. Pop.* And that's what she got for silly wishful thinking.

Giving her tips sounded exactly like something Daniel would do, and he was probably embarrassed in case she might have misunderstood.

"I would appreciate that," she found herself saying. "Should I park the buggy in the field?"

Daniel nodded. "Come back in this way. I'll let Hope know." Then he disappeared inside.

Faith shivered against the brisk wind when she walked back inside after getting her horse and buggy, still hitched, settled for a bit of a wait. Amish horses were trained well to wait like that for some time. She should have worn a sweater today, but the sun was out, so she'd thought she'd be fine. Apparently she had been wrong.

Daniel was walking back through the curtained area when she walked in. "Ready?"

Just a business lunch. He had tips.

She nodded.

Except he frowned, looking her over. "Will you be warm enough?"

He really was such a thoughtful person. "It's a little chilly, but I'll be fine walking from here to wherever we're going."

Daniel grunted, which could have been agreement or disagreement, she couldn't tell. He didn't push, though.

Hope, who was with a customer, waved as they exited through the front onto the street. "How does the Ice Cream Bucket sound?" Daniel asked.

Faith couldn't bite back her smile entirely. "When it's chilly outside?" she teased.

From the corner of her eye she caught the way his lips quirked. "They have the best tortilla soup this side of Texas. Or so I'm told. I've never been to Texas. I just know it tastes good."

"But ice cream after?" Okay, so there was a hopeful lilt to her voice.

The quirk turned into a real smile. No teeth, but his dark eyes warmed like honey on a hot summer day. Kind eyes, she'd always thought. "I thought it was too chilly."

He was teasing her back? Faith almost skipped a step, lurching forward. Daniel's hand on her arm kept her upright, though. Except he let go as soon as she had her balance like he was letting go of a hot skillet.

"Ice cream after," he agreed, continuing their conversation like nothing had happened. "Guess I'm not the only one with a sweet tooth."

"For ice cream, definitely." And chocolate creams.

He nodded slowly. "She likes ice cream," he said, almost to himself, like he was making a list of things she liked.

Only she knew he didn't think of her that way, despite that breath-stealing moment with the butterfly. Daniel was just one of those thoughtful people who liked to keep track of friends' interests.

They fell into a silence that, for once, Faith didn't feel the need to break. As if they were close enough friends that they didn't need to fill every single second with talk. A nice thought. Maybe that's why she was excited to spend time with Daniel. She didn't have many friends.

The soup was ready quick enough that they were seated at a small table with matching chairs almost as soon as they'd ordered. The decorative metal legs of Daniel's chair protested his size, but he didn't seem worried.

Faith had a spoonful in her mouth when he said, out of the blue, "I used to come here with my bruders."

She took a moment to savor before swallowing. He was right. The soup was wonderful gute. "You said you miss them?"

"Jah. It's taken some getting used to." He grimaced. "Don't get me wrong. They are happy, and I love both Hope and Joy. Joshua and Joy even live in my parents' dawdi haus, so we see them a lot, but it's not the same. Especially the shop, with neither of them working there now."

"I imagine it's similar to how I felt when Mercy first left," she murmured, then blinked. Because she didn't talk about that with anyone. Not with her parents because it hurt them too much, and not with others because it brought judgment or questions . . . or both.

No judgment showed in Daniel's expression as he studied her. "I remember how you were her shadow growing up."

Faith chuckled. "That's true. She was always fearless."

"Sounds like Joshua," he murmured.

His youngest brother was several years younger, though they'd attended the same school, so she remembered him well enough. "Didn't he once jump off the merry-go-round and try to land on a . . ." She wrinkled her forehead, trying to remember.

"On a pony," Daniel provided wryly. "Only the pony bolted."

She chuckled. "And he split his lip wide open."

He nodded. "Took six stitches, and Mamm blamed me."

"Why?"

Daniel shrugged over a bite of soup. "Because I was holding the pony."

Faith laughed. "I never got in trouble for Mercy," she owned. "But mostly because everyone knew that she was one who came up with all the ideas." *The wild one. The reckless one.* Most would have used harsher terms.

"And you were the good girl," Daniel agreed.

Until now, it seemed. A baby and no Mercy was too hard to swallow for some, she guessed. "I tried. Breaking rules makes me break out in hives."

Daniel paused with the spoon only halfway to his mouth to stare at her. "Really?"

She laughed again. "Not really. But may as well, the way it feels to me."

His low chuckle warmed her heart. Such a nice sound. She could sit here with him forever. "Do you still miss her?" he asked.

"Every single day." She sighed. "It feels . . . empty . . . without her. After she left, it took me two years to catch up with her, partly because I had to earn my way as I traveled and partly because she kept moving, and I worried every single second." And questioned her sanity for going after Mercy for all that time as well. "Then I found her and stayed close by . . . until she had Rose. Leaving her behind after so long . . . well, that was because Rose needed a home. A better one than either of us could give her out there."

"Mercy asked you to take her."

Not a question, and she wondered how he knew that about her. "Yes. She said she wasn't ready to come back, but that she knew Rose would have a better life here. She could barely keep up with rent for her apartment and worked all the time. She wouldn't have been able to afford or look after a baby yet."

Giving up Rose was the most selfless thing she'd ever seen Mercy do in her life.

Daniel stirred his soup. "She was showing a mater's true heart."

Faith dropped her gaze. All their lives, people had made excuses for Mercy, forgiven her easily. Even now, it seemed. Of course, that included Faith. She'd forgive her sister almost anything if she could see her face again. Know she was happy and healthy and safe.

Maybe someday.

"So . . ." She cast about for anything to change the subject. Or at least turn it away from Mercy. "If you miss your bruders so much, you should do something about it."

Daniel seemed to take the redirection well, nodding around another bite of soup. "We have family dinner night once a week."

"What about brother time?"

He met her gaze, curiosity lightening his eyes. "Brother time?"

She nodded. "Time you spend with either one or both of your bruders, just you. Maybe once a month?"

He considered that for a long moment. "I think that's a wonderful gute idea. It wonders me we never thought of it."

Faith eyed the case of ice cream flavors, finished with her soup. "When I finally found her, Mercy was living with her boyfriend, and I don't think he liked me around much."

Probably because she'd spent hours in their apartment cleaning and picking up and it made him feel guilty that he didn't do that when he didn't have a job. As far as she could tell, Rose's father spent all day every day, and most nights, playing video games. Claimed it was going to make him a YouTube star, whatever that meant. Meanwhile, Mercy worked two jobs to pay the bills while he played.

She shook off the memory. "So Mercy came up with sister days, where she and I would go off together, just the two of us."

"She always did love you," Daniel said.

Yes. She always did.

DANIEL STUDIED FAITH'S expression and worried he'd said something that might have hurt her. While she was still smiling, lips drawn up sweetly, her eyes were . . . sad. Shadowed.

There was probably a lot she wasn't saying about her and Mercy. After five years away, he imagined a lot had gone on between them. Especially for only one to come back with a baby that was the other's. He couldn't imagine his mamm giving any one of him or his brothers away. Ever.

Then again, Mercy had been in an impossible situation, it sounded like. No doubt her choice had nothing to do with not wanting Rose. Besides, Faith seemed . . . content. No, more than that. Rosie was clearly the center of her whole world, and motherhood suited her. She was happy. Maybe more so with Malachi Eash now talking marriage.

Are you going to say yes?

The words trembled at the tips of his lips. He wanted to ask, but it wasn't his place. Not his business. He had the store and the bees to keep him busy enough. He'd missed his chance, if he'd ever even had one. All he could ask for now was friendship.

"I meant to ask," Faith began, perking up, "how is moving the bees going?"

"Slowly." At her raised brows and the sincere curiosity in her eyes, he elaborated. "I have to move them a short distance each day so that the remaining foragers can find the hives when they return. Over the course of the next few weeks I'll have them closer to the Beilers' property line, which is all woods that they won't ever fell. Too many trees. It's not quite as perfect as where I had them—our combined fields were perfect in terms of wildflowers—but it'll do."

Faith reached across the table to pat his hand. "I'm sorry about that."

Daniel stilled under her touch, trying his best to ignore the way something expanded in his chest. "It's your family's property, Faith. You can do what is best for you and the land. My bees will be fine."

Or what Malachi—the man she was probably going to marry—thought best, at least. He owned it now.

He slipped his hand out from under hers and pretended not to see the warmth staining her cheeks or the small gleam of hurt in her eyes. "Where are you working on your flower arrangements? I imagine you need space?"

Faith wrinkled her nose. "I'm still figuring that out. I thought maybe the basement, but it isn't enough space for my drying tables, and the barn is always in use in one way or another. For now, I'm still in the basement and will have to make do."

"You could use my honey room." The words were out before he had a chance to think them through fully. Once they were out, though, he didn't want to take them back.

Faith blinked at him. Such blue eyes. He'd never seen

the ocean, but he'd seen pictures. He imagined parts of the ocean looked like that. "Don't you need it?"

"Not until the summer. My earliest honey harvests are around mid-June and stop by end of September. The room is long with several tables—plus windows, so you're not stuck down in the dark."

For some reason he didn't like the thought of her working long hours in a basement all by herself with no windows or air. She still looked about to argue, so he kept going. "Plus, then Mamm could load things up and take them to the store directly and you wouldn't need to deliver. It also helps that our house is in walking distance from yours."

"I wouldn't want to impose . . ."

He shook his head. "Not at all. That room is empty most of the year and ends up as storage anyway. Might as well get some use out of it. At least use it until you see how much business you're doing and how much space you need to keep up with it."

That did the trick. He could see her shoulders visibly drop. "That would be so helpful. Denki, Daniel."

That same warmth that had filled him when he'd learned his mater had taken his hint to give Faith a chance with her flowers filled him again.

Because I like helping people, he told himself. *And she's my friend.*

Only that reason sounded weak, even in his own head. "Why don't I come over tonight and pick you up? We can move your stuff over so you're ready to get started in the morning."

After only a small beat of hesitation, Faith nodded, then bit her lip. "Is it . . . Is it okay if I bring Rosie with me tonight? And maybe sometimes when I'm working?"

"For sure and certain. Mamm would love to have a boppli around more often. She certainly tells Aaron and Joshua enough."

Faith's laugh sent another wave of warmth through him. She was pretty when she laughed like that, lit up from within. Her light shone, and he wanted to keep it close always. But he couldn't.

Chapter Six

※

IT WAS SILLY to be shy with Daniel, but Faith couldn't seem to help herself. Maybe it had to do with how his knock had come after dark, almost like a date. Or maybe it was the way Malachi had frowned over the situation, making her feel guilt even though she shouldn't, because she was doing nothing wrong. He had even offered to join them to help with loading and unloading of all her flowers.

I should have been excited to have him join us.

She hadn't seen much of Malachi all day. He'd been busy working the farm with her dat—hard work that deserved her respect and gratefulness. But the buggy had filled up with too much stuff for three people to fit in, and so they'd had to leave him behind.

Now Faith sat beside Daniel as he guided the horse down the road, the occasional car zooming past and Rosie in Faith's lap babbling away. She'd brought a bag of things for the baby, who would likely fall asleep on the way back if she stuck to her schedule.

"I'm sorry your fiancé couldn't join us," Daniel said into the quiet of the evening.

The temperatures had dropped and the sky was crystal clear, the heavens showing off with all the stars at their brightest. The air was so crisp around them, the tips of her ears were stinging. She should've brought a scarf to wrap around her head.

"We're not engaged," she said. Then, realizing how that sounded, she tacked on a "Yet."

"Oh." Daniel opened his mouth like he wanted to ask more but closed it after a second.

And she blew out a silent breath of relief, because she wasn't ready to say for sure what her answer as far as Malachi was concerned was going to be. Yes, she'd decided in her head that Gotte had put Malachi in her life for a reason. But to say all that out loud to someone else—especially to Daniel, somehow—that would make it . . . real. She wasn't quite ready for real.

They arrived at the Kanagy house quickly. After hitching the horse and buggy close to a long single-story building behind the barn, Daniel came around to help her down. He eyed Rosie. "My mamm would love to watch over her while we get things situated in the honey room."

Faith bit her lip. Not that she didn't trust Ruth, but she didn't want to be a bother.

Daniel must've read her thoughts, because he crooked a small smile. "She'll be over the moon."

Faith chuckled and gave in gracefully. "Oll recht."

They made their way around the barn and entered the house through the back door.

"Mamm?" Daniel called out.

"In the kitchen. Did you bring me a boppli to hold?"

He shot a wink at Faith as if to say, *"See?"*

She tried to ignore how that wink sent her heart fluttering.

Rounding the corner, she inhaled delicious scents of whatever Ruth was making for dinner. Small and plump, with the kindest brown eyes—Daniel's eyes—Ruth turned from the stove and held out her arms for Rosie, practically bursting with the maternal need to cuddle. To Faith's surprise, Rose went right into Ruth's arms with a happy gurgle.

Maybe she likes the Kanagys.

"Aren't you a darling," Ruth cooed to the baby. "I've been wanting to hold you ever since your aendi brought you home."

Faith tried not to wince at the "aendi" part and chuckled. "You can hold her anytime, Ruth. I don't like to bother anyone."

"Holding a baby is never a bother," Ruth assured her, happily bouncing Rosie on her knee.

Faith kept to herself how different Ruth's sentiment was from that of her own parents. Not that they didn't love their granddaughter. It's just how they were. They'd never been particularly affectionate as parents, and now, with Rosie, they seemed to be of the opinion that they'd raised their own children and so shouldn't have to take part in helping with another one. Instead they'd enjoy her for a few minutes at a time, playing with her and then handing her back for the harder stuff.

Which doesn't make them veesht.

They weren't bad grandparents. They were . . . reserved. Some people were baby people and some were better with older children. Faith had never wanted for anything grow-

72   *Kristen McKanagh*

ing up, and they'd accepted her back home with open arms. That's what mattered.

"Ach vell . . . denki for watching her. Hopefully we won't be too long."

Daniel hefted the baby bag onto the kitchen table with an *oomf*. "What do you have in here? Enough supplies to last the winter?"

Was that . . . Was he teasing her?

Even Ruth looked up from Rose, glancing between them.

Faith tugged the bag closer and wrinkled her nose at him. "You never know what you might need."

"Uh-huh" was his grunted way of saying he didn't believe her. But the way he pressed his lips firmly together—to keep from smiling—was what made her glow on the inside like a lantern under a bushel.

"Run along, you two," Ruth urged. "Faith, I do hope you'll stay for dinner?"

Already halfway to the door, Faith paused. She hadn't thought about dinner. Would it be wrong of her to miss dinner with her own family? Not that they would wait for her. She'd told them she didn't know how long this would take, and she could always clean up—one of her regular chores—when she got home later.

"As long as it's not an impos—"

"You are *not* an imposition," Daniel murmured, cutting her off, but softly enough that his mamm didn't catch it.

Heat surged into her cheeks, though she wasn't sure why. Maybe it was the way he said that, firm and even a little exasperated. Kind of growly, even. Or maybe the way he was looking at her, like he was willing her to believe it, too.

"I'd like that," she said, warmly accepting the offer.

"Wunderbaar." Ruth smiled. "It's family dinner night, so I made a ton. Plenty to go around."

Family dinner night. Wasn't that their special time together with his bruders and their fraas? Daniel's hand at her back hurried her out into the night before she could protest.

"You didn't say it was family dinner night," she accused.

He was walking so briskly back to the buggy she had to jog to keep up.

"Does it matter?"

"Vell . . . jah! This is your special time. I'm not family. I shouldn't—"

"We wouldn't have invited you if you weren't welcome."

Not exactly words to make a girl feel special, but still, they stopped her arguing. Because he was right. Ruth Kanagy wasn't the kind of woman to ever make someone feel unwanted. "I would have brought something if I'd known," Faith grumbled instead.

She was well aware she sounded grumpy, but she wanted to be thought of as someone with manners and who was useful to have around.

"Mamm surprised you. Everyone will understand." Now he was growling again, like a surly bear with a thorn in his paw.

Was she being unreasonable? Maybe she was. So she let it go, grabbing the first batch of flowers she could reach and following him into the honey room in silence. She paused inside the door, gazing around in interest. She'd never tended bees, or extracted honey, or even seen it done before.

The room brought up so many questions, she couldn't decide what to ask first, so she went with, "You have a lot of space."

DANIEL GLANCED IN her direction, trying to decide if she was commenting merely to be polite, but she seemed interested, looking around wide-eyed. Holding two heavy bags of who knew what a person needed to make flower arrangements, Daniel nodded, looking around as well, trying to see it through unfamiliar eyes.

Only recently and with Aaron's help, he'd built this room exactly how he wanted it, including with the capacity to grow his production even more if he decided to. The space was long and narrow and could probably even be used for Gmay services when his family hosted church on their Sunday each year, though they'd always used the barn in the past—a tradition since he was a child.

Counters lined two entire walls in an L shape and had cabinets underneath, where he stored the trays and scrapers and pots they used for the process. He had a deep sink with running water and a handheld sprayer for sanitation and to wash the pots after use. Another wall was lined with three extractors. Hand cranked, they took a lot of work, but the bishop hadn't approved the electric kind that would speed the process. Not yet at least. Daniel would ask again when the business got to a point where they needed the speed to keep up.

"It started out as a shed with only one large potful of honey each harvest, but as I've grown the hives, the business has grown. Now on extraction day, I get the whole family involved."

She turned a sparkling smile his way. "That sounds like fun."

Did she mean that? He pulled a face. "Tell that to my family."

"They don't enjoy it?"

"It's hot, sticky work, especially in the summer. We have to keep the doors closed so bees don't find us and swarm. And I thought the summers were mild enough that I didn't need to build in any fans, but it turns out that was poor judgment."

"I doubt you've had a day of poor judgment in your entire life." Faith crossed to the counter and set down the flowers she was holding.

Daniel stared after her, resisting the urge to hug her for that, but not sure how to respond out loud. "What makes you say that?"

She turned to face him like she was a sinner preparing to confess to her community. "When I first came home with Rose, you greeted me after my first visit to Gmay. Made a point of it, even. Do you remember?"

Daniel nodded. He *had* made a point of it. He'd seen the doubts etched in the faces of his community—people he loved dearly, but some of whom could be a bit hardheaded, not to mention one or two being hard-hearted.

"Well, afterward, I was in the kitchen by myself and overheard Fannie Gingerich saying that if Daniel Kanagy showed forgiveness toward *that Kemp girl*, then the rest of them should, too."

Fannie was one of the older, more curmudgeonly members of their district. One many listened to. Even so, an unaccustomed anger burned in his heart. "She actually said *that Kemp girl*?"

Faith blinked at the question, then waved it off. "That's not important. The point is, people respect your opinion, Daniel. Myself included. You are a gute, strong man of faith who always knows the right thing to do. Steady."

Steady. That's how she saw him? As a steady man who made solid decisions. How . . . boring. "No one's judgment is perfect, Faith. Or Jesus wouldn't have needed to die on the cross to save us."

"I know that." Unaware of his reaction, she was still looking around. "*I* would have put a fan in here." Then she grinned at him.

But Daniel was still smarting over the "steady" descriptor. He fell back on habit and said nothing.

That didn't seem to bother Faith, though. "So what is all this used for?"

Now she was just being polite. "I'm sure you don't want to learn about honeybees."

"Why not?" Her expression was visibly confused.

Which made him frown. Except for a memory. A moment he'd tucked away when she'd run off after her sister all those years ago. A moment when he'd shared about his bees with Faith and she'd been full of questions and let him go on and on, sincerely interested in a way no one else, not even his family members, who loved him, ever was. "Because no one wants to learn about it."

She nodded slowly. "I guess you wouldn't be interested in hearing about my flowers, either," she mused.

Actually, she'd be wrong. But she had an almost-fiancé for that now. "Let's finish unloading."

After a small hesitation that he barely caught, she turned for the door. They worked steadily together until the buggy was empty and Faith was satisfied with where she'd set everything up.

"I'll put some cardboard down on the floor tomorrow morning before I go to the shop."

"Cardboard?"

He nodded. "We do that when we extract the honey. It's easier to clean up afterward."

"That's smart."

Meanwhile, Daniel was still stuck on the conversation. That was him. Steady and practical. Missing opportunities because he waited too long, because he wanted to take his time. Not like Malachi, who proposed on first meeting and had all his big dreams and changes for the Kemp's farm, or like his own bruders, who not only were married to women they loved but had had the courage to leave the steady family business for jobs they loved as well.

Daniel was the boring one.

But she hasn't said yes to Malachi.

The breath locked up in his lungs, or maybe he stopped breathing. Because why couldn't he propose to her, too? Faith would choose, and she might not choose him, but at least he would have tried.

The idea took root, spreading through him fast.

Too fast.

He stared at her as she moved around the room tweaking things to her satisfaction, debating with himself all the while. He should look at this logically. He wanted to marry and settle down with a family. What he felt for Faith wasn't love . . . it didn't make sense that this was love. He didn't know her well enough yet for that, did he? Even if she made his heart beat faster, and was interested in his bees, and was a wunderbaar mater, and made him want to smile all the time. Not love, but a fine start, and they could build on that. Her situation meant he didn't have time to build before he proposed. Despite that, he was certain, in a way he rarely was without a lot more thought and time, that they could build a strong, loving marriage.

She shivered visibly, and Daniel frowned, noticing for the first time how cold it had gotten in here. It wasn't even winter yet. They worked the honey in the summers and never needed heat. He'd have to see about some way to warm the room for her.

He needed to think about this for longer than five minutes. *If I still feel the same tomorrow, I'll propose.*

The decision settled inside him, and he even nodded to himself. "Let's go. I'm sure my bruders and schwesters-in-law have shown up by now."

Faith bit her lip, a show of nerves that surprised him. Was she that anxious around his family? He didn't say anything, though. Neither did she. She just wrapped her arms around herself and followed him back to the house.

Inside, warm laughter filled the rooms and his heart. He would always love that sound. It reminded him of growing up, of being loved and surrounded by love, and of the future he wanted for himself.

A house full of exactly this . . . love and bopplin.

His gaze slid to Faith, who was still cautious, but smiling.

After taking off their coats and whatnot, they emerged from the mudroom to find his mother sitting at the kitchen table holding Rosie up in the air and blowing raspberries on her baby belly. Rosie laughed and laughed and laughed, which made everyone gathered around them laugh right along.

Mamm looked over, flushed with delight, and smiled. "Faith, this child is absolutely precious."

Edging around him, Faith moved closer, chuckling. "She is so like Mercy that way, able to charm the birds from the trees."

Mamm cocked her head, expression turning thoughtful. "Actually, when you were babies, Mercy used to scream until she was red in the face. She never liked to be held or tickled or jiggled. She always wanted to sit quietly by herself."

Faith's mouth opened in a little O of surprise, and Daniel had the sudden urge to lean right in and kiss her. This proposal idea was turning him mushy already.

"Really?" Faith asked. "Mamm never told me that."

"Perhaps she blocked it out," Ruth said in a wry tone of voice that said she wouldn't blame Esther Kemp for doing that. "You, on the other hand, were always a sweetheart. All smiles. Happy to be held by anyone."

"Will wonders never cease." Faith laughed. "Although Rosie is usually particular about who holds her."

Ruth nodded sagely. "She must realize that I love bopplin."

"We call Mamm the Boppli Whisperer," Aaron teased from his place at the table beside Hope.

"Ach, you," Ruth protested, but smilingly.

The egg timer on the counter went off, and Ruth moved to get up. "That will be the casserole."

"I'll get it," Hope and Joy said in unison, and both jumped up, while Ruth happily settled back in her seat.

Faith also moved to help the two other women in the kitchen, going about her business with quiet efficiency to grab a pitcher of water and using it to fill the glasses set around the table. Daniel still watched her, though. That tendency to trip could be worrisome. In fact, when she reached for one of the steaming dishes of delicious-smelling food, he beat her to it, moving it to the waiting trivets. He wouldn't want her burned when he proposed.

When.

Was he already thinking "when" instead of "if"? This was not like him at all. He gave his head a shake as they finished setting the table.

IN SHORT ORDER they were all seated, with Faith somehow ending up right beside Daniel. He was so broad-shouldered, he crowded into her space, apologizing when he brushed against her.

"That's oll recht," she whispered for him alone. "I don't take up much space, so there's more for you."

He blinked warm brown eyes at her. At his dat's cleared throat, together they bowed their heads, each giving a quiet individual prayer before digging into the food.

"Your flower arrangements have gotten a lot of interest, Faith," Joy said as they dished up. "I've already sold several of the smaller bouquets."

"I think she bought half of them herself," Joshua complained with a grin. "There must be one in every room of our house now."

"They make it cheerful, and because they're dried flowers they last." Joy wasn't apologetic in the least. "But I'm not the only one."

A glance in his direction showed Daniel's lips tipped up.

Faith pulled her gaze back to Joy. "I'm glad to hear it, since I just took over Daniel's honey room with my flower-drying racks and ribbons and whatnot."

"Oh, I'd like to see how you make them."

Faith glanced in Daniel's direction again, almost like she couldn't help herself, and in a sparkling instant it was almost as if they were sitting there, just the two of them, sharing a small joke.

See. Someone is interested in your flowers, he seemed

to say with his eyes. And she pretended to silently answer him. *And I'm interested in your bees.*

He cocked his head, which made her own lips tip up. "I can show you after dinner if you don't mind the cold," she told Joy.

"I'd love that."

"Oh my," Ruth gasped. "I hadn't thought of how that room isn't heated. Daniel—"

"I'm already working on a way to warm it up in there, Mamm."

Which earned him a satisfied smile. "Always such a gute boy."

All three brothers groaned in unison, and Faith glanced around. "What?"

Aaron rolled his eyes. "Mamm still insists on seeing us as little buwes. Even with two of us married and Daniel, the oldest, practically considered an old man by the community."

Beside her Daniel stiffened, not that his family seemed to notice, but Faith frowned. "He's not an old man."

Aaron paused, his cheeks turning a little redder. "Daniel knows I don't mean it that way."

But did he? She hoped so.

She wouldn't change anything about Daniel Kanagy. Gotte had made him, and to Faith he was maybe the best man she knew. Hopefully, out there somewhere was an Amish woman who might appreciate everything gute about him.

She ignored the way her heart pinched at the thought. Daniel deserved a gute life with a family. How could she begrudge him that in any way? What was wrong with her?

Chapter Seven

✴

AFTER FEEDING AND changing a squirming Rosie, Faith put her down for her morning nap, then got to work cleaning up from breakfast with her mamm. She was drying the last dish when the back door banged and they both turned to find Malachi coming in.

He was stomping his feet and rubbing his hands together. "It's cold out there today."

"I hope you are warm enough." Faith really was trying. "Maybe you could use a thicker scarf?"

Although the one he had covered the entire bottom half of his face, so maybe not.

"Jah." He beamed. "That would be nice."

She hurried to the hall closet and the basket of hats and scarves there, pulling out a knitted one of wool. By the time she brought it to him, Malachi had unwound himself from his layers of clothes and was accepting a steaming cup of coffee from her mother. "I have some made up for a thermos, if you'll take it to Henry," Mamm was saying.

"Of course."

Faith placed the scarf on top of his coat, which was now hanging on the back of one of the kitchen chairs. Then she glanced up to find Malachi watching her. "I was hoping you might help us in the fields today," he said.

She'd never helped her dat in the fields. She'd never been particularly interested, but Mercy always had been and would beg their fater to go to work with him. *My place is working the land and your place is in the house with Mamm*, he would say. What would he think of this? "I—"

She glanced at her mamm—who knew very well Dat's thoughts on things, and agreed with them as far as Faith was aware—expecting her to speak up now. Only she didn't. All she did was give Faith an encouraging wave from behind Malachi's back.

Faith cleared her throat. "I owe three more wreaths to A Thankful Heart today," she found herself saying. "I'd planned to go over to the Kanagys' to work in the room they set up for me."

That Daniel had set up for her, but that sounded too . . . intimate. Like he'd done it to please her.

What was she doing, anyway? She should be jumping at the chance to spend time with her future husband. Shouldn't she?

The pinching around Mamm's mouth told her she should, but now that the words were out, she couldn't take them back.

"Will he—" Malachi cut himself off. "Will the Kanagys be there?"

It took effort not to frown over the question. "I don't expect so. They're usually at the shop all day, from what I understand."

Malachi's shoulders visibly relaxed. Was he worried

about something to do with the Kanagys? Why? They were gute, faithful Amish people, kind and easy to be around. She couldn't remember a meal she'd enjoyed more than the one with them last night.

"Ach vell . . ." Malachi shrugged. "The way your flowers are selling is gute business. You should definitely work hard to build it. I could never object to that." Then he clapped her on the back like he was praising her. "How about I drive you over?"

"Can Dat spare you?"

"It won't take long, and it's so cold. I'll feel better knowing you're not having to walk in this weather."

But he was okay with her working the fields in this weather?

Stop picking apart everything he says and does. He's trying to be nice.

"Denki. I would be grateful."

Grabbing his coat, but not the scarf she'd brought him, Malachi headed toward the door. "I'll get the buggy hitched up."

"I'll be right out."

As soon as the door closed behind him, her mater's sigh brought her head around to find Mamm shaking her head. "You are never going to catch a husband if that's how you go on, Faith Kemp."

"I promised those wreaths today, Mamm. What was I supposed to say?"

Her mater's sharp gray eyes—Faith and Mercy had both gotten their fater's eyes—turned sharper with disappointment. "He wants to spend time with you. Get to know you. Is that so bad?"

"Of course not—"

Mamm took her hand in a surprisingly strong grip. "I

worry about you. Taking on Mercy's child. Nowhere to go after we move into the dawdi haus. Malachi won't be patient with this arrangement forever, not unless you're planning a wedding. I want to know that at least"—her chin wobbled and she had to take a breath—"at least one of my girls is provided for."

Her parents rarely talked of Mercy, even when they talked about Rose. Faith suspected they found it too painful. So much worry. Rosie wasn't even her child, but she loved that boppli with all her heart as though she were. If anything ever happened and she couldn't see Rose every single day . . . she didn't think she could live through that.

"I'll make it up to him tonight. Maybe a drive into town for dessert at—" She almost said the Ice Cream Bucket, but part of her felt disloyal taking Malachi to the place where she'd gone with Daniel. Which was pure silliness. Daniel didn't own that spot, and they'd gone as business acquaintances. Friends at most.

Her mother's visible brightening lightened her own heart. "That's my gute girl." Mamm squeezed her hand. "Now, don't keep him waiting. He has work to do."

Ten minutes later, Faith got into the buggy with a still-sleeping Rosie wrapped in a blanket in her arms.

"You're taking the boppli?" Malachi eyed the two of them as if Faith were wrong to bring Rose along.

"Mamm is scrubbing floors today and can't watch her," she said. "She'll be perfectly happy lying on a blanket on the floor while I work."

She didn't share her worry about Rosie crawling all over that floor and having to be careful with the flower cuttings and sharp wire she used for her wreaths, making sure she didn't drop any on the floor. She wouldn't want

Rosie to accidentally crawl over something she shouldn't or pick it up and put it in her mouth.

"I'm sure you'll keep her safe," he said, but with a frown that said he wasn't as sure as his words. "Your Dat was telling me that you named Rose."

She wasn't sure that was a question, but she nodded all the same, trying to be more open to his overtures, like Mamm had asked. "Mercy's favorite flower. The rose-bushes around our house are something to see every year, and she loved them."

"That's nice." To give him credit, he didn't hesitate over that or seem to try to avoid the topic of her sister, like many did. "Were you close with your sister? I imagine as twins you would be."

She smiled. "I was. Mercy was always so much braver than I ever could be."

"To go out into the world when the Amish life is all you've known, I would think so." He wasn't looking at her, but she got the impression that he meant that. Admired it, even.

Faith's heart warmed to Malachi a bit more, despite the cold wind beating against the lowered windscreen.

"It must have been difficult for her to let Rose go, yet," he said next.

And she warmed a bit more, because very few people tried to give Mercy any forgiveness or grace when it came to that act. To the Amish, a woman's primary role was in the raising of children, but Faith knew better than anyone that Mercy's making the choice to part with her boppli had been heart-wrenching. Her sister's tear-streaked face, pale even against the white of the hospital bedsheets, was an image that would never leave her. "I think it's the bravest thing she's ever done."

"But you wanted to come home?" he asked.

"Jah. I always loved my life—the community, and my faith, and the Amish church. I know some youngie feel restricted or denied, but I only ever felt safe and cared for and comfortable."

Malachi was nodding along. "I love that we support each other and help each other. From what I've seen of the world—which isn't as much as you, I admit"—he slid her a teasing smile—"it seems to be baze . . . an angry place full of blame and selfishness. Neighbors and families choosing only to help themselves or not know the people they live beside at all."

"Jah. Exactly."

Faith thought about Mercy's boyfriend, Rose's father. He hadn't wanted Faith around, and she suspected that was because he worried she would make Mercy want to leave him. Then how would he pay for things?

"Did anything scary happen to you while you were gone?" he asked next.

Something her parents hadn't ever dared to ask.

"Nae. Not really. I often worked in diners and cafés to pay my way, so I met a lot of people. Most ignored me—either because they simply didn't care or because they thought I was odd with my clothing."

"You wore your Amish clothes?"

"Jah." She'd tried Mercy's jeans and T-shirts, but they had felt so . . . constricting.

"Well, I think you were brave to go after her, and a gute schwester, too." Malachi was entirely sincere. She could hear it in his voice.

I need to give him more of a chance.

Faith reached over and patted his arm. "Denki. That means a lot to me."

Which earned her the warmest smile he'd given her yet. He really was handsome. She didn't even notice the mushy chin so much now. She should make more room for him in her heart.

DANIEL DIDN'T WANT to move the hives. Not today, with the cold wind tearing at the trees and fields. The bees wouldn't be out in this anyway. So instead, he used his day at home to do chores around the house and barn. After the more physical labor, he cleaned up, then did a few things for Mamm, including washing a load of laundry. She hated doing laundry in the late fall and winter, when it was cold out. It made her hands ache when she was putting the wash out on the line to dry, and if he could save her that, then he intended to.

The wind was so bad—rattling-the-windows-of-the-house bad—he wouldn't have heard the buggy pull up if he hadn't been outside. Without being seen, he glanced around the corner of the house to find Malachi holding a protesting, squirming Rose, whose face was turning purple with her fit as Faith clambered out.

Did the way she smiled at the other man hold more than simple thanks?

Last night Daniel had lain awake in his bed, staring at the ceiling, thinking through his proposal idea. Obsessing over it, if he was honest. By the time the rooster crowed, well before daybreak, he'd decided. He would definitely ask Faith to marry him.

But not with Malachi Eash, her other suitor, standing right there.

Which was why Daniel quietly went back to hanging the laundry for his mamm. He couldn't help the way his ears were pricked, though, unable to miss the sounds of Faith going into the honey room and Malachi driving away.

Was it wrong of him to be happy that the other man hadn't lingered?

Not wanting to propose when she was in the middle of working—in fact, he should probably think of a more romantic way to go about it first—Daniel headed back indoors and got started on fixing the broken drawer in one of the bedroom dressers. Not that anyone stayed in that room now that Aaron and Joshua were both gone. They'd shared it before they married and moved away. Daniel had always had his own room, but without his bruders around, even that now seemed oddly quiet.

It was tempting to go check that Faith had everything she needed each time she came over to work. Yesterday, he'd gotten a car ride all the way to the Walmart closest to town and bought a portable indoor propane heater. Maybe he should go make sure she knew how to use it.

Don't be silly. She's perfectly capable. No doubt she'd seen one before, if not that specific one.

Daniel managed to keep himself busy and not give in to temptation the rest of the day, but Faith wasn't far from his thoughts. In fact, he'd come up with the perfect proposal. First, he would talk to her Dat. Then he would take Faith into the field where he'd heard her humming that day.

Or I could take her now.

The sun had come out and was beginning to set, turning everything brilliant orange. It would be perfect. Mamm and Dat wouldn't be home for another hour. Daniel was in the middle of getting out the casserole his mater had already made to pop it in the oven so that dinner would be ready when his parents got home.

As soon as he did, he'd go fetch Faith and Rosie. Because of course Rosie needed to be part of this moment.

Except, as he was closing the oven door and setting the egg timer, a knock sounded at the back door. Frowning, because now wasn't a usual time for visitors to come by, Daniel opened it, only for his heart to flip over.

Maybe Gotte had gotten tired of all his obsessing, because Faith was standing there with Rose in her arms.

Except why was she here?

"Is there a problem?" he asked, mind already going to the propane heater. It was supposed to be for indoor use and safe, but he'd worried about it.

Faith smiled. "No problem. I just noticed you were home, and before I go, I wanted to thank you for all the things you did to make the honey room so comfortable."

Oh. He shifted on his feet. "No thanks necessary."

The look she gave him said she wasn't going to let him get away with that. "You provided an indoor heater—which works wonderful gute by the way—but also a playpen for Rosie so that she can play and roll and pull herself up but is safely out from underfoot. I can't tell you how much I appreciate that."

Right. The playpen. He'd remembered it from when Joshua was a baby. Mamm had probably thought he'd lost his marbles when he'd asked where that thing was, and Aaron even more so when Daniel had insisted he needed to sand the wooden rungs of what essentially was an oversized crib on the floor. "It's old, but I thought it would work."

He'd almost bought a thing called a Pack 'n Play at Walmart when he'd gotten the heater, but he wasn't sure what the Ordnung said about those. The playpen was bigger anyway, as far as he could tell, just not as portable. But Faith didn't need it portable, so that was okay. Wasn't it?

"I need one of those in our house." Faith laughed. "She doesn't stay in one place anymore, so I have to hold her or strap her to me while I do my chores."

"I knew I should have gotten the Pack 'n Play," Daniel muttered, more to himself than her.

Faith's eyebrows rose over twinkling eyes. She really did have the loveliest eyes. They sparkled when she was amused. He could imagine looking into them every day of his life, and contentment filled every nook and cranny of his body.

"The what?" she asked.

Oh, sis yuscht. He should have kept his mouth shut.

She obviously wasn't going to let it go, so he told her about the contraption.

"That does sound handy," she said when he trailed off.

Jah, I should have bought the Pack 'n Play and asked permission from the ministers afterward. He doubted the bishop would have a problem with it anyway. After all, Amish used cribs, and they were allowed to buy things like brooms and cleaning supplies and whatnot from Walmart. At least in their district they were.

It wasn't too late, though. He could get one next time he—

"I'll have to get one next time I'm there," Faith mused, bouncing Rosie. "Then I can keep it at our house and use the one you have here, and I won't have to cart one around."

That was a gute idea, too.

Now . . . how did he move from cribs to a proposal? He didn't want to shock her.

He took too long thinking it over, because Faith nodded, then stepped away, down the stairs to the drive. There was no buggy waiting for her. Wind that had been blowing hard all day—the kind that penetrated clothes and sank into the bones—snatched at her dress as she walked.

Giving a small growl, Daniel bounded down the stairs after her. "You're not planning to walk home in this weather, are you?"

She turned on a gasp, and immediately he put a hand out to steady her before she tumbled over, guilt poking at him for startling her. She could have fallen with Rosie in her arms. What a dumkoff he could be.

"Sorry," he muttered. "I didn't mean to scare you."

She just shook her head. "My fault for being so clumsy. It's why my dresses never last as long as they should."

Daniel bit the inside of his cheek, because he had noticed Faith's tendency to trip over her own feet, and he didn't want to hurt her feelings. Even as a child, she'd done that, while Mercy had been all grace. Why he remembered that, he wasn't sure.

He must not have hidden his thoughts well, though, because she laughed, the wind carrying the sweet sound away sharply. "It's okay. I don't mind so much anymore."

Her smile was pure self-deprecating humor, as though being clumsy was a joke she was letting him in on. Daniel couldn't have stopped his own chuckle if he wanted to.

See? He could tell loving this woman would be wonderful easy. He was making the right choice.

If it had been him, he'd be worrying over his shortcoming, hoping to keep others from noticing. Even one that wasn't all that bad. Was that how she managed to ignore the folks like Martha Gick?

Except ignoring the judgments of others in their community could also lead to sin. For the most part, the Amish were there to help each other stay on the path Gotte had set them on. Yes, to point out the stumbles, but also there to help you get back up. There was wisdom in others, insight when you were too close to see it yourself, gifts Gotte gave them to see the things you couldn't, or look at them in a different way. That was part of what made a close-knit community so important.

He tried not to frown over the thoughts swirling through him. Being clumsy wasn't a sin. No doubt she listened and tried to learn from those she respected, like her parents. He shouldn't worry. Faith had always been a gute girl.

"Daniel?"

Faith's question dragged him out of the noise tumbling around inside his head. "Sorry," he muttered again. He was apologizing a lot today and still not getting to the proposal. Except that with the way he'd asked her about walking in the wind a second ago, proposing in that field now seemed like a stupid idea. Faith was even turned to shield Rosie from the worst of the wind buffeting them.

"Isn't Malachi coming to pick you up?" he asked.

"Nae." She waved a hand. "I didn't know how long I would be. I told him I'd walk home."

"But surely he wouldn't want you walking in this kind of weather." The words were out before his brain caught up.

Faith's frown wasn't appreciative. Far from it. "I'll be fine."

"I'm sure you will," Daniel rushed to assure her. He was stepping on her toes left, right, and center. This was the worst proposal a man had never gotten to in the history of proposing. "Ach vell, I'd feel better if you'd let me drive you home."

Faith opened her mouth, stubborn chin tilted in a way that he knew meant she was going to say no. "Please?" he said, cutting her off before she could get the word out. "I'll worry oll dawg und nocht. Besides, Mamm would have a fit if she saw you walking and came home to me safe and snug. She'll be back soon, so that could happen. You wouldn't want to get me in trouble, would you?"

The stubbornness left Faith in a visible whoosh and was replaced with a laugh. "A grown man afraid of his mater?" she teased.

Grinning, Daniel leaned forward to whisper conspiratorially, "Ruth Kanagy can be terrifying when she wants."

Faith's chuckles were the sweetest sound. "Oll recht," she said, giving in. "I wouldn't want to get you in trouble with such a terror."

Daniel put a hand over his heart. "You've saved me."

The way Faith's eyes widened, even as her smile did, too, told him she'd noticed how out of character that gesture was for him. The thing was, though, it felt right with her. Odd to think that he might act differently around Faith . . . simply because she was Faith.

Clearing his throat, he abruptly started walking toward the barn. "Kumme. Stand out of the wind while I hitch up the small buggy."

By the time he turned the horse's head down the Kemps' drive, Rosie was snoring softly in Faith's arms, warm and happily sleeping away. Little baby snores filled the space of the smaller buggy he'd used, since Mamm and Dat had the bigger one. A sweet sound that tugged at his heart the same way Faith's laugh did.

Daniel glanced at Faith, then straight ahead when she caught him looking, and in his mind, he tried to compose the right words, the right way to start, and the words to convince her. Proposing in a buggy was not romantic.

He turned the horse onto the graveled lane leading up to her house before realizing they'd come so far.

It was now. He needed to ask her now.

Gotte, give me the words to persuade her heart, he silently prayed.

Except Faith suddenly sat forward, staring ahead out the window. For the second time driving her home, they both caught sight of a car parked out front of her parents' home.

Ach du lieva. His chance was gone. He was tempted to stop the buggy right there and ask her, but he couldn't do that. He'd just have to think of another opportunity soon.

"Expecting anyone?" Daniel asked. Or maybe Malachi had given up and was going back home, which would give Daniel more time. He was a horrible person to even think it. He would pray for forgiveness as soon as he had a chance.

"No," Faith said slowly. Then she gasped as a small, jeans- and sweatshirt-clad figure opened the car door and got out. "Gotte in heaven. It's Mercy."

Chapter Eight

✳

FOR THE FIRST time in her life, Faith's first reaction to seeing her sister's face wasn't joy. Which was awful in so many different ways.

Ever since the day Mercy had jumped the fence and left their community—disappearing in the night, leaving only a cryptic letter behind—Faith had dreamed and prayed for this day. For the day her sister returned to the bosom of their family.

But looking down at the precious, perfect baby in her arms, the child she'd raised since birth, the child she'd freely and abundantly given her heart to these last months, she had to physically swallow down the worry that rose on a wave of stinging, sour bile.

Rose was Mercy's daughter.

But I'm Rosie's mater.

The selfish words filled her head, and shame immediately followed, making her shift in her seat. She didn't dare glance in Daniel's direction. What if he guessed her self-centered, terrible thoughts? Gotte would have heard them, and she silently asked for His forgiveness. She wouldn't come between mother and child, of course, but giving Rosie up . . . that would shatter her heart.

Was that why Mercy was here? What did her sister's return mean?

Faith swallowed and tried to pull herself together as Daniel slowed the buggy to a stop behind the car. "Don't get out," she said, as he moved to do exactly that. "It's so windy."

What a pathetic excuse. But somehow, she didn't want him there to witness this reunion. To see how horrible she was. Something about Daniel seeing it would highlight her own shameful worries. Because he wouldn't ever have a thought like the ones she was having. He was the man others looked to for the right way, because he always chose the right way.

Before he could argue, she bundled herself and Rosie out of the buggy. Then, pretending he wasn't still parked there watching, she approached her sister, who stood beside the open trunk of the car, watching the entire thing with wary, tired eyes.

Mercy's gaze dropped to Rosie, and any color left in her pale face fled so quickly, Faith hurried her steps, afraid her sister was about to faint.

She got to her, putting a hand on her arm. "Are you oll recht?"

Mercy was still staring at Rosie. "She's gotten so big," she whispered through lips gone tight and pinched.

Heart cracking at . . . everything . . . at Mercy's expression and the pain in her voice but also the pain in Faith's own breast, she took her schwester by the arm. "Let's get inside, hmmm?"

Thankfully, the driver Mercy had hired had already taken her one dingy suitcase and threadbare backpack up the porch to the front door. Nodding as though she wasn't entirely aware of her surroundings, Mercy allowed herself to be led inside.

Inside, where their mater, coming to see who all the people on her front porch were, yelped at the sight that greeted her. Then Mamm rushed forward in a swirl of tears, arms enfolding her long-lost dochder as she uttered words of welcome and praise to Gotte for bringing Mercy home.

Still holding Rosie on one hip, Faith silently brought in the bags, painfully aware of Daniel's buggy moving off down the lane before she closed the front door on the sight and turned to face her family.

Joy and worry tumbled together in a confusing mix inside her. *Gotte, please show me the way through this.*

As she entered the family room, Mercy turned away from their mother to face her. Her sister's gaze dropped to the baby, her expression impossible to read.

Was she scared? Hopeful? Did she feel the burst of love that Faith did every time she looked at Rosie? Or maybe she wasn't ready yet?

"Can I hold her?" Mercy whispered, visibly swallowing.

Afraid. Her sister was afraid.

Somehow that realization allowed Faith to push past her gut reaction to take Rosie and run far away where no one could take her baby away, and instead cross the room. Luckily, Rosie didn't protest at the transition, though she blinked open sleepy eyes. Then a tiny frown appeared, scrunching up her brow as she stared at her mother.

Her mater.

Mercy is her mater and you are only her aendi.

Faith tried to swallow around the lump that lodged in the center of her chest, making it impossible to breathe or swallow or speak.

Then Rosie, still frowning, reached up and explored Mercy's face with her tiny, chubby hands. Mercy sucked in an audible breath, then smiled tremulously. "I bet my face looks familiar," she whispered to the baby. "And my voice. Because your aendi looks and sounds just like your mater. But I'm your mater."

Faith could tell from her tone that Mercy wasn't saying that to be cruel or even trying to tell Rose that important fact. She said it with awe, like this was the first time she'd realized that she had made this precious soul. Tiny and perfect and . . . Rosie.

The lump turned to an ache inside her that threatened to take her to her knees.

Gotte, it hurts. Help me to do the right thing.

Suddenly, Rosie smiled. A wide, beautiful, gummy smile that lit up her face. The same smile that had won Faith's heart when Rose had been about six weeks old—the age when babies finally start to smile. After weeks of crying, and diapers, and sleepless nights, and spit-up, the baby had smiled, and Faith had melted.

She saw Mercy do the same now, her eyes welling with tears. Then Mercy chuckled, and Rosie gurgled a laugh right back to her. As if mater and dochder knew each other to the core, even though the baby had no idea what was happening for sure and certain.

"She's so beautiful," Mercy whispered, and smoothed a hand over the feather-soft fluff of hair that barely covered Rosie's head.

Mercy lifted her head to look at Faith, and the gratefulness in her eyes made Faith's already weak knees wobble. "Thank you." Her schwester choked on the words. She cleared her throat and repeated them stronger, louder. "Thank you for being the amazing sister you are. She is obviously well cared for and loved."

Faith could only nod. She didn't trust her voice to sustain any words. Plus, if she opened her mouth, she might vomit.

This was right. A mother and child should be together. She should step aside.

It just . . . it hurt so badly.

"Are you here to stay?" Mamm finally broke the moment, the question dropping into a pool of silence.

Even Rosie went quiet, blue eyes wide and trained on Mercy's face, seeming to understand the importance of that question.

Mercy took a deep, shaky breath. "I . . . I don't know."

"FAITH?"

Mercy's whisper wasn't exactly subtle, but Faith kept her eyes closed, pretending like she hadn't heard.

"Fay." The whisper took on a familiar wheedle.

Faith's lips twitched, because she knew what was coming next.

"Fay-fay." Mercy would usually sound exasperated about now, but instead sounded unsure. "I know you're awake. I can tell by the way you're breathing."

On a sigh, Faith gave up. She propped herself on her elbow to check that Rosie, in her crib, wasn't stirring. Then she rolled over to find Mercy lying in the twin bed across the way. To make room for the crib, the beds were so close together, they were almost one bed. Mercy was watching her with that worried wrinkle between her eyes she always got when she'd done something wrong.

"Are you mad at me?" Mercy whispered.

Mad? Faith shook her head. No she wasn't mad. She was confused and scared and trying not to give in to her own selfish wants to keep Rosie as hers always.

"But you weren't happy to see me. I could tell." Mercy was still pressing.

She'd always been that way, needing Faith's reassurance. And Faith had always been happy to be her sister's anchor. The only absolute in her life. Until now.

But even now.

Faith reached across the space between them, and after a small hesitation, Mercy reached out, too, so that Faith could squeeze her hand. "I will always be happy to see you. Always. I was . . . shocked, I guess."

And scared. But she wouldn't put that burden on her sister, who had enough to deal with.

Mercy's lips twisted in a rueful smile that didn't quite reach her eyes. "Me too."

Their parents hadn't pressed her sister for details, probably too happy to have her home to want to probe. Malachi . . . well he'd been unusually quiet after meeting Mercy at dinner tonight. Probably trying to figure out if he had to propose to a different Kemp sister now. But he was the lowest of Faith's priorities at the moment.

"Tell me what happened," Faith said. Then, still holding Mercy's hand, she settled in to listen.

Usually this was when her sister would spill all her secrets in a torrent of words and often tears or laughter. Mercy's emotions were never far from the surface. Faith had always envied that about her sister. That she let herself feel whatever came to her.

"After you left with . . . the baby"—she didn't seem to be able to call Rosie by her name—"after that, I went home to Mason like we talked about."

"What did he say when he found out you'd given me Rose?"

Even in the dim of the moonlit room, she could see the hurt that clouded her sister's eyes. "He said that was probably for the best. Honestly, I'm not sure he would have noticed she was even born and then gone the next day if my pregnancy hadn't gotten in the way of his . . . needs."

Maybe for the first time in their lives, Mercy blushed, the color rushing into her cheeks and making her neck all mottled. "He just went back to his job."

Playing video games didn't count as a job if it didn't make them any money, but Faith had already had that discussion with her sister. Several times. So she didn't bring it up now.

Mercy pulled her legs up, reminding Faith of how she'd slept when they were younger, in a ball. "So I went back to work, too. For months, and I was miserable. Not because of the work, but because I missed my baby. I would be in the middle of cleaning up a table at the diner or taking clothes at the dry cleaner and suddenly wonder if she was crawling yet, or what she was eating, or how big she'd gotten." Mercy paused. The next words came out as a whispers. "The sound of her laugh." Then another pause before she shook her head. "Then one day . . . I just couldn't anymore."

Faith tried to control her own breathing, her lungs tight even as her heart pounded. "Couldn't what?"

Her sister gave a twitch of a shrug. "All of it. You were right. Mason was taking advantage of me, letting me support him. And I don't have any friends. Not really. The people I work with hardly noticed I wasn't even pregnant anymore. Only my bosses asked about the baby, but mostly because they wanted to know if I needed any changes to my schedule. And Mason didn't care. But the baby . . ." Tears welled in her eyes. "I couldn't stop thinking about her. About what a horrible mother I was to let her go."

Faith shook her head, her hair sliding loose from the plait she'd braided it into for sleep. "It was a hard decision, but you're not a horrible mater. You made a choice to try to give your child a better life. That's what a gute mater does."

"Is it?" Mercy's chin was wobbling now. "I don't know anymore."

When her sister got like this, there was only one way to stop her from spiraling through the same loop of questions over and over. "Vell . . . you are here now. Let's think about options."

Mercy sniffed but, looking marginally relieved, nodded. "Okay."

Options. What about Faith's options? Except she didn't have any, because she was only Rosie's aendi.

"The way I see it, you have a few . . ."

"Really?" Mercy blinked as if she couldn't see any.

"Really. First, you have to decide if you will stay here or go back out into the world and start a life without Mason."

Mercy waited, and Faith, once upon a time, would have smiled at the childlike trust her sister still put in her sometimes, the same as when they were kinder.

"If you go, you can leave Rosie here with me. Maybe

you could get a job nearby so you can see her often. I think that would make you hurt less."

"Yeah," Mercy whispered.

Heaven help her, her emotions were being yanked in so many directions. Having her twin sister home with her had been her dream for years. But now that Rosie had taken over her heart . . . she couldn't see any path that led anywhere but heartache of one kind or another.

"Or"—Faith had to swallow before she could force out the next words—"you can take her with you. But can you afford to pay for a home, bills, *and* a babysitter or day care or something like that?"

"No." The single word was uttered on a heavy sigh.

Thank Gotte for that at least.

"Oll recht. The other way would be for you to stay here."

Mercy made a face. "Where, though? There'll be no room with Mamm and Dat in the dawdi haus when they move in there." Her frown grew darker. "I can't believe they sold it, by the way. Without even mentioning it to you, no less." She shook her head. The farm had always meant more to Mercy than to Faith, though. "Besides, if I lived with them, I would have to be baptized Amish."

For the Amish, baptism was done as an adult. A very serious decision and only entered into with the intent to live an Amish life.

"Jah. That is true." Because if Mercy wasn't baptized, eventually Mamm and Dat, and Faith for that matter, would be asked to shun her. That wouldn't help anyone.

"I don't know if I can do that." The wobble returned to Mercy's chin. "I mean, I wouldn't like being in the house all day. I'd feel trapped."

Faith worried at her lower lip, thinking through the jobs

Mercy had had before in the outside world. "Maybe you can get a job as a waitress at one of the places in town."

Mercy blinked again, like that hadn't occurred to her yet. That being stuck in the house wasn't her only option. "I guess that's true. I'm a good waitress. You should have seen the tips I made in Phoenix."

Faith had. So had Mason. Was it horrible of her to hope that he was struggling with the loss of Mercy's income now? She knew it was. Amish life taught her to practice forgiveness the way Christ practiced it. Freely given. No one was righteous in the eyes of Gotte. Even Mason deserved a merciful heart.

She'd have to pray Gotte gave her one where Rosie's dad was concerned.

"So if you don't mind working here in Charity Creek . . ." Faith continued as she warmed to the only idea that had come to her that would allow Mercy to stay and Faith to keep Rosie at the same time. "Maybe we could move to a small place in town together. You could be a waitress, and I'm making flower arrangements for the Kanagys' shop now. We could raise Rosie together."

Then I could be a mother figure to Rosie at least. Keep her close.

Mercy stared at her, eyes wide. "You would do that?"

That wasn't a no.

Hope suddenly cast a ray of sunlight over the pall that had clouded her heart since the moment her sister had arrived.

"I love you," Faith said. "You know that. And I love Rosie. Of course I would do that."

"But what about Malachi?" Mercy asked, tone teasing.

No one had said anything about Malachi's proposal to Faith, but Mercy, while she always had trouble seeing the right paths for her own life, was still sharp as a pin when it came to seeing others clearly. Faith shouldn't be surprised that she'd guessed about Malachi and Faith and a possible relationship.

It was a fair question. One Faith wasn't ready to answer yet. "He and I have barely started dating."

If you could call one picnic that.

"Do you love him?"

"Not yet," she said slowly. After all, she had been seriously considering that proposal.

Mercy nodded. "I didn't think so." Her sudden grin was like a burst of color, flowers in a field in the spring. "No spark."

Faith chuckled. That was true enough. "It wasn't about the spark."

Which sobered her sister right up. "I guess not." She huffed a sigh. "Putting Malachi aside for now, there's another issue."

"What?"

"You've been baptized."

"Jah."

"Would you continue to remain in the Amish community if we lived together?"

"Jah. I love it. I always have. You know that."

"But if I don't, what will they say? They would make you shun me. It's still the same situation."

True. But maybe an exception could be made for twin sisters, and their situation, and the fact that only Faith and not an entire family would be impacted by Mercy's "outsider influences." It was worth asking.

Faith studied her sister's face. "Do you want me to talk to the bishop and see what he says?"

Mercy paused, obviously thinking about it, then nodded slowly. "Jah. Let's talk to the bishop before we make any more decisions."

They stared at each other, and Faith tried to picture their lives together if this worked out. Living together with them both working, both mothers to Rosie. It meant they could both be happy, didn't it? Was it possible this had been Gotte's plan all along?

She prayed it was even as she ignored the small pinch around her heart and a small moment where she could see Daniel's face so clearly, he may as well have been standing there beside her. The knowledge that choosing that path meant giving up dreams of a husband and family of her own one day hurt, but Daniel had never shown any smidgen of an interest in her that way. Rosie was who was important now.

I will have a family. Just not a traditional one.

Chapter Nine

❋

MERCY KEMP WAS back in town.

That fact had knocked his proposal down the road several miles. The situation was as much of a thunderclap three days later as it had been when Daniel had seen her get out of the car. A mirror image of Faith, she'd been dressed in jeans and a sweatshirt that had clearly seen better days, as had the dingy sneakers on her feet.

He couldn't get Faith's tiny gasp of reaction out of his mind.

Maybe because, despite the way she'd arranged her expression so that no emotion showed, that sound had been filled with it—shock, joy, worry, and thousand other emotions all clear as a bell inside that tiny noise.

Figuring out why didn't take much effort, either.

Rosie was coming up on a year old, and Faith had been her mother for all intents and purposes all this time, but she also loved her sister dearly. What had to be going through her mind? And what did this mean for her? Was Mercy staying?

He'd wanted to stay by her side, make sure she was okay, but she clearly hadn't wanted that. Since then, a thousand times a day he'd thought of going over there to check on her. But he hadn't proposed, she hadn't said yes, and that made this none of his business. Even if he wanted it to be his business.

"That's not the right harness," Dat said from behind him.

Daniel was in the barn getting Frank hitched to take them to Gmay. The church service was being held at the Smuckers' today. He looked down at the tangle of leather, buckles, and pads in his hands and hid a groan. Dat was right.

"That's Daisy's," Dat said now, his tone saying that Daniel should have known that, given that he'd been helping hitch up the two horses since he'd been old enough to reach their withers.

"Sorry," Daniel muttered, and put the harness he was holding away, picking up the right one and bringing it over to Frank. The horse actually turned his head to look at him, like, *Even I know which harness is the right one, dumkoff.*

Of course, Frank gave them looks like that all that time. The horse was a bit of a know-it-all.

"What has gotten into you lately?" Dat asked as he stood on the other side and helped strap Frank in. "It's like your head is somewhere else, while your body is here."

Daniel ducked down to grab the belly strap, not looking at his parent. He wouldn't lie. His father knew him well enough to know it for a lie, and besides, he was right. Daniel's head had been with Faith all these days.

What a tangled mess the Kemp sisters seemed to have gotten themselves into. There was nothing he could, or should, be doing to help. This was something the sisters and the Kemp family had to work out among themselves.

Maybe I can pull her aside today and talk.

"See," Dat said, exasperation filling his voice. "You did it again. Mind a thousand miles away and buckling the wrong thing."

Daniel blinked at what he was doing. *Oh, sis yuscht.* He'd messed up the bridle. Frank heaved a dramatic sigh, clearly also unimpressed.

"Sorry, Dat," he apologized again. What else could he say? Nothing.

He hadn't told his parents about Mercy's arrival in town. He figured that was the Kemps' truth to reveal to the community when they were ready.

Maybe today at Gmay?

After all, it had been three days. Three days without a single sighting of Faith or Mercy. Or any of the Kemps. He'd seen Malachi in the distance twice when he'd been out in the field moving his beehives, but he hadn't approached, just lifted a hand in a wave and gone about his business.

The last person he wanted to get the details from was Malachi.

Faith, meanwhile, hadn't shown up at the store or at the honey room to work on her flower arrangements once. Not having a clue about how to make dried flower arrangements, he wasn't sure if that had been her plan anyway. After all, it could take a while to dry the flowers, couldn't it?

He'd been tempted to go in and look around but had resisted the urge.

You're doing it again. Head in the clouds. He shook

himself out of his thoughts and determinedly helped finish getting Frank strapped in.

"I think it's safer if *I* drive." Dat took the reins from him as they were loading into the buggy.

Daniel didn't bother to argue. At his mater's raised eyebrows, his fater just shook his head. She tossed Daniel a worried glance but didn't ask any questions, trusting her husband.

When they got to the Smuckers', Daniel was still standing on the other side of the buggy when he caught his mamm's question to his dat. "Why couldn't Daniel drive?" she asked in a whisper that wasn't all that quiet.

"Have you seen the way he can't concentrate on anything the last few days?"

"Mmmm," Mamm agreed. "Is he sickening for something?"

He almost didn't stick around to hear the rest, but Dat's next words pulled him up short. "I think he's in love."

Mamm's gasp covered Daniel's own grunt of surprise, and he glanced at Hosea Hoffstetter. The boy was helping take care of all the horses and buggies today, but he didn't act as if he'd heard.

In love?

He cared for Faith, of course. He'd had an almighty crush on her when she was nineteen, before Mercy ran off, but love?

"With who?" Mamm asked.

See? If Mamm hadn't noticed, then Dat was seeing something that wasn't there.

"Faith Kemp. The way he looks at her . . ." Dat paused. "It's the same way I look at you."

It was?

"Ach, go on with you," Mamm laughed. "And Daniel is only being helpful to a girl who could use a friend."

Daniel didn't hear much more. His head and heart were spinning. Was that why he'd talked himself into proposing? Faith was a gute and kind woman, for sure and certain. She made him laugh, and probably got him talking more than most did. He was comfortable with her. He liked being around her.

Nae. He knew that he *could* grow to love her, or he wouldn't have considered proposing, but Mamm was right. Besides, Dat didn't know about Mercy's return, and that was the reason Daniel had been acting odd. Vell . . . that and his plan to ask Faith to marry him.

But he would wait on that now until he knew what was happening with Mercy.

Daniel nodded and took himself away. However, inside the barn, he still found himself searching the gathering of men for Henry Kemp. But that was only because he was still worried about Faith and Rosie. That was all.

Her fater wasn't there, though.

And he didn't come while they waited. He wasn't there by the time the men started to filter into the house where the wooden benches had been set up for the service. And Faith and her mater weren't there when the women came in, either.

The rock of worry sitting in his gut grew larger and larger until they opened their Ausbunds to sing the first traditional hymn. In the middle of the song, though, the barn door opened and Faith walked in behind her parents, each quickly taking a seat under the watchful gazes of the entire gmay.

The rock, which had shrunk at the sight of them, grew

again as he realized that Faith wasn't holding Rosie . . . and Mercy wasn't there. In fact, Faith sat with the unmarried girls her age, rather than with the young mothers, where she usually sat.

Gotte in heaven. Had Mercy come home only to take Rosie away? Were they already gone? Faith must be heartsore.

She wouldn't look up, gaze dutifully glued to the pages of the book in her hand, mouth moving, though he couldn't hear from where he sat if she was singing. Maybe he should speak to her after service. Just to be sure she was . . .

What?

Not sad? Not heartbroken? If Mercy took Rosie away, of course Faith would be upset. What good would come of his asking her about it?

What he wanted to do was wrap his arms around her and tell her everything would end up as it should, but he definitely couldn't do that.

With Dat's comments about the way he looked at Faith still ringing in his ears, Daniel made himself look away, focusing instead on Gotte and sermons, which is what he should be doing, anyway.

He managed not to glance at her a single time again throughout the service. Then, outside, he made sure to sit with his back to the tables that held all the food so he couldn't watch as she helped to serve without craning his neck. A small part of him hoped she'd serve his table. Maybe then he could casually ask about Mercy.

But she didn't.

Which was how he found himself still wondering, even after the meal was over and everyone had helped clear up, what was going on. Most of the community had packed up and driven on home to enjoy their day of rest with their families. No one said anything about Mercy, which made him wonder if the Kemps were even sharing about her.

"Where's your fater?" Mamm asked as she bundled her casserole dish into the back seat of the buggy.

"I don't know."

"I think I saw him go around back with Elam Smucker to look at something in the barn. Can you find him for me?"

With a nod, Daniel tromped away, pulling his thick coat tighter around him. The days were getting colder yet. Soon it would be time to do his final winter prep for the bees. Maybe this week on his day to be doing chores at home.

He hadn't yet rounded the side of the barn when voices reached him. Today was still and quiet, rather than windy, which was probably why they carried his way.

"So you see," a woman was saying, "if I am to help my schwester, it seems best to live with her. Except she doesn't want to come back to her Amish roots. What do you think?"

Daniel's steps slowed. He knew that voice. Even more, he knew the question she was asking. That was Faith.

She wanted to live with Mercy? So her sister hadn't gone off with Rosie?

A lump that wouldn't let him so much as breathe lodged in his throat.

"Ach vell, that is a tough one you've brought to me, Faith," Jethro Miller said. The bishop of their gmay, he spoke with a recognizably slow, deliberate cadence. Jethro tended to make decisions the same way—like Daniel himself did. "My greatest concern would be for your own faith," he was saying. "To live with someone who isn't Amish means that you will be around that way of thinking more than you are around the community you've been baptized into. That is why we don't allow non-Amish to live with us. What if your sister, through no fault of her own, were to lead you astray?"

"I was with Mercy for five years in the outside world, though," Faith pointed out. "I never strayed. I obeyed the Ordnung every day. I sought out Amish communities to be part of and worship with every place I went. If Mercy was going to take me away from my faith, I think it would have happened already."

"Mmmm. . . ." Jethro mused. "You do have a point."

"And what if Gotte has given us this chance so that someday Mercy might return to her own faith? What if, rather than her leading me astray, I lead her home?"

A cleared throat sounded. Then Jethro said, "Be careful. That kind of thinking can lead to pride or to heartbreak if it doesn't happen. Let Gotte work in Mercy's heart, jah?"

"Jah, I understand." Faith's response was soft. Even embarrassed.

"Let me think about this some more and discuss it with the other ministers and with your parents. I would also like to speak with Mercy, if you think she'd be up for that."

"Oh, denki." Faith's breathed words sounded almost like a prayer of praise. "I'm sure she will if it means . . ."

If it meant that the sisters could stay together always. Raise Rosie together. Daniel hadn't heard all of the conversation, but he'd heard enough to understand that much.

Daniel turned away, boots heavy on his feet like he'd walked through mud and heart heavy in his chest like it had been hewed of stone. It made sense, what Faith was proposing. Mercy was Rose's true mother, but Faith was her mother in act. As twins, they were even closer than most siblings, and Faith would do anything—*anything*—for the people she loved most. If the sisters lived together and both worked, they could afford to live and share the raising of the baby. Faith wouldn't have to give her up.

It would mean sacrificing other things, like having a family of her own, but that was Faith's decision.

He couldn't propose to her now. He wouldn't do that to her. Rip her apart that way. She'd sounded so . . . happy . . . that the bishop was even considering letting her do this. He would never make her choose between Rosie and him.

Daniel tried to push his way through more pain than he had expected to feel. Dat's words rattled around inside his head.

Would it hurt this bad if I didn't love her? Then, in the next instant . . . *Does it matter?* She'd chosen her path, and it wouldn't ever be with him. Whether he loved her or not didn't matter anymore.

He hadn't realized that he'd stopped walking entirely and was standing there staring at his boots until Faith's voice sounded behind him. "Daniel?"

Faith must've finished her conversation with the bishop. Doing his best to hide his thoughts, he turned. "Wie bischt, Faith?"

"Hi." Her smile was a bit shaky. "What are you doing here?"

"Looking for my fater."

"Oh." She bit her lip, then glanced behind her. "Did you hear any of that?"

He winced, but Faith was his friend, and he wouldn't dishonor their friendship by lying to her. "Jah. A little."

"I see." She stared at her hands, which were twisted together before her. "I—"

"I thought I saw your parents leave earlier."

She raised worried eyes to his but nodded. "I thought I'd walk home."

Daniel smiled. "You seem to like to do that."

"Jah. I like walking."

"Maybe . . ." Maybe his lot in life was to be her friend. Her true friend. That meant being there for her. Would she even want to talk to him? She probably wasn't ready to share any of what was going on with her family with anyone. He closed his mouth.

"Would you want to walk me home?" she asked on a rush.

The way his heart lightened at the question . . . *I'm in trouble.* "Sure. Let me tell Mamm."

"Oll recht."

He hurried around the side of the barn, and Mamm waved from where she sat beside Dat in the buggy. "I found him," she called.

Daniel stopped at the open door. "I'm going to walk Faith home," he told them.

Then he had to hide another wince at the way they exchanged a glance. No doubt they were picturing another wedding soon. He'd have to set them straight when he got home.

"Have a gute time," Mamm said.

"It's not like that," Daniel answered, then turned away before she had a chance to reply.

Chapter Ten

✳

FAITH WALKED ALONG quietly beside Daniel, wondering for the hundredth time since she'd asked him to come with her *why* she'd asked him.

Maybe because after the learning that the bishop wanted to discuss it with the other ministers, and despite the relief that Jethro hadn't said no outright, a pit of worry had still formed in her stomach.

She didn't want to be alone with that worry.

Faith knew from all that time trailing after Mercy how worry could gnaw at your insides until it hurt to eat, hurt to breathe, hurt to think. This felt like that, only worse. Because she had a chance to keep Rosie. She prayed that this was Gotte's will for her life, for Mercy's life.

"I have a confession to make." Daniel's quiet rumble startled her out of her own thoughts.

Despite the gnawing worry, Faith smiled. "A confession, huh?"

"Jah. I . . ." He grimaced. "I overheard a bigger part of your conversation with Jethro Miller than I let on."

Faith might have given in to her own dismay at that, except Daniel rounded his shoulders, hands stuffed in the pockets of his jacket, clearly waiting for the worst. Almost like a little boy waiting to be scolded by his mater. He didn't like to do wrong, did he?

She knew the feeling well. "Ach vell, I don't mind you knowing."

He lifted his head at that, studying her with dark eyes. Kind eyes. And Faith realized all of a sudden that she meant it. That the dismay that had pinched for a moment was more about wanting to hide this plan from others until she was sure of the answer. More than that, she was glad of someone to talk to about it. Someone not quite as invested in the outcomes and answers.

Daniel had broad shoulders and a kind heart. If anyone would understand, he would, and if he chose to give her any guidance, she'd listen gladly. He wasn't one to steer her wrong. She trusted him completely.

"Mercy missed Rose," she said in a rush of words. "She left the man who is the fater and doesn't want to go back to him. And I . . ." She bit her lip.

"You can't give up Rosie?" Daniel said for her.

See? She'd known he would be understanding. The worried knots inside her loosened a tiny bit. "Nae. I've given her my heart, and find I can't . . ."

She couldn't even make the words come out, so shrugged instead.

"So you and Mercy are going to raise her together?"

"Jah. Mercy is a gute waitress, and also worked in a dry cleaner and a gift shop in Phoenix, so hopefully she can get a job in town." Or two, but hopefully that wouldn't be necessary. "And I have my flower arrangements . . ."

"I see." Daniel nodded.

But the bishop's words were still playing through her head. "I just pray the ministers will see that I remained a faithful Amish woman, even out in the world all that time. That my sister's influence would never turn me away from my faith. Never. Neenet."

Another nod as he walked steadily along beside her. Did everyone lay their worries at his feet the way she was doing?

Who did Daniel bring his worries to? He had to have them.

"I'm sure they will realize that." His brows squished together. "Will Mercy let you raise Rosie as Amish?"

Gute question. "I haven't got that far yet. I hope so."

"Is there a reason she kept her home today?"

No doubt it didn't look quite right. Faith had debated long and hard about that. "I wanted to be able to talk to the bishop without distraction, and Rosie can be a big distraction."

Daniel's smile was endearingly crooked. "For sure and certain, but a nice one."

"Do you want kinder someday?" The question was out before she could stop herself, but once it was out, she didn't take it back. She wanted to know.

"Jah. Someday." His mouth pulled down at the corners, that frown back as he seemed to be wrestling with something. "I need to find a wife first."

That was certainly the more traditional, Amish way of things. A sudden image of her standing in a kitchen with a rounded belly and a kinder holding on to her skirts as

Daniel came in the door from working in the shop sent an ache through Joy's heart.

Not for Daniel, she told herself. Then had to repeat it in her head several times. The ache was for the family she was giving up to do this with Mercy and Rose.

"You will be a wonderful gute fater," she murmured. "Look at how Rosie took right to you."

Daniel said nothing to that, and she got the impression he was a tiny bit embarrassed.

"So where will you and Mercy live?" he asked instead. "At your parents'?"

"Nae. That will be Malachi's house soon, so we couldn't do that. Besides, even if we could, our parents, out of love, would drive Mercy up a wall with all their pestering her to return to her Amish way of life."

"I'm sure they only want what's best for her."

Faith nodded. "But Mercy . . . ach vell, she only digs her heels in if you keep after her. She has to figure things out for herself. I'm hoping . . ." *Oh, sis yuscht.* She shouldn't share that. He would think her deerich—foolish—or prideful, which was just as bad.

But rather than take her to task for her hopes, like the bishop had, he only said, "You'll be a gute example for her. Maybe that will lead her heart down a new path."

"Only if it's Gotte's plan." She tried to take her own pride out of it.

Daniel suddenly leaned over to whisper in a conspiratorial voice, "Don't worry. I don't think it's pride."

How had he known? "After being away so long, I'm trying to take extra care—"

Daniel put a hand on her arm, cutting her off as he stopped her to face him. "You don't have to try so hard with me," he said. "Maybe with others who seem to be missing charity in their hearts, but not me."

His handsome face was arranged in an intent expression that only made him more handsome, sending her heart fluttering around inside her like a butterfly newly hatched from its cocoon.

"I believe you," she whispered.

Daniel scanned her features, as if making sure she meant that, then hitched a smile. "Gute."

He started them back down the road.

Faith was tired of talking about her situation. Tired of the worry. "How is moving the bees going?" she asked.

"Slowly, but I'm making progress."

"Maybe I could help you on the days I come over to work on my flowers. I could walk that way as easily as down the road."

His glance was filled with an emotion she didn't understand. Or maybe not, because he nodded. "That would be nice."

"Would it be a long walk from my house?"

"Not far." He shrugged. "But I may need to plant more flowering bushes, trees, and shrubs in the area to make up for losing that field. What do you think?"

Faith's eyebrows winged up. "I don't know much about bees."

"But you do about flowers," he pointed out.

Which was true enough. Should she admit that after Malachi's revelation about plowing up that field, she'd done a little research in the library? It seemed like an overly forward thing for her to do. Maybe she'd keep that to herself. "Vell . . . I think they certainly liked the goldenrod."

"Jah."

"And it seems to me you'd want native plants that don't take much care after you plant them and that grow well in these areas."

"That makes gute sense."

She was on a roll now. "Flowers that produce a lot of blooms might be a gute idea, too, so it would provide a lot of pollen for them."

"Like what?"

Faith bit her lip, trying to remember what was in the book she'd checked out. "Um . . . giant hyssop and milkweed, or purple prairie clover?"

Daniel nodded along to each of those. "I don't know what that first one is, but the others make sense. You're awfully clever, Faith."

Oh dear. That warm surge of pride was going to be her downfall with this man. Plus, lying by omission was still lying. "Actually . . . I checked out a book."

He cocked his head, staring at the side of her face as her cheeks heated at the admission. "A book? What about?"

"Um . . ." Good grief, this was embarrassing. "About good plants for bees in Indiana."

"Really?"

At least he didn't sound horrified that she'd gone and done that—just mildly curious. The way a friend would. She was making too much of thing. "Jah. I have it at home if you want to take a look?"

"That would be helpful."

But what would her mamm say? Or Dat? Or Mercy or Malachi, for that matter? Faith hadn't figured out what was going to happen with Malachi now, though she supposed that was mostly up to him. Maybe he'd still want to marry her. What then? She couldn't say that she was disappointed that her new plan with Mercy would mean marriage to Malachi wasn't as necessary. Maybe he'd be relieved, too, to be able to pick his own bride and still end up with the farm?

She didn't have to wait long to find out her family's reaction.

She and Daniel walked in through the front door, which was never locked, to find them all sitting in the family room together. The scent of Mamm's casserole bubbling away in the oven filled the house. Rosie was pulling herself up on the couch and using it to balance as she tried to take steps. Then she'd wobble and plop back down on her behind, then giggle and giggle, and make the others laugh.

Which is why it took a moment before anyone noticed Faith and Daniel standing there.

"Oh!" Mamm jumped up from where she'd been sitting by Dat on the couch, smiling widely. "You didn't tell us to expect a guest, Faith."

"I'm not a guest," Daniel was the one to rush to reassure. "I just walked Faith home."

"That was nice of you," Mamm said slowly, her gaze sliding to a frowning Malachi.

Faith hid a wince. She'd forgotten that Malachi had offered to walk her home as well and she'd sent him on with her parents.

"Daniel was still there when I finished talking with the bishop," she said in an attempt to smooth any ruffled feathers.

"I was pretty pushy about it," he added.

It took all she had to keep from swinging wide eyes his way. As if Daniel was ever pushy about anything. But she managed to hold her reaction in, and both Mamm and Malachi looked happier.

"I can drive you home to save you more walking in the cold," Malachi offered.

Faith tilted her head, studying the Amish man whom she'd thought she might marry but didn't know at all. He could be a nice man when he wanted.

"Denki," Daniel said. "I would appreciate that."

"Let me get you that book before you go," Faith said as Malachi made to get up.

"Book?" Dat was the one to ask.

"Jah. A book on flowers." There. That sounded as though she had checked it out for her new business. "I thought Daniel might be interested for his bees."

"Oh." Mamm was glancing between them now. Maybe Faith hadn't made it sound as casual as she'd hoped. Then her mother's face cleared. "That's right. You make the honey for the shop."

"Jah," Daniel said. "It was my mamm's idea originally, but I ended up liking working with the bees."

"Do you get stung a lot?" Mercy asked.

He shook his head. "No. I wear special clothes that protect me. Mostly."

"You should see the honey room," Faith said. "It's where he's letting me work on my flower arrangements."

Something her parents knew all about, so they nodded.

"A honey room?" Mercy asked. "A whole room for making honey?"

"For extracting it after the bees make it, jah," Daniel said. "It's nice to see you home, Mercy."

Mercy's smile could have charmed those very bees into making a lot more. "Thanks. Your bees sound interesting. I would love to see you extract the honey sometime."

The immediate "no" that sprang to Faith's lips came with a quick sting of fresh guilt. And confusion. Who was she to say no to that? Just because Mercy tended to flirt with every man she came across shouldn't make a difference to Faith. Mercy didn't mean anything by it, and Daniel was looking for an Amish wife, so he wouldn't take it seriously anyway.

There was no reason for Faith to be bothered. "I'll go get the book—"

In that moment, Rosie gave a tiny gurgle and, as they all turned their gazes to her, took a step away from the couch she was using for balance while they'd been talking. Then with her arms stretched out for Daniel, another step, and another, her bright blue gaze glued squarely on him.

"Oh my God!" Mercy's squeal startled the baby, who lost her balance and plopped down, looking surprised to find herself suddenly back on her bottom.

"I know you've been gone some time, but we do not take the Lord's name in vain in this house," Dat immediately corrected Mercy, but the reminder was in a gentler tone than he would have used years ago.

"Sorry, Dat," Mercy said. "But she walked!" Laughing, she scooped Rose up in her arms and danced with her around the room. "Who is the cleverest baby in all the world?" she cooed.

Faith didn't miss their fater's pinched lips. No doubt he was holding back another rebuke about pride. They were trying so hard, no doubt terrified of losing their dochder again. But living with their parents was definitely a veesht idea. Wonderful bad. They would constantly be correcting Mercy or holding in their upset at her Englischer ways. They might even drive her away again—only this time Mercy would take Rosie with her.

Rosie held up her hands out to Faith with a whine that was impossible to resist.

Heart tumbling over because her baby had walked to her, Faith scooped Rosie up. Except Rosie made a face and reached for Daniel.

Oh. Faith's heart stopped tumbling. Maybe even stopped beating altogether. Because Rosie was not going to her, but to Daniel.

And she isn't your baby. She glanced between Rosie and Mercy, who was grinning so widely her face had to hurt from it.

Trying to hold back tears that burned, Faith handed Rosie over to Daniel.

Face flaring with color, he said nothing. But he did smile at Rosie, who smiled and gurgled right back.

"I'll go get the buggy," Malachi said, his face and voice as stiff as a starched shirt.

Faith cleared her throat, trying to get rid of the lump that had formed there from a thousand different emotions. "I'll get the book."

Chapter Eleven

✳

THE CHARITY CREEK Harvest Festival seemed to grow in popularity every year. Daniel couldn't believe how many more booths, more events, more foods, more rides, and definitely more people there were this year. As a boy, he remembered this festival being half the size at least.

All the people milling about usually made it one of his least favorite events. Not that anyone was very unpleasant. It was just . . . a lot. But there was no getting out of it. Mamm and Dat insisted on having a booth for their shop. Mamm said they sold ten times more goods in the two days of the weekend festival than they did in a week in the store and got returning customers, including online orders. They did gute business in the store and didn't necessarily need more, so he wasn't so sure all this hassle was worth it. After all, Amish were after not riches, but only enough. Enough was as good as a feast.

He didn't argue with his mamm.

Aaron was working in the booth for the Troyers' furniture and woodworking store, so he couldn't help. Thankfully, Joshua, Hope, and Joy were all available to work at A Thankful Heart's booth. That meant Daniel's only job was to help set up, take down, and carry the heavier items each day, and now they were two days in. He was just stowing the last of the boxes under a table covered in a floor-length cloth when a girly giggle reached him.

"Wie bischt, Daniel?" He knew that voice. That was Clara Gick.

Trying his best to arrange his features in an expression that wasn't resigned, he straightened and looked over at her. Pretty as a picture, as always, in a dark green dress under a heavy wool coat, her cheeks were rosy, probably from the nip in the air. At least the winds had died down for the day and the sun was shining.

"Hallo," he said in return.

"I was hoping you'd be here."

Daniel frowned, trying to reason out why that would be. He and Clara weren't particularly close. Unfortunately, she chose to say this in front of Mamm, who flicked him a considering glance before saying, "Daniel is all done for the morning."

Ugh. Why did she have to go and say that? Yes, he'd been a little down since learning of Faith and Mercy's plans, but that didn't mean he wanted to spend time with Clara. Alone.

Clara perked up, smiling prettily while somehow still managing to look appropriately reserved. "Would you like to walk around the booths with me?"

Not really.

"That sounds like fun," Mamm said, giving him a gentle but unmistakable nudge. "You haven't done anything with folks your own age in a while."

Thank heavens Joshua was still busy with the horse and buggy, so Daniel wouldn't have to hear about this from his bruders for the rest of his life. Meanwhile, Hope and Joy, standing behind his mater, suddenly were very busy unpacking and arranging small knickknacks on the shelves that he'd put up for them. Which meant he'd get no help from that quarter, and Dat was with Joshua.

"There's an entire booth dedicated to honey," Clara said in a cajoling voice.

Daniel tried not to visibly sigh. While he enjoyed talking with other beekeepers, he found that others waiting for him to finish talking got bored and left, or dragged him away sooner than he was ready. He was fairly certain Clara would fall into both the bored and dragging categories.

But he couldn't see any way out of this. "Oll recht."

She beamed as he pulled his beanie down over his ears better. The wind might not be blowing, but the nip in the air was wintry. The first snow couldn't be too far away.

Looping her arm through his, Clara walked them off down the aisle, stopping to go into the booths she was interested in. After the fourth booth in a row dedicated to items for the home—furnishings, decor, gadgets, and such—he came to the inevitable conclusion that Clara was going to stop at every single booth like this.

She lived with her parents in a house that was well stocked, and she didn't have any boyfriend as far as he knew. Why did she need home goods anyhow? Was she looking for gifts?

Meanwhile, he stood inside each space, trying his best to stay out of the way.

"Isn't this adorable?" Clara held up a carrier basket that was clearly meant for pies—round with wooden stands on the inside to separate multiple pies in a stack and lined with a simple maroon cloth that fit over the handles.

A person could bring at least three pies to an event with that, which was useful . . . but adorable? "It looks very handy."

She pursed her lips in what he had a feeling she wanted to look like disappointment, but really came across more like she was displeased with his response. She held it up, twirling it and studying it. "It would be handy to bring extra pies when I bake," she mused.

Trying to scrape any kind of conversation into his head, Daniel latched on to that. "Do you like to bake?"

The way her brows drew down, though, maybe he'd said the wrong thing?

"Daniel Kanagy, I bake every time I get a chance. I'm sure you've enjoyed my pies many times. People ask me for them specially."

He never paid much attention to who baked what. How did he get himself out of this conversation without hurting her feelings?

Thankfully, Clara set the basket down and took his arm again. Overly familiar, as far as he was concerned, but he couldn't figure out a way to shake her off without embarrassing her or hurting her feelings. "I'll have to think about it after I look over the other booths," she said.

There had to be at least a hundred booths at the festival. Was he now stuck looking at every single one?

"What do you want to look at, Daniel?" she asked.

He wanted to go home. "I don't have anything to look for."

Clara gave a gurgling little laugh like he'd said the funniest possible thing. "Everybody needs something."

He was tempted to tell her that of all the everybodies out there, the Amish were the least likely to need something. But he had a feeling that would make him sound . . . steady. He was tired of being steady.

Steady had lost him Faith. Twice, if he was honest with himself. He should have courted her long before Mercy ever ran off. Steady wasn't gute. Steady was slow.

"Do you have any suggestions?" he said, just to ask something.

His question seemed to mean a lot more to her than he thought it should, based on the way she brightened and tucked in closer to him, holding on to his arm tighter. This was just shopping? Wasn't it?

"Ach, I have lots of ideas," she said.

Biting back a groan, he let her take the lead. Daniel assumed she would take him somewhere useful, like the honey booth she had told him about, or maybe something to do with items they could sell in the shop, or perhaps a small token for his mother's birthday, or even something like pegs to hang on the wall in his room for his clothes. Come to think of it, he could really use something like that. He was always leaving his clothes strewn across the end of his bed, and it drove Mamm nuts.

But Clara pulled him into another booth full of home-related goods. So he did what he'd been doing before and stopped right inside the makeshift door.

"What are you doing, silly?" Using her grip on his arm, Clara tugged him along in her wake. "You have to look around."

What? In here? He was fairly certain there was nothing

he would find interesting in this particular booth. Most of the items were things Englischers might like. In fact, many were similar to things they frequently sold in his family's shop—signs with inspirational sayings, fluffy pillows edged in lace, clothes that Amish wouldn't wear, and a few larger items, like furniture and so forth. If he wanted new furniture, he'd ask his brother Aaron to make it for him. But he had no place for it, since he lived with his parents.

"Oh!" Clara let go of his arm to hurry over to an admittedly handsome-looking rocking chair. Low-backed and simple, all straight lines with nice broad armrests, it was made of oak and stained naturally. "I can just see you sitting in this after dinner reading the Bible to . . ." She paused, color staining her cheeks. "To your family."

"Dat reads the Bible to us at night," Daniel said pragmatically. That was his fater's joy. "And I sit on the couch with Mamm. I have no need for a rocking chair." Especially not while he had no wife and children.

"I meant after you get married, silly."

Daniel was getting a little tired of being called silly. But Clara was smiling as she said it, so he took it as her way of teasing or showing her amusement. Although he didn't see what was so funny. "Maybe something smaller," he suggested hopefully. "The honey?"

Again her face filled with that expression that looked a lot like disappointment . . . or aggravation . . . to him. Although he wasn't quite sure what he'd done to earn either of those responses just because he didn't want to shop for a rocking chair.

"I'm sure you have all the honey things you need." She waved the notion away with her hand.

"Uh . . . maybe you're right." He shrugged. "But sometimes it helps to talk to other beekeepers to see what tricks they use or how they've solved certain problems that I have been dealing with. They might have ideas that would be helpful."

The disappointment on her face sank into deeper lines that took away some of the pretty. "Oh, oll recht. I'll show you."

This time she didn't take his arm, and Daniel had to follow her out of the booth up and down several aisles. He spotted the honey booth before they got there. It wasn't hard to spot, with its bright yellow tent over the top and a giant honeybee in the center of the sign. The tables were set up with stacks and stacks of jars of honey, beeswax goods, and other decorations. It was manned by an older gentleman whose hair was stark white under his hat and a woman Daniel assumed was the man's wife.

Daniel spotted a row of jars filled with beautifully light-colored honey. Most of his this year had turned out particularly dark. Before he could close the distance between himself and the booth to ask about it, though, Clara, who had been walking ahead of him at a slightly faster clip, suddenly slowed so that he caught up with her. She tucked her hand into his arm like she had earlier. Then, with a blindingly sunny smile, she pointed at the honey booth. "There it is. Are you so excited?"

"Clara!" a female voice called through the crowd. "I've been looking for you all over the festival."

Using her grip on him, Clara stopped them both, pulling them off to the side so that they wouldn't block the path for other festivalgoers. Then she laughed as Susannah Swarey reached them, along with several more friends. "I'm sorry, Susie. Daniel and I have been busy shopping for furniture."

With the way every person in the group did a double

take, staring wide-eyed between him and Clara at that piece of information, Daniel had to bite his tongue to keep himself from embarrassing Clara by denying that. Loudly. The problem was, how could he contradict her? She only spoke the truth. They had been shopping together. And she, at least, had been shopping for furniture. She'd made it sound as though they were shopping to furnish their own house, though. Based on Susannah's wide eyes and a couple of knowing smiles, their friends all thought the same thing.

"Oh," Susannah murmured in a voice that said she wasn't quite sure what to say. "Did you find anything specific?"

Clara pursed her lips. "Ach vell . . . I am trying to convince Daniel to get this rocking chair that would be just perfect for him."

More speculative glances among their friends.

"You like to . . . rock, Daniel?" Susannah asked slowly. Almost bewildered.

Daniel could sympathize. He felt the same way. How had this conversation gotten out of hand so quickly?

"Can't you just picture him reading the Bible to his family at night?" Clara asked.

Daniel wished she'd let go of his arm so he could go talk to the people at the honey booth. It was either that or run a hand over his face and try to hide how uncomfortable he was with this entire conversation.

Susannah nodded solemnly. "Daniel is a wonderful gute reader."

He was? When was the last time he'd read out loud around either of them, anyway?

Suddenly, Clara inhaled sharply through her nose. An angry little sound that reminded him of his bees when he disturbed their hives on accident. "How can she dare to show her face here?" Clara muttered angrily under her breath.

But she still said it loud enough that everybody turned their heads in the direction she was glaring. Daniel straightened when he saw who she was talking about.

Mercy Kemp.

Wearing jeans and a T-shirt, her hair down around her shoulders, she was standing at the honey booth now. Rosie was balanced on her hip, and Mercy was bouncing the baby like she'd held her every day of her short life.

Trying not to be obvious, Daniel craned his neck and finally spied Faith on the other side of the booth. She was carrying a large hamper over one elbow, hooked into the crook of her arm. It was filled up with bags and items. Malachi was not far away, too, standing in the next booth. He must've come with them. Had the sisters gotten permission from the bishop to live together as they wanted to? Were they shopping for their new home?

Beside him, Clara made that angry buzzing sound again. "My mother said Mercy had come back, but I didn't believe her. That girl never wanted to have anything to do with us or our ways, so why would she ever bother to come back?"

Daniel blinked at her.

He had no intention of discussing either of the Kemp sisters with anyone, but especially not with Clara, who apparently had inherited her mother's propensity for meanness of spirit and gossip. What he wanted to say, though, was, *Do you not see the baby she is carrying?* And then point out that that baby was Mercy's child, giving her a wonderful gute reason to return to her hometown.

No one else in the group pointed this out, either. He

wasn't sure if it was because they didn't want to argue with Clara or because they were thinking the same things she was.

"I heard from my dat that Faith and Mercy have asked for permission to live together in a house in town," Susannah said in a voice that she dropped low like she was worried someone would overhear them. Somebody like Mercy or Faith, who weren't standing all that far away. The crowds were loud enough, though, that Susannah probably didn't need to lower her voice at all.

Her dad was one of the ministers, so she would know. But Daniel couldn't say he was too impressed with a man who talked about community business that should have been confidential until a decision was made and communicated to the entire gmay.

"Of course they won't let them do that," Clara said, her voice full of confidence in how right she was.

"Why not?" Abner Miller piped up to ask.

For a brief flash, Clara's face took on an expression dangerously close to prideful judgment, though she wiped it away fast enough that Daniel wasn't sure that's what he'd seen. Maybe he was the one being judgmental.

"I should think that was obvious," Clara said. "My mother says that if Jethro Miller was taking his calling as bishop seriously and listening to Gotte's word and obeying the rules of the Ordnung, he would have the Kemps send Mercy away with her"—she paused and lowered her voice to a whisper—"bastard child. She should be shunned."

The fact that, after a beat, every single person in the group gathered around them nodded their heads in silent but tacit agreement should have been a shock to Daniel. Then again, he found most people took their cues from

those around them, rather than deciding on the best behavior for themselves.

He pulled his shoulders back. "Jesus opened his arms
to the likes of tax collectors, philistines, the poor, and
fallen women. Maybe we should all be a little more like
Jesus." He directed a gentle look in Clara's direction. "Or
would you like to cast the first stone?"

Clara's jaw dropped. Before she could say anything, he
walked away. Straight over to Mercy Kemp, who glanced
up as his shadow fell across her. To the others, her smile
probably looked confident, but up close he could see the
slight wobble. "Daniel," she said in an overly cheerful
tone. "Nice to see you again."

Immediately Rosie let out a tiny baby squeal of delight
so cute his heart lifted at the sound. She reached her hands
out toward him like she always did. Smiling, he accepted
her weight as Mercy lifted the baby in his direction. He
gave her a little cuddle, then looked straight up into Faith's
grateful blue eyes, and his heart turned over.

I love her.

*Dat was right. I'm in love with Faith Kemp. I'm in so
deep, I can't see the bottom.*

He ducked his head to tickle Rosie and buy himself a
moment to hide his emotions. Because he was in love with
a woman he could never have. He would never ask her to
give up Rosie, he already knew that.

But now . . . now his heart was in tatters, and it hurt so
bad he couldn't see straight.

She must never know. It would make things difficult for
her and awkward for them both. *You are her friend, and
that's all you'll ever be.*

Chapter Twelve

❋

FAITH HAD SEEN the group of Amish men and women her own age—some of them friends she recognized from her gmay—standing not far from the honey booth. In fact, she'd spotted Clara Gick long before the others had shown up. When she had, she'd tried to convince Mercy to walk down a different aisle instead. But Mercy had always leaned toward stubborn pride. "I'm going to face their judgment at some point either way," she had pointed out calmly. "Running from it only delays the inevitable."

It hadn't been until the group had moved a little closer that Faith had spotted Daniel among them, standing next to Clara, whose hand was linked through his arm possessively. With no right to be, she couldn't deny a sting of jealousy. He could date whomever he liked.

But not Clara. Didn't he have better sense? As pretty as she was, Clara would be a shrew of a wife.

Trying not to be jealous, Faith had been horribly self-conscious, aware the second she and Mercy had been noticed. Given Clara's scowl, that moment had been hard to miss. Even more so when every head had turned in Mercy's direction. It hadn't taken a genius to figure out they were being talked about, either.

Or at least Mercy was.

Faith had placed herself on the far side of the booth, and it was possible they hadn't noticed her there. Their visible opinions, written all over their faces, had been not unexpected, and yet still had burrowed under her skin like a tick. Her heart dropping, she'd wanted to step between her sister and the others. But at the same time, their concerns were valid. Mercy's choices made her someone who could come between her loved ones and their faith and chosen lives—Faith included.

That wouldn't happen. She knew it wouldn't. Even though she wanted a different life, Mercy had never once belittled or bemoaned Faith's choice to remain Amish. But Faith understood the concern.

How long would it take before she and Mercy were accepted as they were? Years? Decades? Based on the stony, unyielding, uncharitable expressions turned their way, Faith had to wonder.

But then Daniel had come over, and Faith's heart had lifted to the skies at his kindness to her sister. At his understanding. At a display of grace given to another that the others couldn't deny.

Would he be surprised if she ran over and hugged him? Probably. Behavior like that would certainly give the group still watching something to talk about. So Faith managed to hold on to the urge and root her feet where she was standing. Smiling to herself, she even managed to pick up a jar of honey and pretend to study it casually.

Lavender honey.

It took four tries to make the words sink into her head. When they finally did, she wrinkled her nose.

"Is there something wrong with lavender honey?"

Daniel's voice at her side made her jump, and she bobbled the jar. With Rosie held securely in one arm, Daniel still managed to catch it before it smashed on the ground, thank goodness. "Careful." His voice shook with shared laughter. But Faith's smile for him was entirely because of how he'd treated Mercy.

He paused with his hand outstretched to give it back to her, staring back at her with an intensity that stole the thoughts right out of her head. Until he looked away, jaw visibly tense. When he looked back at her, all traces of emotion were wiped clean.

Had she imagined the way he'd been staring?

Rosie leaned forward suddenly, arms outstretched for Faith. Heart lifting even more than it used to when Rosie reached for her, thanks to all the worries weighing it down, Faith happily took the baby in her arms, cuddling her close. She buried her face in Rosie's puff of hair and inhaled.

"So." Daniel shook the jar, raising his brows in question.

It took her a solid stare at the thing to figure out what he was asking. "Oh. Ach vell . . . lavender, the smell of it gives me a headache. I was wondering if the honey would, too."

"Are you allergic to goldenrod?" he asked. But before she could answer, he shook his head. "I assume not, because that's the flowers you made the wreaths from the other day."

He remembered? Faith nodded.

A surprising twinkle entered Daniel's eyes. "Won't you

make arrangements with lavender, though? Or maybe small satchels? It seems to me they would sell well."

Faith chuckled as she dodged Rosie's fingers reaching for her kapp strings. "I figure I can wear a clothespin on my nose." She snuck a look around them, pretending she didn't want anyone else to hear such an embarrassing secret.

"Remind me to drop by and help on one of those days. I just have to see how that goes." Daniel really could be a tease when he wanted to.

Taking the jar of honey from his hand, trying hard not to notice how warm that hand was as their fingers brushed, she set the jar down and moved to follow her sister, who was walking along quietly beside Malachi. Mercy was talking a mile a minute while the man Faith was supposed to have married watched her in what appeared to be smitten awe.

I should be more upset about that. Shouldn't I?

"Thank you," she murmured quietly to Daniel, who fell into step beside her, even though he didn't have to.

Hands clasped behind his back, he tilted a glance her way. "For what?"

"For being kind to my sister."

The way he studied her as they continued walking, she'd guess he was trying to figure out if she'd seen Clara and the others and noticed their reactions. But it didn't matter. All that mattered was Daniel's reaction. Maybe some of the others would learn from his example.

Up ahead Mercy must have said something wild, which wasn't too difficult to imagine, given the life she'd led these last years. Malachi suddenly stopped walking, staring at her sister, who seemed to obliviously continue on without him. Faith cringed as she waited for some kind of scolding from the Amish man whose charity they lived on, since he owned the place where they were staying now. But instead he laughed and followed her sister into the next booth.

He actually laughed.

Faith couldn't remember making him laugh at all. He was never unpleasant with her, or with anyone, really. Malachi had a good heart underneath, but she wouldn't say he was prone to laughter, either. She shook her head. Mercy had always had that way about her.

"I haven't seen your family's booth yet," she said to Daniel, who was also watching the couple ahead of them.

It seemed to take him a moment to shake himself out of whatever thoughts he was thinking. "They are about two rows over from here." Then he bumped her shoulder with his. "Your small bouquets are almost sold out already, and it's only the second day."

A warm glow, like a candle placed in a window of a home full of love, lit in her heart. Not just because people enjoyed the fruits of her labor, but because of the note in Daniel's voice. It was the Amish way to be humble, but just for a moment he sounded as though he was as proud of her accomplishment as he might have been of one of his own.

"That's nice" was all she said. She held back. Faith was afraid that the words that might tumble out of her mouth would smack of her own pleasure both for herself and in his reaction.

"You'll have to make more," he said.

Rosie babbled baby talk that almost sounded as though she was agreeing with him, and he met Faith's eyes as they both chuckled.

Faith sighed at the sudden image of walking with her

own husband and child and almost stumbled at the sudden pain blooming in her chest. Because that wasn't going to happen.

Searching for any distraction, she thought about what he'd said about making more flowers. "They might have to wait till spring. I didn't dry enough flowers, and the last of the late autumn blumes are done for the winter."

"I hadn't thought of that." Daniel actually sounded worried.

"I had. I think I'll try making some items out of mistletoe and holly and some other winter greens. Maybe some evergreen boughs with pine cones. I think they look lovely with candles or as decorations on a mantel or over doorways. But I'm not sure that they'll make good bouquets."

Daniel's nod of approval shouldn't have made any difference, and yet her heart warmed all over again. Then he frowned. "Mistletoe requires climbing high into trees," he mused. "I don't like the thought of you doing that on your own."

She turned to face him, eyeing him mock sternly. "Why? Because you think I'll fall?"

Daniel grimaced but said nothing, clearly not wanting to offend her. Then he leaned forward to stage-whisper to Rosie, "Your aendi has a tendency to trip or fall over. Do you think she knows?"

Faith had to laugh, even through the twinge the word "aendi" gave her. "You're probably right, I would fall or trip or something."

His shoulders fell from where they'd climbed up to his ears. "Let me know when you go out, and I'll go with you."

"Oh, you don't have to—"

"I want to."

And for the briefest second her heart took off like a swallow with a joyful song into the skies.

"We are friends, after all," Daniel said, then moved away to see what Mercy and Malachi were up to.

Friends.

Right. Because that was all they could ever be. Her heart dropped back to earth with a kerplop and she tried to make it stop all of that. Having Daniel as a friend was a wonderful gute thing. She should be grateful.

She cuddled Rosie close.

And I am. Gotte is giving me everything I need.

On that uplifting thought, even if it felt forced, she followed after him.

Chapter Thirteen

✳

DANIEL HAD REGRETTED it the second the words had left his mouth with that offer to help Faith go cut down mistletoe for her creations. He had meant it as a friendly gesture. Actually, he'd been terrified that she would have an accident and be stuck out in the woods with no one to help her. The problem was that spending time alone with Faith was . . . temptation.

Simply being near her made him happy.

Friends shouldn't feel that way about friends. He should leave her to figure out her life and get on with his own plans. Instead, here he was pulling the small buggy up outside her house after having finished all his chores at home on his day to not be in the shop. Maybe Faith would invite Mercy or Malachi along on this holly and mistletoe trip. Or bring the baby.

That would make it more casual.

She was the one to answer the door when he knocked, already dressed in sensible shoes and a warm wool jacket, a scarf wrapped around her head and neck. No Rosie. No Mercy. No Malachi. As far as he could tell, no one else in the house at all.

"Should I bring a ladder?" she asked with a friendly smile, not a hint in her eyes of the same turmoil he was feeling..

Because she only sees you as a friend.

"No. I have one in the buggy." Then, because he couldn't help himself, he added, "You did eat lunch first, didn't you?"

A question that made her eyes sparkle with laughter. "Of course. Did you?"

"Jah."

"Not too much, I hope." Then she held up a jug that he hadn't even noticed was in her hand. "I made some warm apple cider to share."

"Oh. Gute." Now she was making him treats?

Should he ask if she'd brought thick gloves? If they found any blooming holly bushes, he planned to cut those as well, but holly had some wicked spikes. Only asking now would make him sound like an overanxious mama. He'd brought an extra pair of his mater's just in case, so he decided not to say anything.

Ushering Faith into the buggy, he got them started down the road. "I thought we might go to the field where I'm moving my beehives first. We could also move the boxes while we're there. With your help, it will go quickly. Then to Hope and Aaron's house. It backs up to a thicket of woods with plenty of trees."

"Sounds gute."

Then they fell into silence.

Daisy tossed her head after Daniel fiddled with the reins for the umpteenth time, so he quieted his hands. No need to be nervous. This was just Faith. In fact, she seemed perfectly happy to be sitting beside him without saying a word, looking out over the world. Today was rather bleak to be out. A blanket of high gray clouds meant a low chance of rain, but also lent a sort of gloom to the day and definitely kept the sun's warmth away.

First, Daniel took them back to his parents' house, where they had the easiest access to his bees. Faith cheerfully trailed after him to where the boxes were. She asked a ton of questions as he showed her how he moved the boxes only feet at a time. He pointed out where he intended them to end up, at the edge of the tree line to woods that actually backed up to Hope's family's property.

He tried very hard not to picture doing this with Faith all the time—having her at his side chatting away as they worked with his bees together. He really needed to stop picturing anything with her.

Finally they made their way back to the buggy and on to Hope's family home, where she and Aaron lived with her dat and grossmammi. As they pulled up the drive, Aaron came out of the barn brushing off bits of wood chips and dust. No doubt he'd been working on some new piece of furniture.

"I'll take care of Daisy," Aaron said as they got out. "You two get started. Hope's dat thinks worse weather is likely to blow in by sundown."

"We'll be done by then," Faith assured him, coming round to their side as Daniel pulled the ladder he'd brought out of the back of the buggy.

Aaron glanced between them, a sly light in his eyes. "You should take Faith to the bridge."

Daniel stiffened, while at the same time Faith brightened. "Bridge? What bridge?"

"I don't think so," Daniel said. "Come on, Faith."

He hustled her out of there with more haste than kindness before his bruder—who clearly had the wrong idea about their friendship—could put his foot in it even worse than he already had.

"What bridge?" Faith asked as she hurried after him, clutching the empty baskets she'd brought in one hand and the jug of cider in the other.

At a pinch of guilt, Daniel slowed his steps, allowing her to catch up with him. "Aaron built Hope a bridge over the stream that runs through these woods."

"How sweet. I'm sure it's lovely."

"It's a special place for the two of them."

Thankfully Faith dropped the subject. She was even kind enough to not ask why, if it was so special and private to the couple, Aaron himself had mentioned it as a place to go.

But no way was he taking Faith there. It was too romantic a spot to bring a girl who was just a friend.

They walked along in the same silence in which they'd ridden in the buggy. Unfortunately, they walked quite a ways.

"Oh, there's some." Faith finally pointed up above their heads.

Daniel had never been so glad to see mistletoe in all his life. Not that he thought much about mistletoe usually. But then he'd made plans with Faith and decided to look it up in the library. It turned out the plant was a parasite on trees and also poisonous. Wasting no time, he hurried right over, propped his ladder against the tree, and scurried up.

"Did you know," he called down to Faith, who was waiting on the ground below, "they think the reason people kiss under mistletoe is because ancient Druids saw how it bloomed even in the middle of harsh winters, and so saw it as a sign of fertility?"

Realization of what he'd just said sank in, and Daniel paused with the gardening shears he had brought poised to cut a swath from the tree. He had to physically stop himself from burying his face in his hands and groaning. He'd only meant to share interesting facts he'd learned. Why in heaven's name had he thought facts involving kissing and fertility would be appropriate?

"Oh, that's interesting," Faith's voice drifted up to him. "I always wondered about that."

With his head stuck in the branches, grateful that from where she stood below, she couldn't see his face, which had to be ten shades of red, he finished cutting a hunk off and dropped it down to Faith, who scooped it right into one of her baskets.

"Holly makes sense at Christmas, too," she called up, continuing the conversation that he would be more than happy to drop. "The prickly leaves represent Christ's crown of thorns, and the red berries his blood."

"Sounds more like an Easter plant than Christmas," he said. At least it had nothing to do with kissing.

A warm chuckle reached him from the ground. "I thought the same thing. But the red berries only appear in the fall and through the winter, so I guess we make do with what we are given, when we're given it."

"True."

"Or maybe they were also thought to bring fertility like mistletoe? Many Christmas traditions the Englischers still celebrate today have roots in pagan beliefs or practices, which is why Amish celebrate a little differently."

He cringed. Back to fertility. However, he also found himself too interested to change the topic. "Where did you learn that?"

"Mercy told me, the very first Christmas after I found her. She and her boyfriend had this Christmas tree in their apartment all decorated in lights and ornaments, and apparently that was a pagan tradition, too."

He knew of Christmas trees, of course. The Amish didn't celebrate with them, but they sold seasonal decorations in their shop in November and December that the Englischers would like. "I've never heard that before."

He dropped another hunk of mistletoe to the ground, careful he wasn't dropping it right on top of Faith. Vaguely he was aware that she moved to get it.

"Me neither—" A loud gasp was followed by a thump and then whimper of pain that cut off sharply.

He jerked his gaze down to find her crumpled up on the ground, but from this angle, he couldn't tell how or why. "Faith?" he called. The ladder creaked in protest at the speed with which he hurried down it.

"Um . . ." At least she was talking. What could she have done while just standing there?

He hit the ground and dropped to his knees at her side. "What happened?"

She sat up, mouth pinched with pain, which is when he saw that her foot was down what appeared to be a rabbit hole. "I'm stuck," she said with wide eyes, pleading silently for him to fix this.

Taking her by the calf, he began tugging upward but stopped the second a tiny whimper escaped her. Obviously, that wasn't going to work. She really was stuck.

"There's a root," she said.

He reached into the hole, feeling around, and discovered she was right. Daniel tried to tug it out of the way, but the stubborn plant was thick and healthy and wouldn't budge, and Faith whimpered again.

Those small sounds of pain were like pinpricks to his heart. He hated that he was causing them. "It's going to be okay." He tried to assure her in his best calm voice. Then he pulled out the knife that he'd brought along to cut holly and mistletoe in case the shears weren't enough.

Faith's eyes bulged. "You won't be able to see what you're doing."

He was well aware of that, and if he hurt her worse, he'd hate that. But they had to get her out. "You're going to have to trust me."

"I do," she whispered.

Two little words, and they meant so much.

Carefully, he used his free hand to feel down her foot, guiding his knife hand with it so that he didn't nick her accidentally. His jacket tightened against his back, and he glanced over his shoulder only to realize that Faith had grabbed two hunks of it in her hands, holding on to him. Very carefully and very slowly, he sawed away at the root.

With a suddenness that made him grunt, the wood gave way and his knife jerked up into the soil, but at least away from Faith's foot.

With a gasp, she let go of him and drew her foot slowly out. The second he could see it clearly, Daniel winced. Not only was it scraped up—it had already started to puff up. Carefully he removed her shoe, but she was wearing thick stockings to ward off the chill in the air.

"We need to get you to a hospital." Without thinking about it, he scooped her up in his arms and started walking through the woods back toward the Beilers' house.

"Your ladder—" she protested, looking back over his shoulder. "My shoe and my baskets."

"They'll still be there when I come back."

Without further protest, Faith wrapped her arms tightly around his neck, her face close to his. She was so slight in his arms, he actually started wondering if someone should feed her better.

"I'm sorry—"

"Nae. It was an accident." Could she feel the way his heart was pounding? Not from carrying her, but because he could tell by the way she was trying to hold her ankle steady that even the bumping from his steps was hurting her.

He wouldn't hurt Faith for all the world.

They would have to call a car to take her to get treated. Hopefully someone would see them from the house soon and come help.

A splash hit his face, and Daniel almost stopped walking to glare up at the gray skies. But he kept going. Then there was another splash.

This time Faith tensed in his arms. "Oh no. Did you feel that?"

Before he could answer, another splash, then another. Then the skies opened up over them. Not raining so hard that he couldn't see, more like a fine, constant, soaking shower.

"Oh, sis yuscht!" Faith wailed. "Why do these things happen to me?"

Her arms tightened more around him, and the prick of a small, very cold, and now very wet nose hit the side of his neck, almost like she was taking cover under the brim of his hat.

"It's going to be okay," he promised her. "We don't have far to go."

"You're going to get pneumonia and die and it will all be because of me," she lamented in a voice muffled by his neck and coat.

Her ankle had to be throbbing and she was shivering against him so hard now he was surprised her teeth weren't rattling inside her head, but she was worried about him? "I'll be fine."

He was starting to breathe hard as the land angled upward, and he was soaked through, but Faith shivered harder against him even as she grunted with pain every couple of steps, and that's all he could think about. Deliberately he dipped his head so that his hat covered her more. Sure, that meant the rain was now hitting the back of his neck, but that was okay.

They broke out of the trees, and the house immediately came into view. No one came running, though. They probably weren't looking out the windows right then. He made it all the way to the porch steps before the door was thrown open and Joy tumbled out.

His first idiotic thought was, *Is she visiting Hope and Aaron?* Joy didn't live here.

"What happened?" she cried.

Daniel carefully moved sideways through the door. "Faith stepped in a rabbit hole and hurt her ankle."

"Good gracious, in here. Lay her on the couch. I'll go get Hope. Joshua and Aaron are in the barn. Joshua is commissioning something secret. Probably for me."

Daniel leaned over to place Faith on the couch and, as soon as she was settled, dropped to his knees beside her—partly because his legs were tired, but more because she was still clinging to his neck.

"Um . . . Faith . . . liebchen. You have to let go."

On a soft gasp, he found himself released. Only that

might be worse. Because now he was staring into Faith's deep blue eyes, and she was staring right back. Staring at him like he was . . . some kind of wonderful.

"You called me liebchen," she whispered.

He had. The endearment had just slipped out. He didn't want to take it back, though.

"Here's some towels and a blanket," Joy said, rushing back into the room with Hope right behind her.

Deliberately Daniel straightened, pulling his gaze from Faith. He handed her a towel and then moved to her feet, gently lifting her now visibly swollen ankle to prop it up on a pillow.

"I'll go to the call box and get a ride to the hospital," Joy said in a flurry.

Hope was right on her heels. "I'll get Joshua and Aaron."

They were both gone before he could say anything. Needing something to do—anything to help Faith and not address that momentary lapse of judgment on his part—Daniel turned and stoked the fire. Then he picked up the blanket to wrap it around her, only to stop as he took in the wet clothes plastered to her skin. "We should get you something dry to wear."

Teeth chattering, she nodded. "Y-y-you t-t-too."

He'd been so focused on her, he hadn't noticed how he was shivering now, and dripping all over the Beilers' nice clean floor. Tracking mud and leaves from his shoes, too.

"Oh, sis yuscht."

Carefully he pulled his shoes off, and his socks, too, when he found them soaked, then picked them up and walked them back to the front door to put them outside on the porch.

By the time he got back, Faith had company: Joy's two

younger bruders—her cousins, technically, but taken in by her parents years before. Now, where had they come from? They stood over where Faith was lying on the couch, her head on the armrest, eyes closed. Did she look even paler than before?

"Is she dead?" Samuel asked.

Amos reached out a hand to poke her in the cheek, and Faith frowned. "Nae," Amos said. "Just sleeping."

"But why is she sleeping on Hope's couch. And all wet?"

"Maybe she's from that story Joy was telling us last week." Amos leaned closer, his face right in Faith's. "Hey. Do we need to kiss you to wake you up?"

"Ew, yuck." Samuel backed away. "I'm not kissing anyone."

"No one needs to be kissing her," Daniel said, making both boys jump back with guilty looks on their faces.

Only the look didn't last long for Amos. "You're all wet, too, Daniel."

"What is all the commotion—" Hope's grossmammi entered the room. With one swift glance, she took everything in. "Boys, let's get you out from underfoot."

Amos scowled. "We're not underfoot—"

"Our barn cat just had kittens, and the rain has stopped. Go on out there." Rebecca Beiler knew how to deal with stubborn little buwes. Kittens would always be more interesting than a sleeping Amish girl.

With a whoop, the two scrambled out of the house. "Tell Joshua and Aaron to come up to the house," Rebecca called after them in a remarkably robust voice for one as ault as she was.

"Hope already went," Daniel assured her. "And Joy is calling for a car."

Daniel moved back to Faith's side. Taking her hand in his, he gritted his teeth at how cold her skin was and started to chafe her hands between his own. "Are you awake?"

"Jah," she whispered.

But that was all. She didn't open her eyes, and the tense cast to her jaw told him everything. Here he was worrying over a silly word . . . a look . . . and she was just trying to get through her pain.

"The car is only ten minutes away, thank heaven," Joy called out as she banged back into the house through the back door. Aaron, Joshua, Hope, and Hope's dat, Levi, came in from the other way at the same time, all crowding into the family room. It said a lot that Faith didn't even open her eyes.

"We need to get these two into dry clothes before it gets here," Rebecca said.

"If someone can carry her to my room, I'll help her change into something of mine," Hope offered.

Joshua stepped forward, but Daniel, already beside her, beat him to it. "Arms around my neck," he urged her softly.

Then, as gently as he could, watching her face pinch with pain that hurt him, too, he followed Hope and Joy—only he had to leave Faith sitting on the end of Hope's bed. His bruders came, too, and Aaron dug some of his own clothes out of his drawer before leaving the women to it. Daniel hated leaving Faith, but he had no choice.

In no time, he was changed, and thank goodness he and Aaron were close to the same size. But Daniel didn't care about any of that. He was out in the hall, waiting at Hope and Aaron's door. Shouldn't they be done by now? Joshua and Aaron would think he'd gone mad if he put his ear to the door.

"The car is here," Rebecca Beiler called up the stairs.

But still no Faith. By the time Joy opened the bedroom door, Daniel had taken to pacing the hallway. Aaron watched silently, and Joshua, for once, held his tongue.

Rushing inside, he slowed himself when he got to her. She looked like she might be sick at any moment. "Daniel . . . it hurts," she whispered to him, her expression stricken.

He took one glance at her ankle, now no longer covered by a stocking and already turning a deep black and blue with bruising. Helplessness was not a sensation Daniel was used to. If he could, he would have taken all her pain onto himself. But he couldn't. All he could do was get her to help.

"Come on," he said. "Let's go get you fixed."

Again, as gently as possible, he lifted her. He had to be very careful on the way down the stairs not to bang her foot into a wall. When they reached the bottom, he carried her out the door, where—by some miracle—the rain had stopped. He placed her feetfirst into the back of the car, turned sideways so her foot was up on the seat, then strapped her in and got in the front seat.

"Tell Mamm and Dat where I've gone," he told a watching Joshua before closing the car door.

He looked out his window as they drove away, and it was impossible to miss the speculation on both his bruders' faces. Actually, on every single one of the worried faces watching after them.

We're just friends, he wanted to call to them.

But the words "just friends" stuck in his throat and in his heart all the same.

Chapter Fourteen

✳

THE JOURNEY TO the hospital and all the steps of getting through the X-rays and then waiting and waiting seemed to take forever. Forever in a haze of pain.

With Daniel at her side.

He only left her if the nurses made him, and he clearly wasn't happy about it when they did, even though the people were only trying to help her. Had she imagined that look on the couch? The look that said she meant more to him than . . .

He'd called her liebchen. Hadn't he?

Through the throbbing and cold and wet, she couldn't be sure. At least she was dry and warm now, lying on a hospital bed with her foot propped up on a pillow and a heated blanket covering her. They'd also finally given her something for the pain. That had made a world of difference.

Daniel, however, stood by the door, looking out the

small glass window into the hallway beyond. Every so often he would say, "Why is it taking so long?"

If they took much longer, she worried he might tackle the next hospital person who rounded the corner into his line of view and force them to help her.

"It's not so bad now," she tried to assure him.

He glanced back, so she knew he had heard her, but he didn't meet her eyes. Unfortunately, whatever they had given her for the pain was making her sleepy, so she couldn't really focus enough to figure out what was going on with him. Maybe later.

Her eyes drifted shut.

Only vaguely was she aware as nurses popped in from time to time. Eventually she had to wake up enough to hear that her ankle wasn't broken, but badly sprained.

Everything else passed in a blur.

Getting her ankle wrapped up and told how to treat it, then checking out with a lot of paperwork, took forever. Daniel loaded her into yet another car to drive home, then, with Malachi's help, he got her into the house, with her family clucking and fluttering around them like concerned little hens. Then Daniel left.

She remembered that much. He hadn't done or said anything special. Just nodded at her and quietly let himself out of the house while even her family were too distracted to notice.

After that, it had been Mercy getting up with her through the night to make sure she stayed on top of her medication and had everything she needed. It was not the easiest night. The medicine only did so much to ease her discomfort.

Over the next three days—three days that Daniel didn't come to see her or check on her—the swelling went down, and she was eventually able to hobble around and be less of a burden on her family.

But mostly they made her sit on the couch with her foot propped up on pillows. It turned out they could all get along perfectly fine without her help. The baby, the house, the chores, all taken care of. So she was doing oonbunch of reading for her business. At least she told herself it was for her business, and if she got ideas for Daniel's bees, that was just being a gute and kind neighbor.

The way her heart would trip over itself every single time someone knocked at the door was just . . . silly. A side effect of the meds, maybe.

People from their gmay and other Amish church districts nearby in Charity Creek and the surrounding countryside had been dropping by to keep her company, help with chores around the house, and bring food of all kinds for her family.

All the Kanagys had come. Except Daniel.

When his parents had come by, Ruth had commented that he was the one at the store that day but that he would drop by eventually. But after three days had passed, she assumed he probably wouldn't.

Even so, when a knock sounded at the front door, her heart still did that thing. *Pitter-patter, pitter-patter.*

Setting down her book, she tried to arrange herself on the couch in a way that was appropriate, making sure she wasn't slumping and that her dress wasn't rumpled or twisted around her legs. When her mater answered the door and the deep, familiar rumble of Daniel's voice sounded, she frowned at the way the *pitter-patter* of her heart turned into a full *rat-tat-tat.*

Which was why she was frowning when Daniel walked in.

He took one look at her face, frowned as well, and said, "If now is not a gute time, I can always come back."

Faith managed to rearrange her face before Mamm caught her expression, trying for a warm smile instead. "Of course not. I'm wonderful glad to see you."

Daniel studied her closely for a long second, as if he didn't quite believe her. Then he cleared his throat, hands clasped behind his back. "My mamm said you had been getting a lot of visitors and helpers lately," he said. "I would have come by sooner, but I thought I would wait until things slowed down a bit."

Her mother beamed at him. "After the way you helped Faith the other day, even going with her to the hospital, you are welcome here anytime you wish, Daniel."

A statement Faith should have made herself, but if she did now, she would just sound insincere. So she smiled and nodded. Daniel shot her another of those frowning, searching glances. A look she returned with what she hoped was a convincing smile, though it felt stiff on her face.

"Is there anything I can help out with around the house?" Daniel finally asked, directing the question to her mamm, who shooed him away with a wave of her hand. "No, no, no. With Mercy home, we have plenty of hands. But poor Faith. I'm afraid she's been terribly bored just sitting here all day by herself."

Faith tried to hide dawning horror at all of it—Daniel's nearness, her appearance, her mother's words—as her mother then shooed him onto the couch. "You just sit here and keep her company. I'll bring you some snacks."

Daniel shuffled to the end of the couch, beyond where her foot was extended, and sat. Awkwardly. "You don't need to bother with snacks—"

"No bother at all." Her mamm was already moving

away into the kitchen. "I was about to get Faith something to eat anyway."

No she wasn't. What was going on in her mother's head now? She'd been pushing Faith and Malachi together since he'd arrived, but now she seemed to be doing the same thing with Daniel. Though, come to think of it, all the pressure to be nice to Malachi had lessened lately. Thanks to her ankle, Faith hadn't noticed until this moment.

She pulled her gaze away from her mother's retreating back only to encounter Daniel's curious stare, and heat crept into her cheeks. Did he find her mother's behavior odd as well?

As if he had to search for something to say, his gaze skittered away until it landed on the book she had put down on the coffee table. He smiled. "More books about flowers?"

Before she could stop him, he picked it up, leafing through the pages. Her cheeks might as well be on fire, they were so hot, as he paused at the first sticky tab on a page. One she knew was labeled in her neat handwriting. It read, FOR DANIEL'S BEES.

Why did the first one he saw have to be about that?

Mercy had been the one to bring Faith some extra books from the library. And she had been kind enough to also stop in a stationery store and buy some of these little sticky tabs so that Faith could mark anything of interest as she read and then go back and take notes on everything later before she returned the book.

Daniel peered at the note, smoothing his thumb over the paper. Then he glanced up at her. Was that a speculative light in his eyes?

"These are my mater's favorite blumes." That was all he said.

Faith rushed into speech. "I'm researching which flowers to plant for my own business," she said. "But if I see anything for your bees, I mark them. That just happened to be the first thing I saw."

She was tempted to say it didn't mean anything, but that wasn't true. Besides, friends didn't get uncomfortable about doing nice things for each other. Why was she acting so strangely?

Daniel leafed through all her other stickies, pausing at the ones for him, and Faith had to force herself not to cringe as she tried to add up in her head how many of her notes had been for her and how many for him.

But then his lips tipped in a soft smile as he slowly raised his gaze to hers.

What would he say?

He closed the book with a pop and set it back down on the table. "Gute suggestions."

That was it? That was all he had to say?

Then he was looking at her directly. There was no hint of softness in his smile. He was only her good friend. "How is your ankle feeling today?"

It took her a second to catch up to the change in topic and tone . . . then she realized that probably the previous tone was something she'd been imagining in her head all along.

Faith cleared her throat. "Much better, thank you. The swelling has gone down, and I don't need as much pain medication. Now I can walk on it a little with the boot they gave me, although I find that uncomfortable to wear." She pointed at the thick black contraption with its flat rubber sole sitting on the floor beside her next to one regular shoe for her other foot.

Daniel nodded. "I'm glad." Then he added, "I brought you something."

He got up off the couch and went back to the front door, where he picked up a small bag she hadn't noticed before and brought it over to her, holding it out before he sat back down.

Curious, Faith opened the bag, then scrunched up her nose in confusion as she pulled out a box that showed some kind of plastic thing with blue beads inside. She looked at Daniel. "Um . . . what is this?"

He grinned. "The pharmacist at Walmart told me this was the best way to put ice packs on a swollen ankle. You put it in the freezer, and the beads turn purple when they're cold enough. Then you put it on your ankle—you can put it directly on the skin, unlike other ice packs. When the beads turn blue again, it's time to return it to the freezer."

He'd brought her something to help her heal. Why did that make her want to wrap her arms around his neck and squeeze tight, or plant a kiss on his handsome cheek, or burst into tears?

Just say thank you.

Before she could do any of those things, another knock sounded at the door.

"Can you get that, Mercy?" Mamm called from the kitchen, where she was apparently still busy getting them that snack. How long did cheese and fruit, or maybe slices of Mamm's fresh baked bread, take?

"I've got it," Daniel called back as he left Faith on the couch.

But Mercy was already halfway down the stairs when he opened the door, and all three of them blinked at the sight of Jethro Miller standing there, broad shoulders and smiling face framed in the doorway.

Faith couldn't miss her sister's small gasp. The bishop had come. But had he come to give them news about the ministers' decision for them? Or had he come to pay Faith a visit?

Heart in her throat, Faith smiled and nodded at the bishop's greeting. Mamm even came out of the kitchen, wiping her hands on her apron. She cast Mercy and Faith a nervous glance before saying, "How lovely to see you, Jethro. Would you like a glass of apple cider or water?"

Trust her mother to say the polite thing when all Faith wanted to do was ask him why he'd come. That would be rude, though.

Jethro must have seen the question in all their faces, because he shook his head. "Nae, denki. I think I'll just get to the point of why I've come. To check on Faith, of course." He sent her a smile. "But also to tell you that after much discussion and debate . . ."

Was it just Faith, or did he pause a really long time, giving her heart a chance to try to crawl out of her throat and run away? Because what he had to say next would change the course of her life either way.

". . . we have decided to allow Faith and Mercy to live in town together, even if Mercy chooses to remain apart from the Amish faith."

Mercy's gasp was louder this time, and she stepped forward like she might hug Jethro right there.

He held up a hand. "On one condition."

"Anything," Mercy choked out.

Jethro bent a hard look on her. "We would like you to spend one month trying to reconnect with your Amish roots. If after that, you still wish to remain unbaptized, you have our permission to try it your way."

Chapter Fifteen

❋

"MERCY?" FAITH CALLED out ahead of her as she made her way carefully up the stairs toward the room she shared with her sister. She was still hobbling and slow with the boot on her foot, but it was a little easier each day. "Are you ready?"

No answer.

The door to their room was closed, so she knocked. "Mercy?"

Still no answer.

She swung it carefully open to find her sister standing in the middle of the room staring down at herself. She was wearing one of Faith's dresses—this one a deep wine color with a white apron—and her hair neat under the white kapp.

She looked . . .

"Oh Mercy," Faith breathed.

It was like she'd been thrown back five years to just

before her sister had run away from everything they knew and loved.

Mercy looked up, her lips twisted. "I thought I would hate it."

Thought? Did that mean she didn't?

"I used to think these dresses were so dumm. But it's soft. And it doesn't squeeze me. And it feels like . . ."

Like what?

But Mercy didn't finish the thought, shaking her head. "I'm just being sentimental and silly, I guess. After all this time."

Taking her cue, seeing that her sister didn't want to make a big deal of this, Faith moved purposefully into the room and took her by the hand to tug her down the stairs. "We're running late, and it's a surprise party. We can't be late."

But halfway down the stairs, Mercy tugged back, pulling them both to a stop. Faith glanced over her shoulder. "Did you forget something?"

But Mercy wasn't looking at her. She was looking past her. Following her sister's gaze, Faith found Malachi standing at the bottom of the stairs holding Rosie and staring at Mercy, looking utterly dumbstruck.

At Mercy in her Amish clothing.

At Mercy in *Faith's* Amish clothing, and with Faith's face. But Malachi had never, not once, looked at Faith like that.

Mercy's hand tightened on hers. Having no idea what to do, Faith gave her sister another tug and hobbled her way down the stairs to where the rest of the family was waiting.

"We'd better get going," Mamm said, seemingly oblivious to the little moment. If anything, she seemed to be trying to hide her own satisfaction at the sight of both her dochders. Probably she didn't want to risk Mercy seeing and giving up on the entire thing just to be contrary. That had been their mother-daughter relationship since Mercy was little, after all. "It's not every day Stephen Saul turns twenty-one and gets a surprise party."

They all bundled into the buggy, and Dat set them off down the drive at a quick clip. They were the last to arrive at the Sauls' house, so just to be on the safe side, Dat let them all out close to the house before he drove around to the back, where hopefully Stephen wouldn't catch sight of him if he arrived to his own party early. They knocked only to have the door opened to a blast of merry laughing and shouts as at least a hundred Amish jumped out to surprise the birthday boy, only to cut themselves off on a groan of disappointment.

"It's just the Kemps," someone said from the back.

"How embarrassing," their mother muttered, before raising her voice. "Sorry, everyone."

Faith, however, who usually would have been blushing by now, was more interested in the second round of reactions as people got a good look at exactly which Kemps had come in the door and were eyeing one in particular.

Mercy.

A buzz of whispers swept through the room. Beside her, Mercy did what she always had as a girl when she'd done something worth the community buzzing about. She smiled warmly as though she were being welcomed by long-lost friends and sailed right into the room toward the first person in reach.

Daniel Kanagy.

A Daniel who happened to be standing beside a petulantly scowling Clara Gick, who was clinging to his arm like she had every right.

Maybe she does.

But that made Faith—uncharacteristically—want to tell Daniel to shove the other woman aside so Faith could take her place. *What on earth am I thinking? Daniel is a smart man, and this is none of my business.* If he wanted her opinion as his friend, he'd ask.

Despite Clara's scowl, Daniel did exactly what Faith knew he would do in a situation like this. He smiled in his reserved way right back at Mercy, though his comments to her sister were too quiet to hear. Still, his welcoming of her couldn't be denied.

Faith could almost hear the sigh of relief blanketing over the buzzing of speculation throughout the house. Then Stephen Saul's mater rushed forward, arms waving in the air, whisper-screaming, "He's here. He's here, everybody. Places. Places."

Which was how Faith found herself grabbed by the hand and unceremoniously dragged over by Mercy and Malachi and Daniel and Clara, hiding behind the couch. Not only that, she was pressed right up against Daniel, with Malachi on her other side, giving her no room to wiggle any space between either of them. She couldn't have moved if she wanted to anyway, because in this position, she was putting too much pressure on her ankle. She wasn't even sure if she was going to be able to stand up when everybody else did to yell *Surprise!*

"Are you oll recht?" Daniel whispered to her.

"Why wouldn't she be oll recht?" Clara muttered from his other side.

A question Daniel ignored, looking at Faith. He really did have the most lovely eyes—deeply brown, with warmth and caring shining right at her. There went the *pitter-patter* of her heart again, and she bit her lip, which made Daniel's brows twitch in the beginnings of a frown.

Of course, that was when the birthday boy came in and everybody jumped up, shouting, "Gute gubbotta dawg" and "Happy birthday" and laughing at his surprise.

Everybody except Faith and Daniel.

Mostly because Daniel stayed down behind the couch with her, giving her a stern look when she couldn't move. "I knew it. Your ankle is bothering you. You shouldn't have crouched."

Then he wrapped his strong hands around either side of her waist and lifted her right up to standing. Only he didn't let go when they were both up, instead holding on to her to make sure she had balance while she silently gasped around a protesting throb in her ankle from her poor handling of it.

Daniel leaned forward to murmur in her ear over the ruckus. "Will you be able to stand if I let go?"

A shiver chased up her spine—the pleasant kind, though. The kind that had her immediately and silently rebuking herself. Who shivered just because someone was whispering at them about their dumm ankle?

He wasn't asking about anything more than whether her ankle would give out on her, even if Faith's heart wanted to hear something more in his voice.

Suddenly, the next decades rolled out in her head in a flash of images. Decades full of happiness, of course, with her sister and Rosie and living their lives the way that they'd been given permission to do. Rosie would become her world now—watching her grow and laugh and eventually become a young woman in her own right, marry, have children, find her own way. And after that, Faith would become the grossaendi to those children, maybe living in a mammi haus with Rosie's family and with Mercy by her side.

And she was content with that future.

Or she'd thought she was content with it until Daniel asked her that one tiny question. Her heart cried out that no, she wasn't oll recht. She wanted to ask him not to let her go.

Not ever.

Clara suddenly leaned around Daniel with a frown, her gaze pinned to where Daniel was still touching Faith at her waist. Making sure all her weight was on her good foot, Faith shifted away from him. "Jah. Denki for the help."

Then she turned and hobbled off toward the kitchen, because thankfully she was still holding the basket carrying the bread and other goodies she had baked for the party. Mercy found her in there and helped her unload the basket. As they worked, she glanced around and, when she was sure they were alone, said, "Why did you just walk away from Daniel so abruptly like that?"

Faith opened her eyes wide and hoped that for the first time in her life she could fool her twin sister. "I didn't mean to. The basket was getting heavy."

"Well, he certainly took it as you trying to get away from him. You should have seen his face. Like you'd kicked a puppy or something."

He had?

"So, by the way, did Clara Gick. She smiled at me like a cat who didn't just get the cream but stole a bucket of it and drank it all for herself."

Faith turned back to the counter, where she busied herself arranging the bread on a platter she'd brought along with some apple butter in a dish at the center and forced a chuckle. "I'm sure you're just seeing things. Clara Gick has no interest in me."

"No." Mercy snorted, the sound reminding Faith of Daniel's horse Frank, who tended to have an attitude. "Clara has interest in *Daniel*. And Daniel spends time with you. I haven't been around that much, but even I know that."

Faith didn't miss the way her sister didn't say that Daniel had interest in her, just that he spent time with her. "He's a gute friend."

Mercy moved to stand beside her at the counter and bumped her with her hip. "I know."

The discovery of her feelings was still too new and too raw for Faith to face right now in the Sauls' kitchen with her sister. So she borrowed a little trick from Mercy and redirected. "Speaking of funny looks . . ." she said. "What was with that look that passed between you and Malachi when we were leaving the house?"

Mercy backed up a step. "There was no look. I was nervous about coming here tonight. What are you talking about?"

Faith stared at her with her eyebrows raised, because Mercy was babbling. Mercy didn't babble.

"I guess I was wrong," Faith said.

"I guess so." Then Mercy grabbed her hand. "Please don't leave me alone tonight. Maybe people will be more likely to come up and say hello to you and then they won't be able to avoid saying hello to me that way. It'll just be easier for awlee eppa, for everyone. I don't think I could stand it if I got ignored all night long and ended up in a corner by myself."

As if Faith would ever let that happen.

Still, guilt wrapped around her heart and squeezed.

Here she was worried about herself and feelings for Daniel that she knew she would never act on. She would always still have him as her friend, which would be a comfort to her in all her years. Meanwhile, Mercy was facing the community that she had walked away from, had rejected, more than five years ago. Faith had gone through the same process of rejoining the community herself only months ago. Except she hadn't been the one who'd jumped the fence, had a baby out of wedlock, then given that baby to her sister to raise.

Of course tonight was going to be difficult for Mercy.

They had picked this event specifically because it would be casual, and easy, and full of people, including members from other churches in the area. Stephen Saul was well-liked, and no one would want to cause a scene at his special party.

"Let's go help serve the food. That way people don't have to decide to come by and talk to either one of us. They'll have to at least say hello on the way by."

"And meanwhile, my hands will be busy with helping," Mercy supplied, ruefully staring down at her skirt, which Faith now saw was a wrinkled mess. Had she been scrunching it up this entire time?

"Kumme." She handed Mercy one of the platters and took the other.

Luckily, only Sarah and Rachel Price were standing at the tables helping to serve. Both the girls were not only Faith's friends but had been Mercy's, too. Without a smidge of hesitation they both offered her sister a warm greeting.

"It is wunderbaar to see you," Sarah was the one to enthusiastically say. "Although I never expected to see you in Amish clothes ever again."

Mercy glanced down at herself and chuckled. "Me neither. I'd forgotten how comfy these dresses can be."

Curiosity shown in Sarah's and Rachel's eyes. "Are Englischers' clothes really that uncomfortable?" Rachel asked.

"Some can be. Especially jeans. And especially after I had—" Mercy's cheeks warmed with color, and Faith cast a worried glance around them to see if anyone else heard.

This might be the first time in their lives that she'd ever seen her sister blush. Mercy had probably been about to say something about the jeans not fitting well after having given birth, then remembered that Amish didn't talk about such things. At least not at surprise birthday parties, anyway. At least she had stopped herself. Mercy ended a little stiffly with, "They're a little tight, and it makes it hard to sit down or bend over. And they can be hot in the summer. Though they are warmer than dresses in the winter."

Given that the winter was fast approaching and tonight was colder than the last few had been, they all exchanged grins.

"Sometimes I wish I could just wrap my scarves around my legs, because these stockings just aren't enough," Sarah grumbled. Which had them all laughing.

In that moment, Faith glanced up to find Daniel watching her from across the room. With Mercy's questions about her earlier behavior toward him, she didn't want him thinking she was avoiding him. He was her friend. She would never hurt his feelings like that. So she smiled and gave him a little wave, which he returned.

Then they both went back to talking to the people they were with. Though Faith's heart was doing that *pitter-patter* thing again. She really needed to stop that.

Chapter Sixteen

✳

DANIEL HAD NO idea how he had ended up tagging along to look at the only two houses for rent in Charity Creek. The fact that it had to do with Malachi's influence only made him more surprised to be here.

At some point in the middle of Stephen Saul's party, Malachi had approached him. At first, he had just been polite, asking about the store and Daniel's bees. Somehow, that had turned into an invitation to join Malachi and both the Kemp sisters when they went to look at these houses.

The other man had mumbled something unintelligible about Daniel being a gute friend to Faith and how she'd appreciated his thoughts.

Daniel's parents had been perfectly happy to let him go for the day, as there was no heavy lifting that needed to happen in the shop, no goods to be dropped off or organized, and Daniel preferred the back of the store to the front, which they had covered with both Joy and Hope joining Mamm. So here he was.

Still confused.

Up until this point, he had gotten the impression that Malachi didn't want him to have anything to do with Faith. Maybe all of that had changed with Mercy and Faith's new plan? Because here Malachi was, answering the knock at the door to join them.

After a brief greeting, Daniel followed him out to the buggy and got into the back, only to find Faith rather than Mercy seated there. Her sister was up front with Malachi, who was driving.

What is going on here?

Faith offered him her usual warm smile—one he worried was tinged with a tiny bit of the lingering awkwardness that had risen up between them at the surprise party. But she said nicely enough, "Denki for coming with us. We could use an extra opinion on something so important."

Daniel just nodded. He was happy to help.

"Malachi said you were interested in seeing the setup for the houses?" she asked next.

Which made Daniel stiffen—that wasn't the discussion he and Malachi had had. He glanced at the front, where Malachi cleared his throat but said nothing.

For whatever reason, Malachi was obviously the one who wanted him here. Not Faith. Best to keep his mouth closed and ears and eyes open for the reason why. Although it was probably something innocent enough. Maybe Malachi still wanted to marry Faith and wanted another man along to point out the problems with the houses. He'd be disappointed if that was his aim, because Daniel wouldn't do anything to hurt Faith, and he'd never lie to her. Or maybe Malachi really didn't mind Daniel and

Faith being friends and thought she might want Daniel along.

An hour later, after meeting with the property manager to discuss what they were in need of, they were walking through the first house.

Daniel trailed after everyone, but mostly followed Faith as she poked through the rooms more slowly than Mercy and Malachi, who were up ahead of them and already in one of the back bedrooms. Mercy was commenting in rapid bursts, her voice drifting through the house to where he stood. Some of it was positive. Things like, "Oh, what lovely tile they picked." And some of it was not as positive, like, "This bathroom is too small. Where on earth will I put all my things?"

How many things did she keep in the bathroom anyway? It was for relieving oneself and cleaning oneself. That was it. Right? Towel, toothbrush, soap, done.

Faith, meanwhile, opened every drawer, stuck her head in every closet. He could practically see her listing in her head both all the items they owned already and what items they would need to make their home functional at the very least, along with a calculator to add up the cost. Mercy was talking about colors of bedspreads and quilts, but Daniel had a feeling Faith was adding up the money it would take to buy those bedspreads and quilts when really what they needed were pots and pans for the kitchen, a couch to sit down on, a table to eat at, and beds to sleep on. Maybe their parents would help provide some pieces of furniture, though?

Not only that, but this house would have to be retrofitted for their Amish lifestyle—replacing the tile and carpet flooring with vinyl or linoleum, painting the walls white with a high gloss paint, having the electric lines removed, installing a propane tank, and converting all the appliances to ones that ran on propane rather than electricity. The appliances would be the most expensive outlay at the start, and he got the impression that neither Faith nor Mercy had saved much money while they'd been out in the world.

"I think purple would be a lovely color," Malachi could be heard saying to Mercy.

Daniel had to choke back a laugh at the way Faith scrunched up her face. "She's just dreaming out loud," he assured her quietly.

Faith shot him a surprised glance, then chuckled, a tinge embarrassed. "I know. She's always done that, ever since we were kinder. But she comes around to the practical eventually, so I don't let it worry me."

"Then I guess you must not like purple very much to make a face like that," he found himself teasing.

Faith leaned over to check down the hallway before letting herself chuckle again. She lowered her voice, "Not all over my bed, I don't. I outgrew that when I was about five years old and Mamm said a purple bedroom was something only Englischer girls wished for."

Only he couldn't help but hear a wistful tone in her voice. "If it was something Amish girls could wish for, too, would you have?"

Faith moved down the hall to open a closet that held what appeared to be an electric water heater. That would have to change.

"I didn't want all purple, or any other color," she said. "But I saw this quilt once that was mostly white with tiny little pink flowers, and I begged Mamm to make me one like it or buy it. But she said it was too extravagant to spend money or time on. I wouldn't have minded a quilt like that, though."

Her soft smile echoed the wistfulness in her voice.

You don't always have to be perfect.

He wanted to say those words to her. The funny part about that was that until this year he probably never would have thought those words himself. He found it easy to live his Amish life. It was all he'd ever known and all he'd ever wanted. He didn't see how things like all those outside trappings could make anybody happy. What was important were the people in your life, your community, and your faith. His choices and the way he lived his life were easy for that reason. But it seemed to him that sometimes Faith made her choices not because they were easy for her but because they were expected or required of her, at least in her mind.

Sometimes trying to be perfect was also the wrong answer.

They got to the back door and let themselves out into a small backyard, but one that already had a flourishing garden that had clearly been well tended and loved over the years. They'd obviously planted cole crops to harvest in the fall—broccoli, brussels sprouts, turnips, rutabaga.

"Oh, isn't this perfect," Mercy was exclaiming. "Look, Faith. We won't even have to start a garden. It's already started for us. And a clothesline is already set up."

Daniel's eyebrows inched up. Mercy sounded almost as though she planned to live an Amish lifestyle. While living with Faith, who absolutely was, meant she'd have to give up certain things—like electricity—he was still surprised she sounded so happy about it.

"What's in here?" Malachi asked, moving to a decent-sized shed set up at the corner of the backyard.

He and Mercy went over to look while Daniel inched closer to Faith. "Where would you work on your flowers?"

The next second, he felt bad asking the question, as she bit her lip, glancing around with a worried gaze. "I don't think any house we look at is going to have space for that," she murmured in a low voice, probably so neither of the other two would hear. "I'll think of something, though. Maybe I'll rent some space in town?"

The way her voice lifted at the end in question, he knew without her having to say so that she couldn't afford that. Given the way the cost of housing and rent had gone up everywhere recently, he imagined both girls were going to be working very hard just to afford this place if they picked it.

Daniel put his hands on his hips and looked around, trying to picture Faith and Mercy and Rosie living here. They would make it a true home, he had no doubt of that. Luckily, it did have three bedrooms, which meant all three of them would have the luxury of having their own. Or maybe the sisters would share the larger one and Faith could use the third bedroom as a place to work on her flowers—an idea he said out loud to her.

She tipped her head at that. "Vell, there is plenty of room for two twin beds in that large bedroom. Mercy and I have shared a room most of our lives, so it wouldn't be anything new."

Did she sound disappointed? Had she been looking forward to having a room of her own?

"This is the one," Mercy called out as she hurried out of the shed and took her sister by the hands. "I think it's just perfect. You and I can share the big bedroom and you can put your flowers in the smaller bedroom. We will lay down linoleum floors, which will make for easy cleanup in there. And we can keep some of the smaller things we need for the yard, like a push lawn mower and stuff for the garden, in the shed, but there should be plenty of room for you to also keep a lot of your flower-arranging things, I think."

Daniel had to blink at the sudden change in Mercy, who up until this point had only been commenting about things *she* wanted in the house. Clearly, he had misjudged her. She truly did love her sister.

Faith's smile held no reservation. "Let's look at the other house just to make sure," she said. "But if after that you still think this is the one, then this is the one."

Malachi joined them. "Do you have enough money to buy all new appliances?" he asked. "You're going to have to replace just about everything in the house. It's all electric."

Mercy deflated a little bit. "Oh, I hadn't thought of that." She cast Faith a worried glance. "I have a small savings, but if I spend it on the appliances, then we won't have enough for the first month's rent. We would need to go to work immediately to pay for that."

"Let's worry about that after we see the other house," Faith said. Then she bundled all four of them out of the house and back into the waiting buggy.

Only the other house definitely wouldn't do. What was supposed to be a third bedroom was really more of a large closet, certainly not big enough to use as either a bedroom or a workroom. The appliances were all electric as well. And there was no garden or shed.

It was obvious to Daniel that Faith could see this from the second she stepped into the house. She said nothing while Mercy wandered off with Malachi on her heels. But her hands went to her hips as she stared around in dismay.

"Were you hoping that this might have worked better?" he whispered.

She huffed what sounded like a sad laugh. "For sure and certain. But what is that Englischer saying? Beggars can't be choosers." She shrugged. "This house is cheaper rent because it's smaller. I think we're going to have to stay here just so we can afford to pay for all the changes we'll need to make."

Stay in this pokey, dingy little house, the three of them? It might take them years before they had more than beds and appliances to their names. At least her parents had already said that they would give them the twin beds in Faith and Mercy's room, as well as Rosie's crib. But Rosie would outgrow that crib in the next year or so, and then they'd need another bed. That was assuming they could keep on top of all the other expenses with their jobs. Mercy was still in her month of retrying her Amish ways, which meant they had no idea what jobs she could get and what their income would look like.

"I wouldn't start looking for jobs around town until the end of Mercy's month," Daniel said.

"I hope these houses will still be available then." Faith pulled her shoulders back, her expression tightening, turning almost mutinous. Very un-Faith-like. "But we've seen worse. We can make this a home."

Daniel straightened looking around him. "Worse?"

Faith wrinkled her nose, though she laughed. "When I was still tracking down Mercy, I stayed in a tiny town in Kansas, and the only place I could live was the extra bedroom of the woman who owned a diner in town where I worked to make money before I could move on to the next place. It was just one room, and I had to buy this little propane-powered single coil to cook my food on. No refrigerator, so that meant being very careful with what kind of food I bought. Only stuff that could last without being refrigerated or visiting the market each day. The grocer got to know me so well, he started setting aside some of the older fruits and vegetables and sold them to me at a discount, since he said he was going to have to throw them out the next day anyway."

Daniel stared at her stubborn little chin and the light of confidence in her eyes. Neither part of her personality had ever come out before going off after her sister. The woman in front of him had more gumption, more spine, than just about any person he knew, Amish or otherwise. He wondered if Mercy had any idea of the sacrifices her sister had made, first to go out and find her and then to help her come home.

"Ach vell, a woman who can make lemonade out of those lemons should be able to make a feast out of this," he said.

The smile that lit her face may as well have been a bonfire filling him with warmth. If he could make Faith smile that way every time he saw her, he could be a happy man.

Except you won't see her very often once she moves in here.

About as often as any other folks in his community, he guessed. At church every other Sunday, and at some of the social events, assuming they both attended. Maybe in town, since he worked nearby and she would live there. And of course she would have to bring her flower arrangements by the shop.

He brightened. At least he had that.

Chapter Seventeen

※

FAITH SAT IN church with the unmarried women her age. Apart from her mother, who was with the married women. Apart from Mercy, who sat with Rosie and the young mothers. However, even apart from her family, all alone in many ways, something in her heart felt . . . whole.

Her family were *all* here.

They hadn't worshipped together like this since Mercy had run away from home over five years ago. You wouldn't think such small things as sitting on a wooden bench in a room, singing hymns with their community, and listening to the ministers' messages would provide such a sense of rightness with the world, but she couldn't deny it.

Gotte had formed humans to be in community with each other and in family together with Him. Would it be so wrong to pray, just a little, that it was also Gotte's will that Mercy would feel this, too, and want to be baptized? Or was that selfish of her?

Not selfish, necessarily. After all, the story of the prodigal son told them that Gotte wanted all His people to return to Him.

But if that wasn't what Mercy wanted, how could Faith force it on her?

She wouldn't, of course. If at the end of the month her sister still wanted to remain apart and live her life mostly as an Englischer would, with some allowances for the rules Faith would continue to follow, they had permission to live together. Faith would still have her family with her. Just a little more fractured.

She lifted her gaze from the Ausbund in her lap to look directly up into Daniel's stare. She blinked to find him watching her and offered only the smallest hint of a smile. One he returned with a twitch of his lips. It wouldn't do to be found fully smiling during the service, especially not at a man. Her mother would have a fit—and wasn't she getting too old for such things?

After all, Faith and Mercy would be ault maedels together for the rest of their lives.

Following the service, Faith took Rosie while Mercy worked to help serve food. What a luxury to just sit and eat, even while she kept an eye on her sister and corralled a squirming baby. For the most part, the community had been accepting—well, if not accepting, at least tolerant—of Mercy's return to the fold, even it if was only temporary. A few turned their backs or didn't return her smile as she served, but true to Mercy's way, her sister didn't appear to even notice when that happened, moving along with a cheerfulness that would eventually charm the hardest of hearts.

Mercy dropped into the seat beside Faith and filled up her own plate. "Phew. I've been waiting tables for years, and I still forgot how many mouths there were to feed on a Sunday after Gmay."

Faith chuckled, then leaned closer. "Any trouble?"

Mercy shook her head as she chewed. "Nothing I didn't expect."

That didn't mean there hadn't been any, but Faith let it go. Except Mercy suddenly gave a soft sigh that those around them probably didn't catch. "I forgot, Fay."

"Forgot what?"

"I only remembered how all the rules felt like being tied down, and I looked for judgment all the time, so of course I found it, or even forced it with my behavior, I'll admit. But I forgot about how we all care for each other. Despite everything I did, so many here are ready to accept me and treat me as though I never left. I've had offers to help with Rosie or concern over how we're going to fix up one of the houses we looked at. Micah Bontrager even offered us their used stove because they're about to get a new one. I forgot about the kindness."

Despite the cold in the barn where lunch was set up to stay out of the autumn weather, Faith warmed. Maybe what she'd been feeling, Mercy had, too. She'd just have to keep praying.

"Let me take this little mite." Mercy reached for Rosie, who went to her mother willingly, immediately tugging on her kapp strings and then reaching for the plate of food on the table in front of her. With a chuckle, her sister scooted it out of the way. "Has she been fed?"

"Jah, although she'd probably eat a few peas. Do you want me to put some on a plate?"

"Sure. Denki, Faith."

Denki. Now her sister was even sounding more Amish.

Across the table she caught the way their mother was watching Mercy, with so much longing for her child in her eyes that tears stung Faith's own eyes, making her blink rapidly. How hard must these years have been for their mother to know Mercy was out in the world? Faith, too, of course, but Mamm had known Faith would ultimately return. She'd promised.

But to know a child of yours was walking away from everything you'd taught her, everything you'd given her, rejecting what was so important to your life to make her own way and that you might never see her again or know her fate . . .

Oh, Mamm.

Suddenly Ruth Kanagy was standing beside their table. "Hallo," she said with a smile. "Joseph and I were hoping you would like to join us tonight for dinner? The whole family will be there."

Their first invitation as a whole family since Mercy had returned. Sundays were a day of worship and no work, but they were also when many Amish went visiting their friends and neighbors. Trust the Kanagys to show kindness with this invitation. Maybe others would follow and Mercy would . . .

Stop getting ahead of yourself.

"That would be lovely," her mother answered, practically beaming. At least, her subdued version of beaming. "What can we bring? I have newly baked sourdough bread and a chocolate chess pie."

"That sounds perfect. It will just be a ham and butter noodle casserole for the meal, nothing fancy," Ruth assured them.

After they'd agreed on the time, Ruth left, and they

smiled at each other. Even Mercy. Her sister sighed. "The Kanagys are certainly nice. Especially Daniel."

Faith stood up to start clearing the table, pretending not to hear the last bit. She'd managed, all this week, not to think about him. Or not too often. Beyond remarking what a gute friend he was to both of them, Mercy didn't seem overly interested in Daniel.

Suddenly, Faith didn't want her to be.

Mercy had a way about her. She drew people to her. Plus, Daniel loved Rosie. A memory of the way he'd deliberately gone to talk to Mercy at the Harvest Festival took on a new light. What if his kindness to all of them was really because of her sister?

Malachi appeared out of nowhere. "I'll take Rosie so you can help clean up," he told Mercy. Before anyone could move, he scooped the baby right out of her arms and wandered off to where the other smaller children were playing.

"What is he thinking?" Faith thought she heard her mother mutter.

Beyond offering for them to stay in the house, with him still in the dawdi haus, until Faith and Mercy could find their own place, Malachi hadn't said much about his plans. But he had become extra helpful with Rosie. Why, though?

Shrugging, Faith went to turn away, only to pause at a look in her sister's eyes as she watched Malachi and Rosie.

Faith glanced between them, frowning slightly. Was there something there?

She shook her head. Of course not. The last person Mercy would be interested in was an Amish man.

* * *

A KNOCK SOUNDED at the door that had Daniel looking up from the book on flowers Faith had loaned him. He was writing down the various seeds he intended to order from the nursery in town tomorrow during his lunch break.

"Will you get that?" Mamm called from the kitchen. "It will be the Kemps."

Halfway to putting the book down, he paused. "The Kemps?" he called back, confused.

"Jah. I invited them over for dinner."

She had? Since when?

The knock sounded again. If it had been either of his bruders, they would have just come in. "Daniel." Mamm's voice was turning sharper. "Your father will be helping with their horse. It's too cold to make them stand out on the front porch."

Right.

He got up and had to actually take a second to settle himself before opening the door, because his heart was jumping around like a wild beehive knocked from a tree. He opened the door to a large group—Faith's parents, her sister holding Rosie, Malachi, and at the very back, the last to come in, Faith herself.

"Hi, Daniel," she said quietly.

While he knew she'd been to the honey room to work several times this week, other than at Gmay today he hadn't seen her in more than a week. Was it possible for her to have become even more beautiful? "Hi."

After taking coats and bundling their guests inside, where Mamm emerged from the kitchen to welcome them, Daniel hung back quietly. So did Faith, so he moved to stand beside her. "Mercy seems to be doing well," he commented.

She smiled up at him before they both looked to where

Mercy was handing Rosie into Ruth's eager arms, Mercy's laughter warm and natural, in all appearances a happy Amish girl. "Jah. I think it's even surprised her."

"How is it going with the house rental?"

"They want three months' rent up front," she said in a voice threaded with worry.

Before he could answer, the back door opened and both his bruders and their fraas bundled in on a wave of chatter and laughter and greetings and getting the dishes of food they'd brought settled in the kitchen. Then the house was general chaos as the women worked to get the meal on the table, and Daniel found himself holding Rosie, who grinned and gurgled happily at him.

The room only quieted once they were all seated around their kitchen table, which was extended with their folding table at one end in order to be able to seat everyone.

"Oh, the high chair," Mamm had exclaimed just as they were getting settled.

"You don't have to worry," Mercy tried to reassure her. "Rosie sits on my lap, or Faith's."

"No, no. A guest should enjoy their meal. Daniel, will you run down to the basement?"

"Jah."

Except their old high chair had been in the basement for donkey's years. Daniel wiped it clean of spiderwebs once he got it upstairs, but Faith still fretted over it. He was fairly certain she was afraid of spiders, the way she went on.

"Leave it alone, Faith. It's fine," Mercy finally chided gently.

"Don't you remember that spider bite I had when I was little?" Faith demanded.

Which made Mercy snigger. "The one that swelled so big you couldn't bend your pinkie finger?"

"Jah."

"It only lasted for one day," Mercy teased.

Daniel picked up the high chair and wiped it off one more time before setting Rosie in it anyway.

"Denki," Faith whispered to him as they took their own seats. Somehow, they'd ended up beside each other with Rosie on Faith's left and Mercy and Malachi on Rosie's other side.

As soon as they'd all dished up, Joy suddenly broke out with a giggle. "Daniel, why don't you tell your parents about the customer you had yesterday?"

Every eye at the table turned his way, and Daniel hid a grimace. The center of attention wasn't his favorite place to be, even with people he loved. Then again, Faith was watching him with an interested smile. "Was it funny?" she prompted.

Joy and Hope both chuckled. "You would not believe what this woman tried to do," Hope told the table.

Then both his sisters-in-law turned to him with expectant expressions.

He wasn't going to get out of the telling, he could see that much. "A woman came in yesterday. She was dressed in Amish clothing, or at least I think she was supposed to be, but she must have bought a costume that Englischers wear for Halloween or something, because it was like no clothing I'd ever seen before."

True Amish dressed a little differently by order and district, depending on their own gmay's Ordnung, which laid out the specifics and rules they followed. But this woman's outfit had been so far from anything he was remotely familiar with that Daniel had actually stared openly.

"Joy and Hope were in the back eating lunch and I was at the register to check out customers. After this customer had shopped for a bit, she brought up the most expensive quilt currently in the store."

"Not Joy's pinwheel pattern?" his mater gasped.

Daniel nodded.

"Wait," Esther Kemp interrupted. "The one in all those pinks?"

Joy perked up. "You know it?"

Esther nodded. "I was thinking I might buy it for Mercy when the girls move into their house."

Daniel tried not to visibly stiffen, because it suddenly hit him that the quilt in question exactly matched the description Faith had given him of what she would like—white with little pink flowers. There was more to it than that, of course, because Joy's quilts were amazing. That particular one she'd made as a custom order for a woman who'd then had a family tragedy and couldn't afford to pay Joy for it. But the reason he stiffened was because of who her mater thought of it for. For her sister.

Didn't Esther know it would be perfect for *Faith*? Not Mercy.

He didn't glance at Faith, though, and she didn't comment.

"Ach vell." Hope was the one to take up the story next. "She plunked it down on the counter and said, 'I would like to purchase this quilt, and I'm family, so I get a discount.' "

"What?!" His mother sat up so straight she bumped the table, and the dishes of food rattled. No one seemed to notice, though, all staring at him agape. Until Rosie banged her hands on the table like Ruth had started a game.

"Nae, nae," Faith murmured, quieting the boppli's hands with her own.

The little interruption didn't last long, though.

"If we didn't make a vow of nonviolence," Joshua said with a glower, "I would have been tempted to throw that woman out on her—"

"Joshua," his fater warned in a low voice.

Joshua closed his mouth and even stuffed a forkful of green beans in it, but his expression was far from repentant.

"*Was* she family?" Mercy was the one to ask.

Hope snorted. "Nae."

"What did you say?" Faith asked him directly.

Joy laughed this time. "Daniel stared at her with no expression whatsoever—you know that impenetrable thing he does that makes you question what you said in the first place."

He had no idea what she was talking about.

But she wasn't done. "Then he said, 'No, you're not family, and no, you don't get a discount.' Just like that. No tone of voice. Just matter-of-fact."

Beside him, Faith's low chuckle sank right into his chest. "That sounds like you," she said for him alone.

He shrugged. "Then the woman swore at me."

Joshua made a growly noise of frustration but held his tongue at Dat's warning look.

"That's not very Amish," Henry Kemp observed.

"I'll say," Joshua muttered in a dire voice, earning a pat on the hand from Joy.

"Did she leave then?" Mamm asked.

"Ach vell, then she declared that she was married to the owner's son."

Silence greeted that, followed by a burst of laughter from everyone.

"So," Joy jumped in, "Daniel very calmly calls me and

Hope out of the back room, where we were still hiding and listening to all of this. He says that the Kanagys have three sons, and we're married to two of them, then asks us if we recognize our sister-in-law."

"You should have seen her face," Hope sniggered.

Joy was hooting now, she was laughing so hard, and Joshua was grinning at his wife, finally losing his scowl enough to laugh right along with her. "And then Daniel says, 'And I definitely am not married to you.'"

That's when both his bruders lost it, laughing long and loud. The Kemps stared for a minute, and Daniel almost worried that they might be offended by the loudness of his family. But then Henry Kemp's lips twitched right before he let out a guffaw that actually startled Rosie. Instead of crying, though, the baby squealed in delight, which set them all laughing even harder.

Wiping tears from his eyes, Aaron was the one to say, "What happened next?"

Daniel just shook his head.

Hope finished it up for him. "Then Daniel pins her with this look that screams 'stern Amish man' and says . . ." Hope lowered her voice into gruff tones that had Faith chuckling at his side. "'It is a sin before Gotte to lie, and also a sin to steal. I suggest you leave before I call the police.' I've never seen someone leave our store so fast."

Which set everyone off laughing again. Daniel looked around, for once enjoying every second of it, even though he was the center of the story. He just liked that they were all enjoying themselves. Together.

Especially Faith.

The rest of the night wasn't quite so loud, but otherwise about the same. Even so, the quieter Kemps fitted right in with the louder Kanagys as though they'd been enjoying Sunday dinners together all their lives and not just from time to time.

After they'd cleared up and his mater had put the pies in the oven to warm, Daniel approached Faith where she lingered at the edge of the kitchen, poised as though she might fly into action at any second. He couldn't wait anymore to give her his surprise. He'd planned on showing her the next time she came to work on her flowers, but this was better. "I have something to show you."

She glanced over her shoulder at the group like she was debating if leaving them would be polite or not. Daniel reached out and gave her apron a gentle tug, pulling her focus back around to him. "We have time before dessert."

She lowered her gaze to where he still held the material between his fingers, and he let go. More reluctantly than he cared to admit. Actually, what he yearned to do was reel her in closer, but of course he couldn't.

"Oll recht," she said in her soft voice.

Then she blinked at him in owlish surprise when he led her to the back door, where he wrapped her up in a woolen coat. It was his coat, and too large on her, but he used the excuse that her own things were hung up in a closet on the other side of the house and this was more convenient to justify doing it. Naturally, it didn't have anything to do with enjoying seeing her in his coat. Before she could protest, he also wrapped a scarf around her neck and head, then wanted to chuckle. She suddenly looked like a young child, all bundled up to play outside on a cold school day.

When he'd bundled himself up similarly in his Dat's coat—not that he told her that—she followed him out into the night and across the yard to the honey room.

"Why are we coming here?" she asked as he ushered her inside.

The light of his oil lamp set a warm glow around them that hardly penetrated the shadows of the room. He took her by the hand, and even through the thick mitten he'd insisted she wear, her hand warmed his.

Daniel's heart tripped over itself, and he wanted to close his eyes and savor the small contact.

Friendly contact, he tried to convince himself. "I know you've been here this week, but I wanted to wait until your ankle was all better."

"Wait for what?" she asked, voice doused in confusion.

He lifted the lamp. The glow hit the countertop and she gasped, hurrying over to find it covered in holly and mistletoe. He'd been storing it in the barn but had brought it in here today after church so that if she came over to-morrow, she'd find it. But that was before he found out the Kemps were coming for Sunday dinner.

Staring at the heaps and heaps he'd gathered for her, Faith's mouth hung open in utter shock and made him want to gather her up in a hug and laugh at the same time. They'd only collected a few hunks before she'd ended up in that rabbit hole, so her surprise was all the more satisfying.

"Did I get enough for what you want to do?" he asked.

"Daniel," she whispered. Then turned a smile on him that stopped him in his tracks.

She . . . glowed. Not from his lamplight, but from the inside. From her heart. That glow reached down deep and wrapped around inside him, lighting an answering warmth. Faith Kemp was beautiful and wonderful and . . . oh, help.

"When did you do this?" she demand on a gasp.

He shrugged, a little embarrassment creeping in. Was it too much? "Just when I've been out and about." He tried to dismiss the effort he'd taken.

All those cold days and the pricks and scratches from the holly were his secret to keep. He wouldn't want to make her uncomfortable. She'd never given him any cause to think that she saw him as more than her friend. Except . . . there had been that moment at Stephen Saul's party. He'd looked into her eyes and forgotten they were in the middle of everyone. They could have been alone in the woods, the way he'd felt.

Which was wrong.

He shook himself out of the memory. Faith's path was set, and it didn't include him as anything more than a neighbor and friend.

"I thought it might go faster for you to work on the wreaths and things for Christmas if you didn't have to go back out to gather more," he said.

Faith looked away, staring again at the plants he'd gathered, her expression unreadable. What was she thinking? Was she embarrassed by his gesture? Then, with a suddenness that had him stiffening, she stepped close and wrapped her arms around his middle, her head laid against his chest. After a shocked second, Daniel lowered the arm not holding the lamp around her, hugging her back.

"No one has ever done something like this for me before," she murmured into his coat. Then she lifted her head to smile directly into his eyes. "Denki, Daniel. You are a kind and gute man."

Her words were soft and sweet, and so was the look in her eyes.

And Daniel couldn't have stopped himself even if gute sense had intruded into that moment. Without a second thought, he lowered his head and pressed his lips to hers in a warm kiss that reflected the glow in her eyes. It wasn't quick, either. He lingered, breathing in the scents of wind and shampoo that lingered around her.

Faith didn't pull away.

She stilled against him at first, a small gasp escaping her, but then she sort of sank into him, her eyes fluttering closed. And he kissed her again. Then once more.

Gotte couldn't have gifted him these feelings for no reason.

Daniel lifted his head to stare down into her face, smiling at the way she stared back at him with a sort of hazy kind of happiness.

"Will you marry me, Faith?"

A bang of a door, followed by Joshua's voice calling across the yard that dessert was ready, was the only thing that could have doused the light in her eyes.

And it did.

With a jerk, she stepped back, and they stared at each other, wide-eyed. He was breathing hard. So was she.

Then Faith swallowed and licked her lips, her eyes darkening with regret that was unmistakable even in the dim orange glimmering of his lamp.

"Daniel . . ." Her voice was a stricken whisper. "I can't . . . Rosie."

Then she hurried out of the room, her head bent low. And Daniel stood there, watching her run away from him.

Chapter Eighteen

❋

ROSIE'S HIGH-PITCHED SQUEAL of delight was probably Faith's favorite sound in the entire world. Though Daniel's low, soft chuckle came in a close second.

Will you marry me, Faith?

She closed her eyes against the memory, but it wouldn't leave her alone. Every nuance of that night—the mistletoe, the dark room, Daniel's voice, the look in his eyes, the feel of his lips against hers—wouldn't leave her alone. An ache had taken up residence in her chest, and she tossed and turned at night, so much that she was shocked Mercy hadn't said anything about it.

Why couldn't Daniel have asked me sooner—

She cut that thought off for the hundredth time. Gotte had already given her a path. She had plans. She couldn't lose Rosie.

With another delighted squeal, the baby slapped the water with her hands, splashing it all over Faith, yanking her out of her thoughts. Rosie was sitting in the tub for an impromptu morning bath and having a grand old time. Given how much the baby loved baths, Faith wasn't entirely sure she hadn't deliberately smeared herself in oatmeal at breakfast.

"I don't know how you got this in your ears, Rosie Posie," Faith teased as she took a washcloth to the spot.

Faith, meanwhile, was now soaked from the top of her head to the upper part of her apron and dress that showed over the edge of the tub. Not that she minded a bit. She was splashing just as much as Rosie.

Creating little waves to the rhythm of her words, she chanted the rhyme she remembered from her own childhood. "One. Two. Three. Four. Five. Once I caught a fish alive." She pretended to scoop up a wriggling fish from the water. "Six. Seven. Eight. Nine. Ten. Then I let him go again." The fish swam away in the form of Faith's wriggling hand under the water, and Rosie's eyes got big. "Why did you let him go? Because he bit my finger so. Which finger did he bite?" She picked up Rosie's chubby hand. "This little finger on my right." Then she pretended to nibble her finger.

The baby guffawed and chortled and squealed, then said a bunch of nonsense words in baby talk. She was babbling more and more every day.

Has it really been almost a year?

Draining the tub, Faith grabbed a fluffy towel from where she'd left it on the floor, folded Rosie up in it, and hoisted her out of the tub, gently talking to her all the way into their room. There she laid her on the bed, heedless of the damp towel, and pretended to tickle her as she dried her off. Rosie came out with her fluff of hair sticking up everywhere and a big old grin. Then she held her arms out to Faith and said, "Mamamamama . . ."

Faith gasped, straightening abruptly. Pure happiness could apparently steal her breath and leave her on the edge of tears. Or maybe that was the immediate, gut-clenching realization that she shouldn't be this happy.

Because she wasn't Rosie's mother.

Forcing a smile, she leaned over the baby. "Nae, liebling. I am your aendi." Just saying that out loud hurt so much more than she'd thought it might. "Let's get you dressed and go find your mamm."

"I'm here." Mercy's voice behind her was unusually quiet, and for the second time, Faith straightened on a gasp.

Then, forcing her stiff smile wider, she pointed at Rosie. "Did you hear her? I think she's warming up to say real words."

Mercy's smile seemed equally forced. "I heard." She went to the bed and scooped her baby up. "She is just the smartest, most beautiful, most wonderful baby in the whole wide world."

That sounded more like her sister.

Faith relaxed a little bit as she moved to gather up Rosie's clothing, along with a cloth diaper. Mercy took it from her and got started dressing her, blowing raspberries on Rosie's tummy and legs as she went, drawing even more giggles.

Then, to Faith's great relief, Rosie said to Mercy, "Mamamamama."

Thank you, Gotte, for giving her that so quickly.

Any remaining stiffness disappeared as Mercy swung Rosie up into the air. "Yup. Just the smartest baby ever."

"Don't let Mamm or Dat hear you," Faith hushed her sister with a wave.

Mercy settled the baby on her hip and headed out of the room only to stop at the door to face Faith. "I need to ask you something, and I need a straight answer."

Faith wasn't entirely sure what a "straight answer" was, but it didn't sound like a gute thing. She nodded anyway.

"Will you resent me for this?"

Faith frowned, not following. "For what?"

"Living with me? Giving up things like a family of your own."

"You are my family, Mercy," Faith said, hoping her sister couldn't hear her heart pounding. Because she'd asked herself these things already, and she already had her answers. But after Sunday . . . after Daniel's kiss . . . after he asked her to marry him. After he dangled the life she'd always wanted right in front of her, but one without Rosie . . .

"It's not the same," Mercy insisted. "You know it's not."

"Will you resent me?" Faith asked back.

The question had Mercy staring at her with her mouth open. Apparently, she hadn't considered the same thing for herself. After a second Mercy finally closed her mouth, then shook her head. "I could never resent you, Fay-fay."

Faith crossed the room and wrapped her arms around her sister. "Me neither. I love you, and I love Rosie, and we'll figure it out as we go."

Mercy chuckled. "You don't like to figure things out. You like to know what's going to happen fifty years from now."

"Maybe I've learned to be more . . ." She wrinkled her nose as she searched for the word. "What do you call it?"

Mercy laughed. "Flexible."

She used to say that to Faith after Faith had finally caught up to her but was still living her Amish life in the Englischer world.

"Jah. I guess I learned how."

Mercy sighed and strolled out of the room. She leaned her face near Rosie's and whispered words Faith didn't quite catch, though it sounded a lot like, "Maybe I should learn, too."

Mamm was still cleaning up from breakfast, but Malachi was waiting at the bottom of the stairs in his coat, hat in his hand. "Redd up?"

He and Mercy were going into town to pick up new seeds he'd ordered, and they were going to drop Faith off at the Kanagys' on the way. She was heading to the honey room to work, though she wasn't sure she was entirely ready to face Daniel yet.

She'd sort of been avoiding him, which she knew was cowardly. They needed to talk, and she would make sure they did. But she'd needed time to sort out her heart and her head.

She wasn't sure she had yet.

There'd been no church service last weekend, and Sunday was in three days, so she'd be sure to see him then. But what if he happened to be at the house today? She hadn't let anyone know she was coming. The Kanagys had told her to come and go as she pleased.

Being alone with Daniel was . . . Her stomach clenched.

What if he tried to kiss her again? She didn't see Daniel doing that. He would respect that she'd said no to him and why. He knew what was going on in her life.

The real trouble was, if she was being honest with herself, she was scared to see him because she was the one who might cross the line. Might be the one to kiss him.

Might ask for things she shouldn't ask of him. Daniel deserved a life with a woman who could give him everything.

I wish I could give him everything.

He deserved it. He deserved to have his bees, and his store, and a wife and children, and happiness. He was the best man she knew.

Luckily, she didn't see any sign of him when Malachi let her out by the honey room. She worked quietly through her day completely alone and undisturbed. There was no sign of any of the Kanagys, actually, though she looked out the window toward the house more often than she meant to. Maybe today wasn't one of the days when one of them stayed home to do chores.

At least she got a number of wreaths and other arrangements completed. The holly was horrible to work with, but worth it because it made such lovely decorations. Still, her arms above the long, rubber gloves she wore had little bleeding nicks all over the place, and she'd snagged her clothes more times than she wanted to think. Maybe this would just have to be her work dress from now on.

Except then Daniel would only ever see her in one dress.

Not that that mattered.

The *clop, clop, clop* of horse hooves had her looking up from her work. She ignored the dip of disappointment in her belly as she recognized her parents' buggy. Mercy and Malachi were back to pick her up.

With a sigh she finished cleaning up. So nice not to have to put everything away each time, but to be able to leave mid-project and just take it back up the next day. She was debating leaving a note for the Kanagys about which arrangements were ready for the shop. She'd left the finished ones on one of the countertops by themselves.

The door opened with a rush of chilly air, and she shivered, turning to reach for her cloak. "I'll only be a second—"

"Oh, these are lovely!"

Ruth Kanagy's exclamation had Faith turning back with a surprised little squeak. A glance outside showed her that Ruth and Joseph must've arrived right behind her sister and Malachi. Gathering her wits, she moved to stand beside Ruth as the other woman admired Faith's work.

"Denki," she said quietly. "I was hoping you would like them."

"I love everything you do, Faith," Ruth said without looking up. She picked up a small sprig of holly meant to go around the base of a candlestick. "But these are perfect for the season."

"I hope your customers like them."

Ruth shot her a smile. "Your customers, yet."

The door opened and Joseph ushered Mercy and Malachi inside, all of them taking time to exclaim over Faith's work.

But there was no sign of Daniel.

Maybe he was unhitching Frank?

Mercy turned away from the counter with a huff. "Faith, I have bad news."

Malachi turned toward her sister with a stern frown. "Mercy—"

"I'm sorry." Her sister's chin wobbled. "I should wait to talk to you about this when we get home, but I'm just too upset."

Ruth's motherly heart obviously couldn't stand it, and she took Mercy's hands. "What's wrong?"

Mercy clamped her lips together and breathed in through her nose, then looked right at Faith. "Both houses in town have been rented."

Ach du lieva. The air in her lungs deserted her in a whoosh. *What are we going to do now?*

For once, though, Mercy was the one worrying. Maybe her life in the world had taught her that things didn't always work out the way you wanted or hoped? Either way, there wasn't much they could do about it. "I guess we wait for another house to go up for rent, and this time we don't wait. Jah?"

Mercy took another shaky breath. "But poor Malachi. He's been waiting for us to move out so that he could finally live in the house that he paid for. It's unfair to him."

"Nae," Malachi suddenly said in a tone Faith had never heard from the man.

They all turned to face him and found him standing in the center of the room, hands in fists at his sides, face turning redder by the second.

"Malachi?" Mercy was the one to ask slowly. "What do you mean, no?"

If he didn't take a breath in a moment, the man was going to pass out. That or blow a blood vessel in his eye. Mamm had done that once, though she never told Faith how it happened. But her eye had looked angry and bloody for a month afterward.

Mercy took a step toward him, visibly alarmed. "Malachi, take a breath—"

"Marry me."

They all stilled. Even Mercy, who'd been walking toward him, though her chest rose and fell with rapid, jerking movements. "What?" she asked through lips gone white.

Malachi jerked his black felt hat off his head, mangling the poor thing in his hands. "I want you to marry me, Mercy."

"I—" For once in her life, her sister was at a complete loss for words.

Faith glanced at the Kanagys to find Ruth had taken Joseph's hand, and no one in the room seemed to know what to do next.

"I don't know what to say," Mercy whispered.

Oh, help. "Why don't we get home," Faith said. "Then you can find a private place to . . . talk. Jah?"

Except neither Mercy nor Malachi made a move to go, standing across the long room from each other, just staring.

Faith bit her lip.

"We can go inside the house and leave these two to it," Ruth suggested instead.

Faith almost hugged the woman. With a nod, she grabbed her cloak and winter bonnet and followed Ruth and Joseph outside, the cold barely penetrating her state of shock, and into the house. At some point Ruth must have coaxed her into one of the chairs at the kitchen table, because she found herself sitting there with a mug of steaming hot chocolate in her hand.

What was Mercy going to say? Did she even want to be baptized and marry an Amish man and live an Amish life? Sure she'd seemed more and more content as her month had gone along. If she said yes, what would that mean? For all of them? Faith closed her eyes against the selfish realization that if they married, she would lose Rosie.

"Is Daniel taking care of Frank?" she asked, just for something to talk about other than Mercy.

The quiet that greeted her question, though, had her lifting her gaze from her mug to find Ruth and Joseph looking at each other strangely.

Then Joseph cleared his throat. "Daniel has gone to stay with friends in Shipshewana."

In Shipshewana . . . with friends?

"Oh?" she asked faintly.

Which was when Ruth hit her with a gentle smile. "He's hoping to find a wife there."

Chapter Nineteen

❈

DANIEL LOOKED ACROSS the group of die Youngie scattered through the house where he'd just arrived. A nice girl who couldn't be more than fourteen smilingly offered to take his coat, which he shrugged out of, all the while regretting coming.

Why am I even here?

Granted, he was visiting the Schrocks, who operated a quilt shop out of their family farm, the given reason being so he could meet Amish women and hopefully find a wife. He'd vaguely meant to do that but gave up on it pretty quickly. He'd been here eleven days.

He hadn't told his family about proposing to Faith, but he'd needed to get out of town. To get some distance from everything and clear his head. But when he'd said that he wanted to go visiting in Shipshewana, Mamm had taken it as courting. He hadn't bothered to correct her, because it got him out of town like he wanted.

It had been the longest eleven days of his life.

"Wie gehts, Daniel?" a soft voice sounded from behind him.

He focused to find Amanda Eicher standing in the hallway, balancing a plate of brownies as she struggled to take off her coat.

He'd met Amanda his first day here. She was one of the quilters who worked for the Schrocks. Younger at only eighteen, but sort of quietly solemn with it so that she came across as older, and very nice, she was one of the few girls who didn't giggle and blush around him.

"Here," he said, taking the plate from her.

"Denki." After getting her coat off, she took the brownies back and looked past him into the house full of Amish youths ages fourteen on up to midtwenties. "I'm running late because the wheel on our buggy broke," she said. Then grinned. "What's your reason?"

Which made him chuckle. He might have expressed to her his doubts about being here at all, especially attending a frolic just for die Youngie.

"Kumme," she said. "Walk me to the treats table so I can set this down, and then you can sit by me. I'll make sure no girls bother you unless you want them to."

"In that case." He scooped the plate out of her hands and waved for her to go ahead while he followed behind.

"Who is your friend, Amanda?" A girl about her same age sidled up to her after they'd put the brownies with the other treats. She had two other girls in tow. Girls that reminded him of Clara and her friends. Not that they were bad or anything, just . . . too immature for him. They always had been, even when he was younger.

After a brief round of introductions that Amanda hustled them through before pulling him away, he found himself sitting beside her toward the back of the room. One of the boys started singing, and all joined in.

Except Daniel. *I don't belong here. This isn't where I'm supposed to be.*

He glanced at Amanda, studying her as she sang. With dark hair and blue eyes and a welcoming smile, she was lovely, and he found her easy to talk to. If he'd come here before Faith, he could maybe even have considered marrying her.

That's why everyone thought he was here, after all.

He wasn't being fair to himself, or to nice girls like Amanda, either. Why he'd thought distance and time were going to make any difference to how he felt about Faith, he didn't know.

The problem was, he didn't want to push Faith out of his life or his heart. He could still feel Faith's soft lips under his. Could picture the dreamy look in her eyes as he'd lifted his head. That was, until he'd proposed and she'd blinked herself into shock and then walked right out of his life.

But other memories of her were right there, ready to fill his mind at the most inconvenient moments. Faith humming happily as she picked flowers in a field. Faith bouncing Rosie and laughing. Faith in his honey room cheerfully working at her craft. Faith laughing with him over just about anything.

Faith who he couldn't have. So he'd run away from his feelings and the situation.

Now here he was, attending a frolic in a church district not his own, surrounded by girls who were too young, but even more important, weren't Faith. The evening stretched out before him. Unending. Not that these people weren't perfectly nice, he just . . . he shouldn't be here.

He turned to Amanda, who had stopped singing to look at him with wide eyes. "I just remembered something," he said.

"On Sunday night? What?"

"That I'm in love with a girl from home."

Her mouth formed a perfect O of surprise and then stretched into a kind smile. "Then you're in the wrong place, Daniel Kanagy."

He let out a breath of . . . what? Relief? "You are a gute friend, Amanda."

She sighed. "I know."

With a squeeze of her arm, he got up and hurried into the room where they'd been putting all the coats and hats. He found his coat and whipped it on, along with the beanie that he fished out of the pocket. Then he was out into the cold night. It took a while to locate his horse and buggy, but eventually he was on his way back to the house of the kind people hosting him. He needed to pack and call a car to pick him up in the morning. Early. As early as they'd allow.

He couldn't wait to get home.

THE TRIP HAD felt like wandering the desert for forty years, but eventually Daniel walked into his parents' house, the sound of tires crunching on the gravel fading away as the car he'd taken drove off. He hadn't had time to mail a letter ahead of his return to warn his parents to expect him. Of course, they were at the store right now, given that it was a Thursday.

The quiet of the house closed around him.

What he wanted to do was hitch up the smaller buggy

and drive over to Faith's house and see her. Talk to her. But he didn't. Common sense prevailed, and he headed upstairs to unpack his belongings and think over what his next step with her should be. Because there was going to be a next step, without a doubt. He wasn't giving up. Not yet.

He chewed over idea after idea—thinking of one before discarding it for this or that reason, then moving on to another before discarding that one in turn.

He'd been long done with unpacking and was sitting on the side of his bed thinking when he happened to glance out his window and catch movement in the honey room. Everything inside him stilled.

Faith. She was there.

She was the only other person who would be in that room at this time of year. Was this Gotte's way of providing an opportunity for him? Daniel didn't think so. Not entirely. Because he still didn't have an answer for Mercy and Rosie and for Faith's need to keep them so close.

Even so, he was down the stairs and across the yard, forgetting his coat entirely. He only paused when he got to the door of the honey room. The last thing he wanted was to put her off, and the way he was feeling after rushing home, if he didn't have total control over himself, he might sweep her right off her feet and talk later.

After a deep breath, he knocked and let himself into the room.

Faith turned, a sprig of holly gripped in her rubber-gloved hands, and her eyes went wide. "Daniel?" she whispered his name.

"Hi." *Ach du lieva.* Was that all he had to say to her? Only he couldn't seem to make his mouth work. She was just so lovely, standing there with her fine brown hair sticking out from her kapp in whisps and her large dark eyes trained on him.

"You're. . . ." She paused to lick her lips in a nervous little gesture that made him frown. Had he ruined everything with that hasty proposal? "You're back," she finally said.

"Jah."

"Did you . . . did you bring your fiancée with you?"

His fiancée? Now he was frowning out loud, as his mater would say. "Who?"

She hesitated, then pulled her shoulders back. "You went to Shipshewana to find a wife. Didn't you?"

His parents told her that?

"I assume you've come home with gute news already."

Any words he might have said lodged in his throat. It would be gute news to her if he found a wife?

"Nae," he finally said. "I did not find a wife."

Faith didn't react to that at all. Not a blink, not a breath even. She just stared at him across the room. "Oh."

That was it? Oh?

"Are you sad about that?" she ventured next.

"Nae." What else should he say? He wasn't sad. What he was right now was confused. Verhuddelt.

This was not how he'd pictured this conversation with Faith going at all.

She'd kissed him like she loved him. He could remember every detail of her face as she'd gazed at him in that moment before he'd proposed. But she was acting as though him marrying someone else, so soon after asking her, would be a . . . relief?

Maybe she isn't bothered about it one way or the other.

In which case, he'd read that kiss they'd shared all wrong. Had he been the only one who couldn't get it out of his mind and his heart?

He opened his mouth, with honestly no idea what was going to come out, and found himself saying, "If I ever marry it will be for love."

He willed her to hear him. To know that he meant he loved her.

Faith stared at him for a beat. "That sounds wise" was all she said. She turned to put the holly down and take off her gloves. "If anyone deserves love, it's you."

What does that mean?

She turned back to face him. "Ach vell, we missed you."

Who was *we*? Because if she had missed him . . . "I'm sure no one noticed I was even gone," he mumbled.

"That's not true. You're important to a lot of people around here." A teasing glint entered her eyes. "Clara Gick, for instance."

Clara Gick. He couldn't help the face he made, which made Faith chuckle. "I heard that she was wonderful disappointed that you'd gone to find a wife away from Charity Creek. In fact, she was very loud about how you had your pick of so many wonderful maedels here, and how she just couldn't understand you."

Ugh. Hopefully Clara didn't get the idea that because he'd returned still single that meant he was interested in her in any way, shape, or form. And why were they even talking about Clara when he'd proposed to Faith, something neither of them had brought up yet? His heart was Faith's. Didn't she know that? Didn't she realize that he wouldn't have proposed if that weren't true?

"Malachi proposed to Mercy while you were gone."

Daniel closed his mouth shut with a snap. Malachi had proposed . . . to Mercy?

So many questions chased themselves like dogs chasing their tails around and around in his head. Had Mercy said yes? Would she? Marrying an Amish man meant she had to be baptized. What did that mean for Faith? And for Rosie?

What do I do?

HE'S NOT ENGAGED.

He's not getting married.

He didn't find a wife.

He came home.

The longest days of her life. And now here he stood before her, back in her life and unmarried, and . . .

All sorts of confused and befuddled thinking was filling up her head like a clogged kitchen sink. She'd spent this week worrying over Malachi and Mercy and how she might be about to lose everything. Lose Rosie. She couldn't even begin to figure out where she might go after they married. Mamm and Dat would be in the dawdi haus, after all, but she couldn't afford a place on her own, in town or out of it.

But if Daniel wasn't married . . .

Faith Kemp. How selfish could you be, wanting to marry simply to have a home. Daniel deserves better. So much better.

Except that wasn't why she wanted him. Her heart was being pulled in a thousand directions, and she was so confused.

The door suddenly banged open, making her jump and Daniel turn, putting himself between her and whatever had opened it so violently.

"What did you say to her?" Malachi demanded.

Faith choked and leaned around Daniel to find Malachi filling up the doorway in a towering rage, his face a glower as dark as a thunderstorm.

"What are you talking about?" she asked. "Say what to who?"

Was Malachi here because he knew Daniel was home? What would Daniel have said to anyone?

"You," Malachi practically spat at her.

Me? What could I possibly have done?

"Calm down," Daniel said in a voice that made her turn her surprised blinking from Malachi to him. Daniel never used tones like that. Like he was actually angry.

Reaching out, she took his hand in hers, waiting for him to uncurl his fist and grasp hers. "It's okay," she told him quietly.

Finally he looked down, first at their hands, and then into her eyes with so many questions in his that she wanted to wrap her arms around him. She'd put those questions there. The doubts and worries.

Not letting go, she faced Malachi. "I'm still not sure what you're talking about."

"Then explain why she's gone."

Gone.

The word rattled around in her head like the last donut hole rattling around in a box. He had to be talking about Mercy, but . . . "What do you mean *gone*?"

"Gone as in vanished. In a car. She left me this." He jerked his hand in the air, waving what appeared to be a letter. "Said she couldn't marry me when I was meant to be with you."

"What?" Faith squeaked.

"She left you one, too." He fished another crumpled letter in an envelope from his coat pocket.

Daniel let go of Faith to cross the room and take it from him, then hand it to Faith, who opened it with shaking hands, because suddenly she was back almost five years ago, to the day Mercy had run away from home, abandoning Faith to follow her own life.

I can't go through this again.

She paused pulling the letter out of the envelope as realization dawned and horror made her hands shake even more.

Rosie. Had Mercy taken Rosie with her? She had every right to, as her mater. *Please, Gotte, this isn't happening.*

"Faith?" Daniel's large hand fell over both of hers, clasped around the letter in front of her. It said a lot about her state of mind that she lifted her gaze to his, but didn't really see him, or feel his touch.

But she latched on to the steadiness of his gaze like wrapping herself around a tree trunk in a storm.

"She wouldn't," she whispered.

Daniel gazed back. "It will be oll recht." He mouthed the words just for her. His quiet assurance somehow reached through the darkness that threatened to pull her under, and Faith managed to suck in a shuddering breath.

Her lips moved, forming words, and she even heard her own voice telling him, "Okay. Okay."

Giving her hands a squeeze, he let go of her, and she managed to finish opening the letter. It took her a moment before she could focus on the words. They were definitely in Mercy's handwriting, all loopy and girly.

Dear Faith,

Last time I left you a letter like this, I couldn't bring myself to ask you for your forgiveness. You are the most important person in my life, and I left you because I just couldn't face a life the way we'd been raised. I knew even then that I was being selfish, and maybe even a little overdramatic.

This time, though, I can ask your forgiveness with my whole heart. I am making this choice for the right reasons. For you and not for me. I feel I owe you at least that much.

When I came home, it was because I couldn't bear to be away from the baby I had given birth to. I needed to see for myself that she was safe and loved and cared for, even though I knew, giving her to you, that I was giving her to the best mother possible.

But then, when I got to Charity Creek, everything just seemed to fall into place. As if God had a plan for me in the community that He had put me in at birth. Everything felt right, and natural, and I realized how much I had missed my life here. But even then, there was always this sinking feeling in my gut telling me that something was wrong or off. It wasn't until Malachi proposed and I saw your face that I realized what it was.

My being here ruins everything for you.

You were all set with a husband to care for you, and a home to grow old in, and a baby who you are more mother to than I am no matter how much I love her. And then I had to show up and ruin that for you.

In all of our years on this earth together, you have never asked for anything for yourself. You were born

*second, and I have to believe that it was because you
let me go first, even in the womb. You always let me go
first. I already took away years from you, making you
follow me across the country. Please don't do that this
time. I want you to stay and marry Malachi and raise
Rosie. Please live every one of those dreams of being
an Amish wife and mother and eventually grandmother that you've ever had.*

*I love you, and I want only the best for you. For the
first time in my life I can be the one to let you go first.*

*Don't worry about me. You know I can take care of
myself. Somewhere out in the world I will find a man
who loves me and wants to work beside me rather than
off my back, and maybe I'll get those two-point-five
kids and the charming house with a white picket fence.
I will write often and send you pictures so that you
don't worry and always know where I am.*

*Tell Rosie every single day that I love her with all
my heart. Mom and Dad, too. I love you, sister.*

Mercy

"Not like this," Faith whispered to the letter in her hand
as if it might send her words directly into her sister's heart.

Didn't Mercy know that she couldn't be happy without
her? Whatever way that looked. With Mercy married to
Malachi, Faith would find a new path. Would it be hard?
Yes. But she would find her way eventually. She looked up
at Daniel, hardly aware of the tears streaming down her
cheeks except that they made him fuzzy to look at. "Not
like this," she whispered again to him alone.

She held out the letter to him. "You can read it."

In fact, she wanted him to. Because it seemed to her that of all the people in the world, including Malachi, Daniel was the only one—the only one—she would want to talk to about this, want to find comfort from, or advice.

He was her rock, even though she knew she was a terrible person to lean on him when she'd already caused him pain.

"See," Malachi ranted. "She left because of *you*."

But Daniel ignored him, keeping his head bent over the letter, silently going over her sister's words.

"You must have said something to her," Malachi accused.

Daniel lifted his head. "Go home, Malachi," he said in a voice that brooked no argument.

And for once, in the short time she had known him, Malachi did as he was asked. Although it took him a moment of openmouthed gaping, followed by stomping away and slamming the door closed behind him, before he did.

He was hardly out of the room before Daniel gently walked her to the hook on the wall where she hung her coat. Somehow, without her help, he managed to bundle her into it and her scarf and put her black bonnet over her kapp, and then urged her out to the barn, where he hooked up the Kanagys' smaller buggy and settled her in it. It was warmer today, the sun shining with a bright happiness that seemed to mock her.

"Where are we going?" she finally roused herself from her shock enough to ask.

"I'm taking you home" was all he said.

She wrinkled her nose. "It would have been much more efficient to send me home with Malachi."

He shook his head. "He is not fit to be around right now.

He would spend the entire drive berating you and then regret it when he calmed down."

He wasn't wrong about that, but she felt bad all the same. Daniel had only just gotten home. He didn't need to be carting her around when she had a perfectly good ride. She could even walk, but it was too late to protest now, so she didn't.

They didn't talk all the way back to her parents' house. He slowed in the circular drive, pulling back on the reins to stop the horse. They just sat there, neither speaking, for the longest time, until finally Daniel turned to face her. "Do you trust me, Faith?"

There was nothing he could do to fix this, nothing he could say, but that didn't matter. The strength in him lifted her up. "Jah. For sure and certain."

He gave a jerking little nod. "Do you trust Gotte?"

"Of course."

"Then pray . . . and wait."

Faith took a deep breath. "I feel like I've been waiting all my life," she whispered, entrusting one of the darkest secrets about herself to him.

Daniel smiled as he reached out to tug the tie of her kapp gently. "Trust in the Lord with all your heart and lean not on your own understanding; in all your ways submit to Him, and He will make your paths straight."

"Proverbs," she murmured.

Daniel nodded. "Take care of Rosie," he said. "And try not to worry."

He got out of the buggy came around to slide her door open and help her out. Then he was back in the buggy and trotting off down the lane while she was still standing on the first step leading up to their front porch, watching him leave her.

"Trust in the Lord with all your heart and lean not on your own understanding." She whispered the words he'd given her as a comfort, and they were snatched away by a sudden gust of wind. For a brief moment before his buggy turned the bend in the drive, she felt a little less hollow.

Chapter Twenty

✳

THERE WAS ABSOLUTELY nothing Daniel could do, and the weight of that uselessness pressed down on him hard. He'd told Faith to trust in Gotte, and yet he felt compelled to somehow fix this for her.

But how?

"You're back! When did that happen?" Joshua's voice broke into his thoughts.

Daniel looked up from where he was sitting at the kitchen table brooding to find both his bruders standing there staring at him.

"What are you doing here?" he asked—probably with more brusqueness than he meant to, given that they both frowned.

"Joshua asked me to make a new set of drawers for Joy as a Christmas gift," Aaron said. "I'm here to take measurements and talk about what she might like."

Oh. "Mercy Kemp left town and Faith is devastated." The words burst from him.

He knew he wasn't making sense. At least, not to anyone who didn't already know the details of what had happened. His bruders glanced at each other, then each pulled a chair around to sit in front of him in all seriousness. Even Joshua.

"What happened?" Aaron prompted.

Daniel filled them in. On everything. Not only on Mercy but on kissing Faith and proposing and why he'd come home so quickly. On Malachi's proposal and what had happened this afternoon. When he was done, he flopped back in his chair. He was usually the one who knew what to do, the paths through any obstacle always clear to him, and he'd told Faith to trust him, but he was lost right now.

"Do you think Faith will marry Malachi?" Joshua asked, only to grunt as Aaron elbowed him. "What?" he demanded, rubbing at the spot. "It's a legitimate question."

"He's already asking himself that, dumkoff," Aaron muttered under his breath, his concerned gaze resting on Daniel's face.

Aaron wasn't wrong.

Daniel sighed. "Faith might marry a man she doesn't love just for security and to raise Rosie, and maybe even to make Mercy happy. That's just who she is."

Joshua let out a low whistle. "And I thought Joy was all about making others happy."

Aaron, though, was still watching Daniel, who took another breath. "I love her."

Joshua sat up so fast his chair scooted back with a screech. "Wait. What?"

"Ach du lieva. Keep up, Joshua." Aaron rolled his eyes. "That's why Daniel kissed her, and proposed, and had to run off to lick his wounds when she said no, and now he's so worried about this."

Daniel ignored them both, still working through everything in his mind. "I love her and all I can think is that someone needs to tell Mercy that she made the wrong choice, leaving the way she did. Again. Even if it was for the right reasons."

"What would that accomplish?" Aaron asked. "Just go propose to Faith . . . err . . . again . . . and then everything will be fine. She doesn't have to marry Malachi."

Daniel shook his head though. "Faith won't be right in her heart, married to me or Malachi, while she believes her sister is alone and sad. I have to bring her back." Then he frowned hard. "Am I just being selfish to want to bring her back?"

Aaron shook his head. Actually, so did Joshua. "You've never made a selfish decision in your entire life," the youngest of them said in all seriousness.

"I've never been in love, either," Daniel muttered.

Both his bruders fell silent.

"I guess," Aaron said slowly, "what you have to ask yourself is, would Faith be easier in her mind with Mercy here, even if it means making difficult decisions? Or would she be happier if you left it alone?"

"And when I figure out the answer?" Daniel asked.

Aaron shrugged. Joshua didn't. He sat forward. "Then do something about it, if you can."

WITH ROSIE ON her hip, Faith made her way through the Yoders' house to the kitchen, where she watched as her mother set the dishes they had brought for the after-church meal on the counter.

She didn't pretend that she didn't hear the whispers following her through the house. They were worse this time than before, even. More speculation about Mercy, and Rosie, and Malachi, and even about Faith herself. For once though, rather than rounding her shoulders and ducking her head, she did what her sister would have done in her place. She pulled her shoulders back and met each gaze as she passed, smiling and pretending she didn't hear a single word uttered about her or her family.

The speculation would die down eventually, and she had a child to raise if her sister didn't come back.

Had Mercy been gone only a day?

Rosie had cried all night long, saying, "Mama, mama, mama" over and over again. But when Faith would reach for her or try to soothe her, she'd shake her head. Which maybe hurt more than anything else could have.

"Why don't you take Rosie up to Amos and Samuel's room?" Anna Yoder, Joy's mamm, urged her.

That would probably be best for everyone.

With more smiles and more nods, Faith made her way upstairs, where the other mothers with little ones had gathered together. They all looked up and looked . . . guilty? Had they been talking about her, too? Faith closed the door behind her so that none of the new crawlers and walkers could make their way out of the room easily. She set Rosie down gently on her unsteady feet. Normally, Rosie would toddle right over to the other babies and start babbling away. Instead she plopped down on her well-padded backside right where she stood, then stuck her fingers in her mouth, mumbling around them, "Mama, mama, mama."

Faith was pretty sure every woman in the room winced, shooting first Rosie and then Faith looks filled with speculation and sympathy.

Faith swallowed a sigh and the urge to go lie down.

A second later, the door opened too quick for her to

move out of the way and bonked into her. Without any apology, Clara Gick stepped inside, no baby on her hip—after all she didn't have any nieces and nephews, or even children of good friends, to be toting around yet.

Her gaze landed on Faith, and she didn't even bother to hide the look of utter disdain twisting her face from beautiful to something ugly.

Faith had no energy left to deal with Clara and her judgments. "What do you want?"

The other three ladies in the room gasped softly, but in a way that told Faith that what she'd said, or more likely the impatient way she'd said it, was downright rude. She was beyond caring at the moment. She would probably regret it later.

Except, with the way Clara's remarkable green eyes sparked with her irritation, Faith revised that to regretting it now. Maybe being a peacekeeper would have been easier in the short run.

"How can you show your face here after driving away one of the best men in the district?" Clara demanded.

Faith frowned. Men? She couldn't be talking about Malachi, because he had come to Gmay with her and her parents today. So who—

Apprehension tiptoed with icy steps up her spine. *Do you trust me?* Daniel had asked her that. "I'm not sure what you're talking about."

"Oh, I just bet you don't," the other girl snapped. "Daniel Kanagy."

Faith tried to quiet her heart, which was thumping heavily as her fear was confirmed. "I thought he came back from Shipshewana?"

That was what he had told her that day, wasn't it? Everything had gotten so muddled up with Mercy's letter and

Malachi so angry. He still wasn't talking to her, blaming her for everything.

Clara gave a derisive snort. "Don't pretend you don't know."

"I don't know."

Clara gave another snort, then, crossing her arms, seemed to decide that she'd let Faith in on the secret. "Everyone knows how Mercy left town—again—but so did Daniel. Yesterday. I heard he talked to your parents first, so you have to know." The tone she used dripped in accusation.

Faith wasn't paying attention to Clara, though. She was battling the urge to scoop up Rosie, run downstairs to plop her in Mamm's arms, find out what he'd apparently said to her parents—and when had that happened, anyway?—then hightail it to the nearest phone to call a car and try to follow him.

But she could fix this. She'd found Mercy eventually, after all. She could find him. Bring him home to his family and the community and his bees. He loved Charity Creek and his life here too much to leave. The problem was, she had no idea where he might have gone. Mercy hadn't left any clues in her letters about where she was headed.

"His parents are beside themselves." Clara's words broke into her thoughts and cracked her heart wider.

She could only imagine. She was, too.

Clara must've felt she'd done her duty as the community shamer. With a self-righteous little nod, she flounced out of the room. Thank goodness for Annie Allgyer, who followed and closed the door behind her softly.

"Don't listen to Clara," she urged Faith. "For a month at least, she's been telling anyone who'll listen that she's going to marry Daniel. So his leaving, first to go to Ship-shewana, and now to go after Mercy, has stung her pride."

Go after Mercy?

Faith's lungs froze before expanding suddenly in a painful rush. Was that why he'd left? Her sister had that winning way. Had Daniel fallen in love with her?

In the same breath, though, Faith was shaking her head. Daniel didn't love Mercy. Not that way, at least. She was sure of it. *He would never, ever propose to me if he did.* Which meant . . .

Did he go after Mercy for me?

Her legs turned wobbly with the thought, and she just managed to get to the bed and sink down onto it. Thoughts flew around her mind like starlings in a summer sky.

Do you trust me? she could hear Daniel asking her. The words took on a different meaning now. Not just of comfort, but the conviction that he could fix this.

For her.

She'd laid all her problems at his feet in the most selfish of ways, and he was such a gute man, of course he wouldn't have left this alone.

Oh, Daniel.

Chapter Twenty-One

✳

"HEY, BUDDY. WHAT'S with the getup?"

Daniel looked down from the street sign he was reading to find a man standing at the corner of the busy street where he stood, staring pointedly at Daniel's clothes.

"Are you in cosplay or something?" the man asked.

He had no idea what cosplay was, but he was fairly certain that he wasn't. "Nae."

The man's bushy eyebrows shot straight up. "Hey, Merv. Get a load of this guy with the hat."

Another man who was leaning against the building smoking a cigarette grinned. "I'm looking."

"Weird, right?"

Had these men bothered to look in a mirror? Figuring he had two ways he could address them, Daniel tried on what he hoped was an easy a grin. "I guess my clothes are weird around here," he said, channeling the way Faith was extra friendly to people sometimes. "Where I come from, everyone dresses this way."

It did the trick. Both men appeared to relax, grinning back at him. "What are you?"

What a rude question. Thank goodness he worked in a shop and met Englischers all the time. Nice ones. Mildly curious, sure, but kind yet. Otherwise he would wonder if all of them were this obnoxious.

"I'm Amish," he answered, rather than give them a lesson in manners. He just wanted to get where he was going.

"Amish?" Merv came up off the wall. "What is that?"

"You know, Merv," the other guy said. "They live without electricity and stuff."

Merv's head went back, but he stopped moving toward Daniel. "Oh, right. I heard about them." Then he relaxed again, shoving his hands into his pant pockets. "What do you do at night?"

Daniel chuckled. "We go to bed."

Both men made faces, and the other guy, whose name he still hadn't heard, said, "Sounds boring."

Daniel just shrugged. "Actually, maybe you can help me. I'm looking for the Sunset Diner?"

Merv made a face. "Why'd you want to go there? Their food will just give you a bellyache."

"I'm looking for a friend, and I think they work there." Deliberately, he didn't say "she." No need to court more questions.

Both men burst out laughing. "I don't think so," the other guy said. "No one who looks like you works there."

"They wouldn't wear Amish clothes like this," he said.

"Oh." The two men looked at each other, then shrugged. Merv said, "Yeah, you good."

Daniel had no idea what that meant, but Merv kept on. "Go two blocks that way. Past the L." That, at least, Daniel had learned meant the elevated train. Merv pointed. "Hang a left and go three blocks down. It'll be on your right."

"Denki for your help," Daniel said with an automatic tug on his hat. "Much appreciated."

Then he started walking briskly in the direction they'd steered him. Their voices followed him down the street. "Get a load of that guy," Merv was mumbling. " 'Much appreciated.' Who says shit like that?"

Daniel winced at the profanity. His mater would wash that man's mouth out with soap.

But at least they'd helped him out. He had a feeling they'd been on the fence about doing that or beating him up. His vow of nonviolence was something he'd never had to stand up for before. Not in a peaceful, quiet community like Charity Creek. Given the urgency of why he was here now, he was glad he hadn't had to today, either.

How had Faith done this, especially on her own, for so long?

She said she'd always remained true to her Amish faith, wearing her clothes, and not trying to blend in with the rest of the world. Daniel had been in Chicago for only five days, and he just wanted to be home. Most of the people he'd run across were perfectly nice, even those who stared. But this was his third encounter that could have gone differently. Why was it so hard for people to just accept and respect anyone different from them?

A harder question to swallow loomed large in his mind. Had anyone ever hurt Faith? The thought strung out his insides and tied them into knot after knot just thinking of her on her own. Without him. Without Mercy for much of the time.

She was so strong.

Even now, knowing she was safely home in Charity Creek, he wanted to wrap his arms around her and tell her that he would take care of her for the rest of her life. That he would never let anyone hurt her.

Up ahead he saw the diner, and all thoughts beyond what he was about to do left his head.

Mercy's letter that she'd left for her parents had said she was headed to Chicago. Since she was a waitress, he'd been methodically making his way through any restaurant or diner or bar that employed them. But last night he'd managed to talk to Dat on the phone at the shop and learned that Faith's parents had received another letter saying where she had ended up with a job and a place to stay, and that she was settled nicely, and not to worry about her.

Now here he was.

Gotte, please let my words to her be Your word. Open her heart to hear You.

Daniel stepped inside the diner with a ring of the bell hanging on the door that had the waitress—not Mercy— behind the counter glancing up. "Take any seat you want, honey," she offered in a distracted manner before returning to pouring coffee for a man sitting at the counter.

This was not a conversation to be had over a counter, so he chose to sit in the booth in the back corner. But when another waitress came to serve him, she wasn't Mercy, either.

"What can I get you, hon?" she asked.

"Is Mercy working today?"

She studied him for a moment. "You know her?"

He nodded. "We're friends from childhood."

In a long sweep, her gaze took in the way he was dressed, even seated at the table with his hat off. "Well, that explains a lot," she murmured, more to herself than to him. Then, louder, "I'll go get her."

Daniel was facing the swinging door the waitress went through. A second later it opened, much more slowly this time, as Mercy stuck her head out. As soon as her gaze landed on him, she blanched, paling so much Daniel got up from his seat to go to her. But she waved him back down as she crossed the room to slide into the bench across from him.

Then she stared at him with wide eyes. "Why are you here?"

No use beating around the bush. "To talk."

She went rigid in her seat, expression turning stony. "Go home, Daniel."

"I'm in love with Faith."

She was halfway out of the seat but froze at his words, then slowly slid back to face him, searching his gaze. "You are?"

He gave a single, brisk nod.

Blowing out a long breath, Mercy looked away, gaze focusing somewhere outside the window in the street beyond for a long moment before turning to face him again. "Why are you telling me? Shouldn't you be telling her?"

"I'm telling you because I think you are the only person who loves Faith as much as I do."

She fiddled with the napkin-wrapped pack of silverware on the table. "I still don't see—"

"You broke her heart, leaving the way you did, and even if she does love me, I won't be able to make her happy until you are happy."

Mercy's gaze dropped away from his, and she plucked at the paper glued around the silverware. "I'm happy here."

"No. You're not."

She jerked her gaze up. "You can't tell me—"

"You were happy home with your family, and Rosie, and Malachi. Everyone could see it."

"I—"

"Are you going to lie to me again? Gotte is listening, Mercy. Tell me you weren't happy and I'll leave."

After a pause, she gave her head a shake. Then another. Then took a deep breath. "If I come home, I'll just mess everything up for Faith again."

"If you stay here, she might marry Malachi, a man she doesn't love and who I'm fairly certain is in love with you, and raise Rosie, who asks for you every day. She won't be happy."

Mercy visibly flinched with each point. "Rosie asks for me?" she whispered, her voice cracking.

He nodded.

"Faith doesn't love Malachi?"

He shook his head. That much he was absolutely sure of.

"Does she love you?"

Daniel thought of the kiss they'd shared. Of the way she had kissed him back. Of the way her words afterward weren't rejection of his proposal but of the situation. Because of Rosie. Was he taking Rosie away from her by doing this? Maybe, but he'd seen her after getting Mercy's letter. Being Rosie's mater at the cost of losing her sister was breaking her heart. "I don't know. I pray she does."

"I left because—"

He reached across the table and covered her fidgety hands with his, stilling her. "Faith let me read your letter. I know why you left."

She took a shuddering breath. "I've hurt her so much," she whispered. "I need to give her a chance to figure out what she wants, without all her considerations for me getting in the way."

Daniel squeezed her hands. "Don't you see? You staying away to give her those options is still taking away her choices."

Mercy frowned. "What do you mean?"

"I mean that with no one to care for Rosie except for her, Faith will make choices based on what she feels is best for Rosie."

"Isn't that what she wants, though? To be Rosie's mother?" Mercy's frown was ten colors of confusion.

"I'm not saying her choices will be easy." Faith's love for that child was the only thing that had made Daniel think and rethink about what he was doing right now. For five days straight he'd been second-guessing himself. But his gut told him he was doing the right thing now. He'd pray and leave the rest in Gotte's hands. "But isn't it better to give her all the options to pick from, rather than take some away?"

The way Mercy quieted, her eyes unfocused and far away, he could tell she was thinking that over. Then she took a deep breath. "What do you think I should do?"

Daniel's breath left him in a hard whoosh. Until this second, he hadn't been sure he could convince her. "Between you and me, I think we need to show Faith that she has a lot, oonbunch, of options, and make sure she knows that if she picks the option that will make her the happiest, all those she loves will have options that make them happy, too."

He knew his Faith. She would sacrifice herself every time. But if she knew all outcomes were gute for everyone . . .

"Maybe between the two of us, we can figure this out."

* * *

FAITH TROMPED THROUGH the fields of dried autumn grasses—all browns, and with the gray skies above, very dull. Rosie was strapped to her front, all bundled up in the baby scarf thingy Mercy had bought them to use. Faith was huffing and puffing, because she was carrying the collapsible travel crib Mercy had bought, too.

No one was available to help her watch Rosie today, and she was determined to do this thing for Daniel. He was off doing something for her out of the goodness of his heart. The least she could do was try to repay that kindness. But she couldn't have Rosie toddling off in fields of brambles and stickers while she worked. There were other critters to worry about, too, though the cold would probably drive them to seek shelter.

By the time she got to the beehives, she was starting to shake a little with the effort. Maybe she should have come a different way, but she'd figured she would take care of this chore on the way to the honey room. After all, she had her own business to tend to as well.

Her Christmas season arrangements were selling like hotcakes. She was blessed and she should be grateful. And she was.

Except she couldn't make herself feel it. Feel anything.

It was like Daniel and Mercy both leaving had doused the light inside her. She went about her day. She loved Rosie and made sure the baby stuck to her schedule and was fed and clean and got her naps and was cuddled and played with. She made her flower arrangements. She did her chores around the house.

And all of it she did in a sort of numb haze.

As if her mind was somewhere else. But it wasn't just her mind. It was her heart. Her heart was somewhere else. With someone else.

Even Mamm had noticed. Just this morning over breakfast she'd said, "You look pale, Faith. Are you sleeping?"

Faith had forced a smile, not wanting to add to her mater's worries. "I sleep fine."

If you counted lying in bed staring at the ceiling sleeping. The last time Mercy left she hadn't come home for five years. Now Daniel was out there, away from his home and his loved ones. And a sick sort of clenching had taken up residence in the pit of Faith's stomach and wouldn't go away. She suspected if she opened her mouth a keening wail might crawl up her throat and never stop.

Please, Gotte, keep them safe.

She wanted to ask Him to bring them home. Both of them. Only that felt selfish. So instead she would pray. *Please show us all the path. Show us Your will in our lives.*

Gotte knew her heart. Every bit of it.

Once she got close to the hives, she stopped far enough away that if she set up Rosie here, she'd be able to keep a close eye on her, but if the bees were too disturbed by her moving them, Rosie wouldn't be in danger. Then, struggling around the almost-toddler strapped to her chest, she managed to set up the travel crib. So far, Rosie hadn't figured out how to climb out.

Making sure the baby's winter clothes were all buttoned up, she popped her in the crib with blocks and her favorite Amish doll and a thick quilt. Then Faith made her way over to the beehives, only she stopped when she got close enough to realize that they didn't need to be moved another time or two like she'd worried.

They were already where Daniel had showed her he wanted to place them that day she'd helped him move them.

Plunking her hands on her hips, she looked around as if she'd find him lurking in the woods ready to jump out and tell her he was here and had done it himself. But she knew he wasn't home yet. Ruth had told her so just yesterday.

His parents didn't seem to blame Faith like Clara and Malachi both had. A small part of her worried that they were just being polite. But Ruth kept insisting that Gotte would work everything out in His way and in His time.

I wish I had the same strength of courage in Him.

Ach vell . . . if the beehives were where they were supposed to be, then there was no need for her to interfere. As she went to move away, she caught sight of a white sheet of paper suck to the top of one, flapping in the wind.

Curious, she moved closer to find that it was a note in Daniel's scrawling, masculine hand. One with her name on the outside. Frowning, her heart tripping inside her, she plucked it off the lid and opened it.

I knew you would try to help me with the bees while I was gone because that is the kind of heart you have. But I went ahead and took care of it before I left because you are too small to try to move these without help. I hope you trust me to always take care of you, Faith.

That was it. No signature. And yet her heart was jumping around inside her like a jackrabbit bursting from its warren.

Always take care of you.

Always. He'd used the word "always" even when he'd

left town because of her. She read the words, then read them again, and again, and again. Smoothing her hand over the rough scrawl, she closed her eyes and tried to picture him writing this and sticking it here for her to find.

"I love you," she whispered.

Words she hadn't dared allow herself to think let alone say out loud.

But the second her lips formed each sound, the truth of it settled so beautifully in her heart, it was like when the chaos of her flower arrangements finally came together and suddenly she could see the entire bouquet completed. Every color and line and piece in harmony as a whole.

Faith fell to her knees, staying still in silence, giving all her emotion and worries to Gotte.

She loved Daniel. With all her heart. And she wanted to spend the rest of her life doing little things for him, making him happy, and making sure he knew he was loved. Always.

If he came home, she would wrap him in her arms and tell him that and let him decide what happened next. He might never forgive her stubborn heart for taking this long to admit the truth of what she wanted. What she longed for.

For him.

But if Daniel succeeded in bringing Mercy back with him, that meant giving up a different dream.

Being Rosie's mater.

Except now that Gotte had softened her heart she could see more clearly. Since Mercy had come home and become part of their lives again, Faith had gladly shared the baby with her. It hadn't been as hard as she thought to think of Rosie as Mercy's. Could she change to just being the aendi? What kind of mater did that make her? That she could change her heart so easily?

Please, Gotte, what is right? What role do You want me to play in this life? Show me the way.

Of course, all of her prayers would be useless if Daniel and Mercy never came home. She glanced over her shoulder to find Rosie standing in the travel crib, watching her. A tiny, solemn figure with big blue eyes and cheeks red from the cold.

Pushing herself to her feet, Faith dusted off her skirt and her stockings underneath, then wiped the dampness from her cheeks. Gracious. She hadn't even realized she'd been crying. At least the cold air would make her swollen eyes look normal by the time she got to the honey room, just in case any Kanagys were around to see her.

As Faith got nearer to the baby, Rosie lifted her chubby little arms with a smile as wide as the sky and as brilliant as the sun. "Aendi," she said in her high baby voice. A single word, clear as day, looking right at Faith.

Faith stilled and waited just a second for the pain. The knowledge that she wasn't really the mater to this child she loved so much. But it didn't come. Instead, she felt . . . right. Content.

Scooping Rosie up, she cuddled her close. "That's right, Rosie Posie. I am your Aendi Faith, and I will always, always love you and always watch out for you."

Suddenly Faith knew exactly what to pray for.

Bring them home, she silently called out to Gotte. *Bring them both home so that Mercy can be a mater, and maybe marry Malachi if that's what she wants. Bring them home so that I can tell Daniel I love him and ask for his forgiveness and take care of him the rest of his life. Bring them home.*

Chapter Twenty-Two

❋

DANIEL CLIMBED OUT of the car and could hardly stop himself from sprinting to the barn to hitch up a horse and go straight to Faith. He hadn't seen her in a week, and yet it felt like years. Years off his life.

It wonders me if I haven't sprouted gray hairs over this.

Because while he may have convinced Mercy to come home and at least discuss all the options they had come up with, that didn't mean Faith would choose any option that involved him. In particular, the one where she would become his wife.

But she will be happy. He kept trying to convince himself that would be enough.

And she might be, but he would be shattered if she didn't choose him. For sure and certain a broken man. So he'd prayed all the way here in the car that Gotte would lead them all. He put his faith in Gotte and in the woman he loved with all his heart.

Mercy had asked to come to his parents' house first.

They had called ahead, asking that the bishop meet them there so that she could discuss everything with him before she went home to her family. She wanted to have answers for them.

Something Daniel understood. But the fact that it added more time before he could see Faith, talk to her, made every second crawl.

He'd moved around to the back of the car to get his suitcase and Mercy's out of the trunk when a flash of movement from between the honey room and the dawdi haus where Joshua and Joy lived caught his attention and he glanced over. Then he went utterly still.

She was here. Faith.

Had Gotte heard his prayers, seen how his heart yearned for her, and sent Faith to him?

She was trudging through the tall autumn grasses in his direction. Daniel's heart clenched then unclenched in an ache of longing so strong it stole his breath. She was here. He didn't have to wait. He didn't have to crawl through more time without her. Faith was here.

She must be coming to work on her flower arrangements.

She was far enough away that she hadn't seen him yet. Her head was down, gaze pointed at her feet. Probably so that she didn't trip or stick her foot in another rabbit hole, yet. She clearly had Rosie strapped to her front with that funny scarf thing that Mercy had bought. And what was she lugging? She clutched something large and bulky that knocked against the side of her leg with every step.

Also, why was she coming from the direction she was? Her house was not in that direction. It was almost as if she was coming from . . .

My bees.

Had she seen his note? His heart warmed at the realization that he knew her well enough to be certain that she would go out there to try to help him while he was gone. That was just something his Faith would do.

She was so beautiful, even all wrapped up in a winter coat with her black bonnet over her prayer cap, and the baby, and whatever that thing was she was carrying. He should let her reunite with her sister first, but Daniel couldn't help himself—he started walking toward her.

She didn't look up.

He kept willing her to raise her head, to see him. But she didn't. Between both of them walking, they closed the distance quickly. In fact, she was almost at the back of the house when she finally lifted her head. Faith's gaze connected with his and she jerked to a stop, her eyes going wide. He should have been close enough to hear her, but no sound reached him. He could read her lips just fine, though, as they formed the shapes of his name.

Daniel watched her expression closely for any sign of her feelings, but she just stood there staring at him as he continued walking toward her. Was she happy to see him? Would she be happy once she saw Mercy? One of the hundred different worries he'd had since the moment he had left Charity Creek to go find her sister hit him with force.

Maybe Faith had been perfectly happy with things how they had been with Mercy gone. Maybe he should have asked her first what she wanted. Too late now. His heart clobbered against the inside of his ribs so hard he pressed his hand to his sternum. Faith still hadn't moved by the time he made it to her, tipping her head back to look up at him, her gaze searching his.

"Faith, I—"

The sound of a car door closing had her dropping her

gaze slightly to look behind him. He could see the moment she recognized her sister. She took one look at Mercy, dropped the bulky contraption she was carrying with a thud, then buried her face in both her hands and burst into tears.

Great racking sobs that tore his heart out and ripped it into shreds.

Careful not to crush Rosie, Daniel did the only thing he could—he stepped into Faith, wrapping his arms around her. Cupping the back of her head with one hand, he ran the other down her back in soothing motion. "Don't cry. Don't cry, heartzly."

But the tears didn't seem to be letting up. Still holding her, Daniel was starting to panic. Did she hate him for bringing Mercy home? Was she overjoyed? He'd seen his mother cry enough to know that tears could come with all forms of emotions, and he had no idea which one he was dealing with right now.

Rosie, who he was pretty sure had been asleep when all this started, protested being smooshed between them with a small whine, pushing against his chest.

"Here. Let me take the baby." Mercy appeared out of nowhere. Or maybe she had been there the entire time.

Faith didn't so much as pause in her sobbing, merely let go of him to wrap her arms around her sister's neck and hold on tight, the sounds coming out of her in great gulping rushes, her shoulders shaking. After a small hesitation, and adjusting herself around the baby, Mercy's arms tightened around her sister and her own shoulders started to shake as both the Kemp girls cried together.

"I'm sorry," Mercy mumbled between sobs. And then again and again.

And every time Faith shook her head, but she couldn't seem to get any words out around her cries.

Daniel stood there, utterly helpless, as the woman he loved above his own life poured out everything he knew she'd been keeping inside. Years and years of worries that she hadn't let anybody know she carried. Not even Mercy. Her tender heart had wanted to save them their own grief.

He should probably go inside and give them time together, but Daniel was not leaving her side. If he had his way, he would never leave her side again.

"Here, here, here. What is all this about?" Jethro Miller boomed out in a jovial voice.

It worked, too. Both girls stopped crying and lifted their heads to look at the bishop. Faith with a thousand questions in her eyes. Mercy with hesitant hope and not a little bit of fear. Unwinding her arms from around her sister, Mercy said, "Let me take Rosie. I need to talk to the bishop for a little bit. Why don't you take that time for Daniel to fill you in?"

Eyes all puffy and red, and tears streaking her cheeks, Faith glanced between Mercy and Jethro. Daniel could practically feel the worry coming off her in waves. Finally she nodded and started unwrapping the monstrosity of cloth that held the baby to her chest. A giggle even escaped her when she got tangled up in it and he and Mercy had to work together to get both her and the baby out. For the first time since she'd looked up and seen him, Daniel gave in to a small amount of hope.

Faith couldn't be laughing if she was angry, could she?

She watched as Mercy took the baby and followed Jethro across the yard and on into the house. She watched her sister as if she was worried that if she took her eyes off her, Mercy would disappear again. When they were out of sight, Faith still didn't look at him for the longest time, and Daniel waited.

It seemed as though he'd been waiting for Faith his entire life, but this moment—this one stark moment—was the most important.

Finally she moved her gaze slowly to his. Daniel clenched his hands into fists at his sides. He wanted to take her in his arms with a desperation that threatened to take him to his knees. To hold her, and never let her go. But he would only do that if she wanted him to, and he couldn't tell what she wanted right now.

Faith visibly swallowed. "I knew you left to get her," she said so softly he had to bend his head closer to catch the words.

The answer to that comment seemed pretty obvious, so he remained silent, letting her work through it.

"You did that for me?" This question was even smaller. As if she was afraid to hear his answer.

Nothing could have stopped the words on his lips. "I would do anything for you, Faith. I—"

She surged closer, reaching up to cradle his face in her hands and lift her lips, pressing them to his in a kiss filled with gratitude and love, breathless with hope, and damp from her tears. Grief he hoped she would never experience again. He would never let anything in this world hurt her if he could help it.

Her breath hitching, Faith pulled away, but only slightly, just enough to look him in the eyes. "I love you, Daniel." Then a smile broke out over her features—sheepish and fearful and hopeful all at the same time—and as beautiful as the sun breaking over the horizon with a new dawn.

"I'm sorry for any pain I caused you with my stubborn heart. Will you marry me?"

Four simple words. And yet they hit Daniel so hard, he grunted.

It was all there for him to see now, the emotions freely shown in her eyes. Love, need, partnership, laughter, understanding—but mostly love. She hadn't even heard all the options he'd discussed with Mercy, and that Mercy was now discussing with the bishop.

Faith was choosing him, no matter what else happened.

"What about Rosie?" he asked. He knew how much the baby meant to her, and he would never ask her to trade one happiness for the other.

Faith took a deep, shuddering breath. "Gotte has showed me that He has a plan for my life, and for Rosie's life, and Mercy's life. And if we get out of our own ways, He'll show us what that plan is. I know with everything inside me that *you* are the path He wants me to take. If Mercy decides to leave again, and Rosie stays, then we'll raise a beautiful dochder with our own children and love her all the ways that we love them."

Daniel nodded, his heart lifting with each word.

Faith's smile turned soft and only slightly tinged in sadness. "And if Mercy decides to stay, then Rosie will be raised by the mater God blessed her with . . . and I will love her as an aendi. She'll grow up with our children as cousins. And all will be well."

Could Gotte work these kinds of miracles? Just for him, and for Faith, and Mercy, and Rosie?

Daniel knew the truth of it before the question even solidified in his mind. Because Gotte had made Faith in His image and with His heart.

Faith wrapped her hands around his suspenders and gave him a tiny shake that barely nudged him. "A girl can only wait so long for an answer to a proposal of marriage, Daniel Kanagy."

He wanted to chuckle at her teasing, but he could see the worry in her eyes, and he wouldn't make her worry one second longer. "Yes, I'll marry you, Faith Kemp. With all my heart."

Chapter Twenty-Three

✳

DANIEL TOOK FAITH by the hand, and together they walked to the house to see how Mercy and the bishop were getting along. Faith thought her heart might float the rest of her body right off the ground. Happiness like this . . . she wished she could bottle it, like the scent of flowers, to be taken out during the hard times and reminded of how incandescently, beautifully happy she was in this moment.

Hard times were unavoidable in life. She knew that. She might even be facing one of those hard times with her sister right now. But somehow, facing those moments with Daniel at her side, together and in partnership, and with their eyes lifted to Gotte always, they would get through whatever came their way.

Inside the mudroom, Daniel helped her out of her coat and scarf, sneaking in a quick kiss as he did. Cheeks warming, she tried to shake her head at him, nodding in the direction of the kitchen, where she could hear her sister's voice. But Daniel's answering grin was so wide, his eyes so bright, that she had to clamp a hand over her mouth to hold in the sounds of happiness that wanted to burst forth.

She still needed to talk to Mercy.

Sobering, she walked ahead of Daniel into the room, only to stumble to a halt at the sight of Mercy's wet cheeks. Fresh tears, she could tell.

All of Faith's peace and contentment deserted her at the sight, and she rushed over. "What's wrong?"

Only Mercy didn't answer right away. She looked at the bishop, and Jethro nodded with an unreadable expression. Was he . . . concerned? Stern? What?

"Sit down, Faith," Mercy said. "I need to talk to you."

Taking a bit of a shaky seat, she was grateful when Daniel scooted his chair right beside hers. He even reached for her hand, but at a look from Jethro stopped himself. Bolstered by even that small show of support from him, Faith kept her gaze on her sister's face and waited patiently.

Mercy flicked a glance to Daniel, then Jethro, then back to Faith.

"First, I want to say how sorry I am for running away." She grimaced. "Again. And I will apologize to Mamm, and Dat, and Malachi when we get home."

She called it *home*. Was she staying?

"I thought I was doing the right thing. That there wasn't a place for me here, because things were obviously simpler for you if I was gone."

Faith shook her head, but could tell Mercy wasn't done, so she buttoned her lips around a denial.

"Daniel convinced me that it would be better to discuss all my . . . *our* . . . options with our parents and with Jethro and the ministers and then make a decision that is hopefully best for everyone."

She paused.

Faith nodded to encourage her to go on.

"Before I say more, I have to ask you a question. And I need you to be completely honest, even if you think it will hurt me or make me leave again. Okay?"

Faith's heart shrank in on itself. She would never do anything to hurt Mercy. She would rather rip out her own heart than do that.

Except her sister reached under the table to wrap her hand around Faith's, which were clenched tightly together in her lap. "Promise Gotte, Faith. Promise that you'll be honest. It's important."

Faith looked down at their hands. Then Daniel's larger, capable hand landed on top of Mercy's. "Trust us," he whispered. "And trust Gotte."

She raised her head to look at him, only to find that steadiness and something else staring back at her . . . a kind of peace that all would be well.

Swallowing heard, Faith nodded as she turned to face Mercy. "I promise. Total honesty."

Her sister paused, then rushed into her question. "Is my being here . . . does it make it harder for you?"

Faith pressed her lips together. Honesty. She'd promised total honesty. "When you first came home, I would have said yes," she confessed quietly.

She hated the way her sister flinched, but Mercy's gaze remained fixed on hers. So Faith took a deep breath and kept going. "Except if you hadn't come home, I would have married Malachi and raised Rose as my own. Maybe I would have been at peace with that life, but I wouldn't have learned what love—true, deep love for the man I marry—could be like." She turned to face Daniel, who smiled back at her the way sunflowers turned to the sun.

Then back to her sister. "I would have married Malachi out of necessity or my need to do the right thing for everyone around me, and that wouldn't be fair to him or me."

Mercy's gaze flicked between Faith and Daniel, and a smile tugged at the corners of her mouth but didn't quite make it to her eyes. "You could still marry Daniel and keep Rosie if I left," she said quietly.

Faith's heart cried out for her sister and she scooted forward in her chair, bringing Mercy's hand to her breast, because she'd promised Gotte she would be honest, and the first part of her answer would hurt.

"When you showed up here, I was heartbroken," she admitted, and felt her sister flinch. "I was torn into selfish pieces because you are my precious and most loved schwester and I want you home safe and sound where we can laugh together, and raise our families together, and grow old together."

Mercy took a shuddering breath, her eyes welling.

Faith offered her a smile. "But I had also spent eight months of sleepless nights, and feeding, and watching Rosie's every breath, hearing every giggle, seeing her crawl and now walk, and waiting for her smiles. I was her mater in my heart, and I knew that if you stayed, I wouldn't be that anymore. That's why my heart was broken."

"Oh, Fay," Mercy whispered, her chin wobbling.

Faith pressed on, though. Now that she'd started, she needed to say it all. "How could I choose between the two people . . . three, once I fell in love with Daniel . . . who I love best in the world?"

"See," Mercy said. "I was right to leave."

Faith shook her head, squeezing her sister's hand hard. "Nae. Nae. I was the one who was wrong."

"What?" Mercy frowned.

"I was wrong to think I had to choose at all."

Mercy searched Faith's expression. "What do you mean? If I stay, then you do have to choose."

Faith smiled on a long breath, feeling nothing but peace in the knowledge that what she was about to do and say was right. "Nae. While you've been gone, I realized something important. So maybe you leaving again was Gotte's plan after all, for me—because He changed my heart, softened my hardness."

"You are never hard, Faith," Mercy insisted.

"Jah, I am in my heart, even if I don't show anyone. I was only looking at everything one way. Desperate to keep both you and Rosie but knowing I would give up love and a family of my own if I did, so I couldn't let myself love Daniel the way he deserves. When all along, you being Rosie's mater without me was the right path."

"But then you won't be her mater," Mercy whispered.

"But I will still get to love her every single day. In a different way, jah. But I still get to love her. And I get to love you. And that's as it should be. I think Gotte gave her to me, just for a little while, so that you could find your way home to us. So that your heart would finally lead you back to where you are loved and wanted and needed."

Mercy stared at her in total silence, searching her face as if she didn't quite believe her. Then, with no warning, she flung her arms around Faith's shoulders. No sounds came from her, but the way she shook, Faith knew she was crying.

A fresh set of tears silently trickled down Faith's own cheeks as she cried for her sister's pain and held Mercy as she let out all her emotions. Eventually Mercy quieted and sat back, giving a rueful chuckle as she wiped her palms across her cheeks.

"I can't believe it," she said. Then laughed. A sound of joy. Then sobered again, turning to Jethro. "Now that I know what Faith wants, and what is in my own heart, I'm ready," she said.

Ready? Ready for what?

Faith glanced back and forth between them, trying to push her own fear down deep while Jethro's features remained set in stern lines. "It will take time, and hard work, and true repentance," he said to Mercy.

He seemed to be warning her sister. What was going on?

"I know," Mercy said. "But I believe with all my heart that Faith is right. Gotte brought me home. This is where I want to be." She took a deep breath. "Who I want to be. I want to be baptized in the Amish faith and life."

Faith gasped out loud. Just like she had when she'd seen Daniel walking toward her through the field, she covered her face with her hands and burst into tears.

At this rate, her soon-to-be-husband was going to think he was marrying a watering pot.

But Mercy's words were just too much. Faith would never have pushed her sister to a life she didn't want, but she'd prayed and prayed and prayed—most of her adult life—that Mercy would choose this. Would find her way home. She'd lost all hope for years, even as she'd still prayed, wondering if she was praying for something He didn't want. But here her sister sat, her beautiful, tear-streaked face content—joyful, even—with her choice.

Gotte had truly wrought a miracle today, and Faith's grateful heart was full to bursting.

*   *   *

DANIEL KNOCKED ON the Kemps' door, his heart fluttering like a thousand butterflies had taken wing. He'd come to take her to the frolic. Their gmay were gathering in the Kemps' field—the one near where his beehives used to be—for a big bonfire. Malachi had finished clearing that large field for planting his new crops come spring and had invited the gmay to come roast hot dogs and toast marshmallows as he burned the pile of trees and other debris he'd created.

Malachi was the only piece of the Mercy-shaped puzzle that Daniel wasn't sure about. He'd been there with Faith and Mercy and Jethro as Mercy had filled Esther and Henry in on everything, setting off another round of joyful weeping. Especially from their mater, who might be stiff as a poker in general, but clearly loved both her dochders. They had cried again when Daniel had asked for their blessing to marry Faith.

But Malachi hadn't been there for that. Mercy had asked that he be left in the field where he'd been working until she'd talked everything out with her parents and the bishop. Faith said that Malachi had agreed to stay in the dawdi haus longer while Mercy worked through returning to her faith and being baptized. Beyond that, he hadn't proposed again, or said what would happen after Mercy's baptism, but his generosity made Daniel appreciate the man much more than he had let himself before.

Faith opened the door, and her smile, her beautiful face, but most especially the love gleaming at him from her eyes, knocked the breath right out of him. It did every time.

"Hi," she said. Almost shyly.

None of that now.

He cocked his head, then stepped over the threshold

and right into her, taking her face in his hands to place a gentle kiss on her lips before lifting his head. "Hi," he whispered back.

She grinned, hands circling his wrists—not to tug him away, but to hold him there. "Our first official date. I've been so excited, Mamm told me to go outside and hang all the laundry in the cold, just to calm down."

"Mamm made me work the front of the shop," he admitted.

Which made Faith laugh. "I guess we better get married fast, or we'll both be worn out by Christmas at this rate."

Oh how he loved this woman.

"Redd up?" he asked.

Faith nodded. With visible reluctance that warmed his heart, she let him step away so that she could gather up the basket of goodies she'd made for the two of them to share. Only he plucked the basket—which was decently heavy— right out of her arms and handed her the lighter blankets he'd brought to carry instead.

They walked together with a lantern for light, crossing behind her house and into the fields that would lead them to the bonfire.

He wished he wasn't holding so much stuff so that he could take her hand while they walked. Once they got to the bonfire, he wouldn't be able to. Amish did not show public affection. That was reserved for private moments. Maybe he could take her into the woods to steal a kiss or two.

"When did you know you loved me?" Faith's question came right out of the blue.

Daniel smiled at his feet. Confession time. What would she think when he told her the truth? "The year before you left to find Mercy."

Faith jerked to a stop to swing a wide-eyed stare his direction. "What?"

Stopping beside her, he chuckled at the dumbstruck look on her face. "Do you remember the Hostetlers' reroofing frolic?"

She blinked, then . . . "When you fell off the ladder?"

Another nod. "Someone helped me inside to lie down, and you sat with me, holding a cloth with ice to the bump on my head I'd gotten on the way down."

"And we talked about your bees," she recalled.

He huffed a laugh at the memory. "For two hours. I had just started my first hive, and was in the thick of learning things, and went on and on and on. But you never once seemed bored with the topic."

"I wasn't," she said. "You impressed me with how much you knew."

He knew he'd been right that day to believe she was the girl for him. "Ach vell, my heart just sort of tumbled over inside my chest. You were always the kindest girl I knew, but suddenly to me you were also the most beautiful. I remember watching how your smile lit you up from the inside. Because of my silly bees."

She gave him a stern frown. "Your bees aren't silly."

"See," he said. "I fell head over heels that day, but then, for a whole year, I fell more and more as I watched you from a distance."

She shook her head, looking a little dazed in the warm glow of his lantern. "Why didn't you ask me on a date?"

He tipped his head, not wanting to hurt her, but wanting to be honest. "It's not my way to rush, and . . . I thought I had plenty of time yet."

Faith winced. "Then I left."

Daniel couldn't stand it anymore. He set the basket

down, balancing the lantern on top, and wrapped her up in his arms, holding her tight. "I thought I'd missed my chance forever," he murmured in her ear. "You were gone so long, and my regrets piled up as high as mountains."

"Oh, Daniel," she sighed against him, then burrowed into him. "I'm sorry. I'm so sorry for ever being part of your hurt."

He took her by the shoulders and held her away so she could see him shake his head. "Nae. Like you said, Gotte set you on that path to bring His stray sheep home." He dropped his forehead to hers. "Even though I didn't know if you would ever come back, He gave me the patience to wait for you. That's why no other girl ever quite measured up. Because Gotte knew and He told my heart. Even then, I almost messed it up by taking too much time again."

"Oh, Daniel."

He didn't like the wobble to her voice. The regret. "You were worth the wait. I love you so much, liebchen."

Her sigh was so big, his hands moved with her shoulders. "I love you so much, too, Daniel. So much I think I might burst with it," she whispered. "And I will spend every day of our lives together trying to make you happy."

To make up for the waiting she'd put him through? He knew his Faith. He had no doubt that's what was going through her mind.

"Just love me, Faith. And I will love you. With my whole heart. That's all I could ask for."

She gazed at him with a growing smile, then lifted her lips to his for a kiss he was happy to give. "Jah. I can love you forever," she said when they opened their eyes. "And if you love me the same way, Gotte will take care of the rest."

Epilogue

✳

RUTH KANAGY SAT on the narrow bench with the other married ladies whose children were all grown. She watched contentedly as the bishop approached the group of young men and women who would be baptized today. They'd all sat on the front row in a bent posture during both of the morning sermons—a sign of their yieldedness to Gotte and willingness to submit to the authority of the church.

Beside her, Esther Kemp gave a deeply contented sigh, because her dochder was among those men and women. Mercy Kemp was being baptized today.

A true miracle.

Jethro had the candidates kneel and asked each the four baptismal questions. Then, as they remained kneeling, the congregation rose to their feet. Jethro read a baptismal prayer from the prayer book, and Ruth smiled at the solemn memory of her own baptism.

She returned to her seat with the rest of the congregation as the bishop made his way down the line, baptizing each person with water, in accordance with Gotte's word, individually. She allowed her gaze to drift, just for a moment, to those she loved most.

To her son Aaron across the way, strong and thoughtful. His business was going so well, busy making more and more furniture for the Troyers' store, and he and Hope were expecting their first boppli in a month or so. Then to Joshua, who, even during such a serious rite of passage, still had an irreverent twinkle in his eye. Gotte had found him the perfect wife in Joy, who was bouncing her niece— her older sister's baby—on her knee. Ruth suspected that Joy might be expecting a little one of her own as well, but that was news that the couple hadn't shared yet. Ruth's gaze moved on to Daniel, who Gotte had truly blessed this year. He continued to work in the family shop while his new wife, Faith, helped him tend the bees, and harvest the honey, in between making her beautiful flower arrangements. They lived at home with Ruth and Joseph still, but already had plans to buy a house of their own as soon as the right one came on the market.

Ruth had worried about Daniel the most.

So quiet and tending to keep to himself, her oldest son seemed to have been on a path to remain alone all his life. But since finding Faith, he'd opened up more, and she'd never seen him so happy. Faith was holding Rosie in her lap, content to be the child's aendi in a way that showed the true depth of her heart for others, because she was happy in that role, too. Ruth had worried needlessly about that.

Truly Gotte's path for each of her children was a blessed one.

She glanced across the way to find her husband's gaze on her and blushed a little to have been caught with her mind wandering during the baptism. But instead of frowning, Joseph tipped his head in question, making sure she was fine. She offered him a tiny smile, because a big one wouldn't have been appropriate in Gmay.

He answered with a tiny one of his own, and she knew he understood what she'd been thinking about, and that they were both filled with the same gratefulness.

The bishop finally made it to Mercy, who was last, asking her to kneel. He cupped his hands, resting them on top of her head, and the deacon poured a small amount of water into them, which Jethro then opened, allowing the water to dribble over her head, baptizing her.

"Rise," the bishop invited her, so that she could receive a handshake and a kiss of peace from the bishop's wife.

From her seat, Ruth could see the tears in Mercy's eyes, and she felt her own sting as her heart swelled. Those who wandered farthest brought the most rejoicing when they returned. Mercy had worked hard to repent and resume her Amish life with a sincere and cheerful spirit, winning over even the hardest of hearts in their community.

Then Jethro said to all of the newly baptized, "You are no longer guests and strangers, but workers and members in this sacred and godly fellowship."

Ruth met Joseph's gaze across the way again as the service was concluded, and she could see in his eyes that he was as moved as she had been. She always found baptism to be a beginning, a time to look toward the future, and what she saw for her family was bright. Did Joseph see it, too? She could see in his smile that he did.

They were both filled with joy in this moment of new beginnings, hope for the futures of all three of their boys and their wives, and faith that Gotte would lead them through whatever was to come.

Acknowledgments

No matter what is going on in my life, I get to live out my dream surrounded and supported by the people I love—a blessing that I thank God for every single day. Writing and publishing a book doesn't happen without the support and help from a host of incredible people.

To my readers (especially my Awesome Nerds Facebook fan group!) . . . Thanks for going on this ride with me. Sharing my characters with you is a huge part of the fun. Faith and Daniel always were going to have a heartfelt if somewhat rocky journey, but I didn't realize how hard until Mercy came to life in the words. I hope you love their story as much as I loved writing it. If you have a free sec, please think about leaving a review. Also, I love to connect with my readers, so I hope you will drop a line and say "Howdy" on any of my social media!

To God . . . thank you for the journey and the blessings of imagination and words.

To my editor, Kristine Swartz . . . thank you for your support and picking up this series I love so much!

To my Berkley team . . . thank you for the amazing and appreciated support and all the hard work to make these books the best they can be.

To my agent, Evan Marshall . . . thank you for everything!

To my author friends . . . you are the people I feel most me with, and you inspire me every single day.

To my support team of beta readers, critique partners, writing buddies, reviewers, writing groups, friends, and family (you know who you are) . . . thank you, thank you, thank you.

Finally, to my wonderful husband and our awesome kids . . . I don't know how it's possible, but I love you more every day.

Love,
Kristen McKanagh

Amish Words & Phrases

THE AMISH SPEAK a variation of German called Pennsylvania Dutch (some speak a variation of Swiss) as well as English. As happens with any language spread out over various locations, the Amish use of language includes different dialects and common phrases by region.

As an author, I want to make the worlds I portray authentic. However, I have to balance that with how readers read. For example, if I'm writing a romance based in Texas or in England, I don't write the full dialect because it can be jarring and pull a reader out of the story. Consequently, for my Amish romances, which hold a special place in my heart, I wanted to get a good balance of readability and yet incorporate Pennsylvania Dutch words and phrases so that readers get a good sense of being within that world. I sprinkled them throughout and tried to use what seem to be the most common words and phrases across regions, as well as the easiest to understand within the context of the story.

If you read books within this genre, you'll note that different authors spell the same words in several different ways. Each author has her or his own favorite references, and not all references use the same spellings. I preferred to go with a more phonetic spelling approach.

The following are the words and phrases most consistently used in my books:

WORDS

ach jah—oh yes
ach vell—oh well
aendi—aunt
appenditlich—delicious
Ausbund—the Amish hymnal used in worship services
boppli—baby, babies (alternate spellings: bobbli, bopplin)
bruder—brother
dat—dad (alternate spellings: daed, daadi)
dawdi and/or grossdawdi—grandfather (alternate spelling: daddi)
deerich—silly, idiotic, foolish
denki—thank you (alternate spelling: danki)
dochder—daughter
dumm—dumb
fater—father
fraa—wife
Gelassenheit—yielding or submission to the will of God. For the Amish, this is a central tenet to living their beliefs. Translations in English include serenity, calm, composure, and equanimity—essentially the result of that yielding.

Gmay—capital *G* when referring to worship / church
    services held biweekly

gmay—lowercase *g* when referring to the Amish
    community who worship together (alternate spelling:
    gmayna)

Gotte—God (alternate spellings: Gott, Got)

gute—good (alternate spelling: gut)

jah—yes (alternate spellings: ja, ya)

kinder—younger children

kumme—come (alternate spellings: kum, cum)

liebling/liebchen—darling (term of endearment)

mamm—mom (alternate spellings: maem, maam)

mammi and/or grossmammi—grandmother

mann—husband

mater—mother (alternate spelling: mudder)

nae—no (alternate spelling: nay)

narrish—crazy

Rumspringa—"running around," the term used to
    describe the period of adolescence starting at around
    age sixteen with increased social interaction and
    independence (alternate spelling: Rumschpringe)

scholar—student

schtinke—stink

schwester—sister

singeon—a Sunday evening social event for the older
    youth / teenagers / unmarried young adults. They
    bring tasty food, play games, sing hymns and other
    favorite songs of faith, and enjoy other social activi-
    ties. Often part of courtship (especially offering to
    drive a girl home in a buggy).

sohn—son

vell—well

wunderbaar—wonderful (alternate spellings: wunder-bar, wunderlich)

yet—used at the end of a sentence in place of words such as "too" or "still"

youngie/die Youngie—young folks, usually referring to teenagers or unmarried young adults

PHRASES

for sure and certain
it wonders me
oh, help
wonderful gute ("wonderful," as a way of saying "very," can be placed in front of many words)

PHRASES IN PENNSYLVANIA DUTCH

ach du lieva—oh my goodness
Er is en faehicher schreiner—He is an able carpenter
Gotte segen eich—God bless you
oh, sis yucht—oh no, oh darn

SAYINGS & IDIOMS

"Blowing at the smoke doesn't help if the chimney is plugged."
"Difficulty is a miracle in its first stage."
"If you aim at nothing, you're bound to hit it."
"If you want a place in the sun, you will have to expect some blisters."

Keep reading for an excerpt from

The Gift of Hope

Available now!

THE KNOCK AT the door was expected, but a bit early.

"I'll get it," Hope Beiler tried to quietly shout down the stairs from her doorway. Her sister was always saying she was too loud, but she was trying. She needn't have bothered this time. The front door squealed a protest at the use. Over the indistinguishable murmur of voices, Hope mentally added the task of oiling the hinges to her unending to-do list.

She would just have to hurry to finish getting ready. Hopping around her room, she put on her shoes as quickly as she could. Voices drifted up to her, but she couldn't make out the words. Hopefully Mammi wasn't in one of her moods and was keeping her comments to the weather—or something equally neutral . . . or normal.

Her grandmother had moved in this year. While Hope loved Mammi with all her heart and was grateful for her cheerful if somewhat scattered presence every day, she was also never entirely sure what might come out of Mammi's mouth, particularly when guests arrived.

Snatching her hard-saved money off the dresser, Hope hurried down the stairs to find Mammi standing there with her hands on her hips, talking to Sarah and Rachel Price. Tucking back an errant strand of her wayward strawberry-colored curls, which never wanted to stay pinned under her white kapp, Hope made her way to Mammi's side in time to catch the words "Find my Hope a husband."

She had to hide her snort of laughter.

A husband wasn't exactly high on Hope's list of worries, not these days at least. That topic was better than last week, when Mammi had asked Elam Hershberger if he thought he saw a turkey every time he looked in the mirror. To be fair, the poor man had a hunk of skin that sort of hung under his neck, but still . . .

"We'll try," Sarah said, glancing at Hope over Mammi's shoulder, eyes twinkling with amusement. "But she is wonderful picky. She seems almost . . ." She paused and wrinkled her nose in thought.

"Hopeless," Mammi filled in. Then nodded solemnly as though her granddaughter weren't standing right there listening. "There must be *some* young man."

As if men grew on trees like apples, and you simply had to pluck one from its branch, rotten or not.

Hope lifted her gaze heavenward, sending up a quick prayer for patience. She was always praying for patience but found that to be more and more the case lately.

"Dat needs me at home too much," she said firmly. "A husband can wait."

Her mamm's sudden passing last year had been hard on them all, but hardest on her dat. Levi Beiler had shrunken in on himself without his fraa at his side, turning into a ghost of the strong, dependable provider and father he'd always been. With only the two girls—she and her sister, Hannah—he had to work the family farm alone. Hannah was getting married, focused on preparing for the wedding. Mammi was a dear but getting older and less able. Which left Hope, who tried to help in her own way.

Speaking of which . . . "Where is Dat?" she asked Mammi.

"He's already in the north field," she was informed.

She exchanged a quick glance with her grossmammi that said everything. Every day her father went to "work the fields," but as far as she could tell, not much was getting done.

She hadn't voiced her concerns out loud, though. No need to burden others with worry when little could be done. The signs hadn't become obvious until recently because, after Mamm's passing, the community had gathered around them in so many ways. The blessing of a close-knit community. Their Amish neighbors and friends had helped get the farm through summer and fall harvest, after which winter had been relatively slow with no need for extra hands. But now that spring had come . . .

Unfortunately, Hope was fairly certain Mammi had noticed as well.

Mammi might be prone to saying odd things and having an outlook that bordered on overly optimistic, but beneath that, she was surprisingly sharp. Not much got by Rebecca Beiler. While neither Hope nor her grandmother had voiced any of their concerns outright, they'd both done their best to fill the gap left by both of Hope's parents.

The general air of neglect in the fields was equally true around the house. Not the cleanliness or tidiness, which the women were on top of. But the place was quickly falling into a state of disrepair—the roof needed patching, a gutter was hanging on by a thread, and there were various other fixes that they were waiting on Dat to get to.

Hope tried her best. In addition to her usual chores, she'd been trying her hand at repairs, but she could only do so much in a day. Also, several larger repairs needed a man's muscles, like digging up the massive dead rosebush in the front yard. She'd reminded Dat about it until he'd asked her not to repeat herself, but still the rosebush sat outside, untended.

Nothing she could do about that either.

In addition, the wedding preparations were a lot. Getting ready to host and feed over three hundred people took planning, coordinating with their close community of friends and neighbors, and money they didn't have, which meant getting creative.

Things would get better, though. Dat was in mourning and would find his way home again eventually, with Gotte's help, the wedding would pass, and everything would get back to normal.

As her mamm used to say, "Difficulty is only a miracle in its first stage."

"Can I get anything from town for you, Mammi?"

"Nae, denki." Her grandmother patted her shoulder. "Enjoy your outing with your friends."

"I will," Hope promised.

Other than Gmay every other Sunday, and the daily walks to her spot in the woods where she went to think, this was the first she'd been away from the house in some time. She'd stopped attending singeon with the other youngie Sunday evenings. Enjoying the social time felt selfish when so much needed doing at home.

She leaned in and placed a kiss on her grandmother's

cheek, the skin soft and paper thin under her lips, a reminder her mammi wasn't as young as she liked to act.
"Keep an eye on Dat?"

"I always keep an eye on that boy. It's what gute maters
do, even when their sons are grown." Mammi winked.

Hope chuckled at the image of her strong, silent father
as a boy.

With a deep breath, trying to rid herself of the anxious
feeling that the house might collapse without her there to
hold it together, Hope followed Sarah and Rachel down the
stairs. As she hit the third step, she wobbled slightly. Peering closer, she discovered the wooden tread was starting to
split right along the overhang. Yet another thing to add to
her list of concerns and fixes.

Maybe while she was in town, she could ask about how
to fix a breaking stairstep and even get the supplies she'd
need.

Except there was no money for it. So perhaps not.

"Your grossmammi is precious, Hope," Sarah said,
pulling her from her thoughts.

Giving herself a mental shake, she smiled. "Yes, she is."

Sarah and Rachel lived just down the lane and had been
her closest friends, along with Hannah, since childhood.
They knew about many of the troubles in the Beiler house.
Dawdi had passed away a few years ago, leaving her
grandmother alone, and after Mamm . . . Regardless of the
sad circumstances leading to it, having Mammi here now
was a blessing in the midst of sorrow.

"Denki for the ride," she said to Sarah and Rachel's
father as she climbed into the waiting buggy.

"My pleasure, Hope." He pulled the wide brim of his
hat lower over his eyes to shield against the bright sun and
snapped the reins to set the horses to an easy pace.

Intending to enjoy the day shopping for wedding gifts for Hannah, the girls planned to walk the three-mile trip home afterward.

Hope turned her face to the warmth of the sun and let the pleasant chirping of the birds sing her worries away. While the air remained brisk in mid-spring, which meant she'd brought a sweater with her, the sun would keep them warm well enough. This was always Hope's favorite time of the year, when small green shoots sprouted in the fields and the last of winter snow, clinging to the shadowy bases of trees, melted away. Soon enough, flowers would bring color to their community of Charity Creek.

Many blessings to thank Gotte for today. Hope laid her worries aside, determined to enjoy her outing.

"How did you keep Hannah from coming with us?" Sarah asked. "It wonders me she could not join us today?"

Wedding shopping meant keeping her schwester away. "She and Noah are looking at a house he wishes to buy for them."

"How wunderbaar!" Rachel clapped her hands. "Hannah is lucky to have caught Noah Fisher."

"I think he's lucky to have caught Hannah," Hope said, though in her sweet way. Hannah was perfect. Exactly what Hope tried to be, though she often fell short. Especially in the kitchen.

"True," Rachel agreed easily. "Too bad he is an only child."

All three of them nodded. Poor Noah's mamm had died in childbirth when he was born. Hope had wondered if Noah and Hannah had bonded over that small sadness they had in common. The loss of a parent.

"I wish I was picking a house with my handsome husband," Sarah sighed.

She earned a sharp glance from her dat for the trouble. "I hope I've raised dochders who wish for helpmates, men who can walk beside them in life and faith, rather than wishing for houses or material things."

Sarah lowered her eyes. "Yes, Dat."

Rachel wasn't as meek as her younger sister, and merely chuckled. "Handsome wouldn't be so bad."

"Ach." Zachariah Price shook his head, though Hope caught a small twitch of his beard that she thought might be hidden amusement.

"What do you think you'll get for Hannah?" Rachel asked Hope.

"Something she could use in the new house maybe. Or in her garden."

Thankfully, talk turned to the wedding and gift ideas and plans for the future. Hope let Sarah and Rachel's cheerful chatter pour over her as she debated her own purchase in town today. The Amish lived a plain and simple life with not a lot of fluff, but a new house would require many useful things. They planned to visit A Thankful Heart—the only Amish-owned and -run gift store for several towns around, popular with the Amish and Englischer locals and tourists alike. Granted, the Kanagys owned it, and Dat wouldn't care for her giving them any business. She could hear his gruff voice now saying, "No dochder of mine should have anything to do with the Kanagys, even if I *have* forgiven them."

He said he had, but anyone in their family could tell he still harbored bitterness. Not that her parents had ever explained why. As far as Hope could tell, the Kanagys, whom she knew because they were part of the same church, were honest people of faith. Well . . . all except Aaron Kanagy maybe. Granted, she didn't know the Kanagys

well, mostly because of the tension between the two families making them acquaintances more than friends. Still,
their shop had to have some small item appropriate for
Hannah on her wedding day.

The way Hope saw it, she had no other choice. Given
the pittance in her purse, saved over time for rainy days,
finding anything would be difficult. She'd thought she
might paint something, but Hope's paints had dried up
these last months, thanks to lack of use, and she hadn't
wanted to waste money on new ones.

She straightened in her seat, determined to find at least
a little something.

Despite it being a Wednesday in the middle of spring,
Charity Creek was as busy as she'd ever seen, bustling
with cars and people on foot, as well as several buggies. The
town itself was small enough to recognize most anyone—
both Amish and, to a certain extent, Englischers—who
lived in the area. Everyone in everybody else's business,
especially within her Amish community. However, they
were in the heart of Indiana Amish country of the Elkhart-
LaGrange counties and drew tourists and outsiders for
various reasons. Especially their lovely little downtown
with its shops and places to eat. But this was more than
usual. Perhaps the weather had drawn people out—a hint
of coming warmth and skies as blue as she remembered
her mother's eyes.

Zachariah pulled his buggy up right outside A Thankful
Heart, and Hope jumped out, giving a quick wave to Luke
Raber, who stood across the street and thankfully nodded
in return but didn't come over. As she waited for Sarah and
Rachel, Hope peered in the shop window, already mentally
discarding items as inappropriate wedding gifts.

Then a small, simply carved chair, obviously intended

for a child, caught her eye and sparked an idea. Perhaps the new couple could use a simple piece of furniture for the new home. Noah's family were selling their farmland, as most of his sisters had married and moved away and his dat had started working in the nearby factory, as many Amish men in this area had out of necessity. A farmer born and raised, Noah intended to move to the Beiler farm and help her dat, who'd only had two girls. Luckily, a small home on three acres that backed up to their southern border had been put on the market. If that didn't work out, Noah intended to build eventually.

"Did you hear me, Hope?" Sarah's voice pulled her from her thoughts.

She turned away from the window with what she hoped was an interested smile plastered to her lips. "I'm sorry. I was caught up with this little chair."

"Which one?" Sarah and Rachel pressed closer to peer through the glass and Hope pointed it out to them.

"Oh," Rachel said. "That is sweet. Aaron must've made it, for sure and certain. He does all the woodworking for the store."

Hope tried not to let her smile slip at the sound of Aaron's name, and a picture immediately formed in her mind. Dark hair, laughing dark eyes, a too-easily-given grin, and strong hands made for hard work. Why couldn't it have been one of Aaron's brothers, Joshua or Daniel, who'd carved the chair? She could've dealt with one of them much better.

"Why do you need a child's chair, though?" Rachel turned to her with a frown.

Hope quickly shook her head. "I don't, but I was thinking I could have whoever made that build a small table or a rocking chair perhaps. For Hannah."

"She would love that," Sarah enthused. "I'm sure Aaron could build you something right quick."

Hope shook her head.

She had no intention of asking Aaron Kanagy any such thing. Just the thought of him still made her wince, the sting of her hurt pride not dimmed by time. No doubt he hadn't meant for her to overhear him telling his friends that he had no interest in her after singeon one night about a year ago. He hadn't known that Hope had been standing outside to escape Barnabas Miller's attentions. She'd been taking a needed break around the corner from where the group of boys he was with had gathered, mid-conversation, talking about girls they were interested in. One of the boys brought up her name.

"Hope Beiler is okay, I guess," Aaron had said, his voice unenthusiastic.

Hope's heart had shriveled in the same way she'd shrunk herself into the shadows, the burn of mortification heating her skin.

True, her curls were a tad unruly and brightly colored, and she was on the short side and skinny with it. Next to Hannah, with her golden hair and flawless ways, Hope had often felt inadequate. Regardless, Aaron shouldn't have said such a thing to all those other boys. No one would want to show interest in her after that.

The memory still had the power to turn her ears hot and no doubt bright red, and she was suddenly grateful for her kapp, which covered them.

"I'll ask at the Troyers' store where they make larger furniture," she said firmly, glad for the excuse. "They might have something already finished."

"I guess so." Sarah puckered her brows, but then a sly

glint came out to play. "But wouldn't you want to spend time with Aaron? I would."

Hope was well aware how all the Kanagy boys—men in their early twenties now, actually—were considered quite the catches. They never wanted for girls to talk to at the various community events and frolics. Even Daniel, who tended to keep to himself.

Rachel widened her eyes dramatically. "Hmmm . . . But think if it led to more, and he fell hopelessly in love with you, and you married him."

When they turned to Hope with such expectant expressions, words of denial popped out of her mouth. "Aaron Kanagy is the last man I could ever think to marry."

The instant she'd said it, Hope clapped a hand over her mouth and wished she could pull the words back in and swallow them whole.

Unfortunately, Sarah and Rachel, instead of appearing shocked, exchanged glances filled with a knowing that set Hope's teeth on edge. "What's wrong with Aaron?" Rachel asked.

Hope lowered her hand. "Nothing. That was an unkind thing to say. Please don't repeat it. I would feel terrible."

The words spoken in haste made her no better than Aaron telling those boys she was just okay. Worse even. Hope glanced around, relieved to find no one else close enough to overhear.

"But you don't like him?" Sarah prodded, confusion evident in her tone.

"Nae. He's . . . fine . . ." Hope stumbled over herself to get words out. "He's not who I would . . . choose, is all."

She barely kept from closing her eyes in despair. What could she say to fix this?

"You're so picky, you don't choose anyone," Sarah pointed out. "I, for one, wouldn't mind his interest."

"Me neither." Rachel waggled her eyebrows.

Hope managed a laugh that sounded just the right type of light and airy. "Then *you* commission him. Let's save the gift shop for last and see if anything in Troyers' will do?"

At least her friends allowed her to lead them away. Hope couldn't possibly go in there right now. Not with them watching her extra closely, especially if Aaron was working today. Given her behavior, they no doubt assumed she either disliked him or harbored a secret crush.

Too bad, since she'd so wanted a closer look at the little chair. Affording anything in Troyers' was not an option. She'd have to be extra persnickety and reject everything in there, which no doubt would earn her more teasing.

Or maybe she'd manage to find a small item. Probably tiny. Because asking Aaron Kanagy for anything was not an option.

Ready to find
your next great read?

Let us help.

Visit prh.com/nextread

Penguin
Random
House